Graham's
Charlotte

Advance Review Copy
This is an advance review copy.
Please excuse any remaining errors.

Graham's Charlotte

Drew Farnsworth

www.ColumbusPressBooks.com

Columbus Press
P.O. Box 91028
Columbus, OH 43209
www.ColumbusPressBooks.com

Editor
BradPauquette
www.BradPauquette.com

Cover Artwork & Design
Columbus Publishing Lab
www.ColumbusPublishingLab.com

Print ISBN 978-0-9891737-5-9
Ebook ISBN 978-0-9891737-6-6

Printed in the United States of America
1 3 5 7 9 10 8 6 4 2

Chapter 1

Madison watched her feet move under her flowery yellow sun dress as she lifted her sandal over the threshold between the airplane and the jetway. A breeze blew her hair into her eyes creating a halo of frizz around her caramel cheeks. It was her first step into another country since she'd moved to America for good.

When her foot landed it felt like freedom. The voice over the intercom said, "*Bienvenido a Costa Rica.*" It was just an airport and the PA announcements just happened to be in Spanish but to Madison it was like she'd arrived home. Her eyes usually stared ahead with grim tenacity, the whites peeking out from behind her darkened brow, but she was suddenly overcome by a need to look up and around. She widened her eyes from their usual slits into an expectant gaze that for once actually made her look fourteen, instead of like an adult.

The class huddled together. Señor Dipson, lacrosse coach turned chaperone of the Spanish class field trip, waved his hand in the air for them all to follow. When they didn't respond he yelled, "Come here!" Madison was happy to hear he'd already given up speaking Spanish. At least it was his outfit and not his accent that would embarrass him.

Hannah Chanel, Carolyn Kaplan and Jillian Jacobs walked in a line in front of her, all wearing almost identical outfits: a too short skirt and a flirty blouse. Those clothes probably cost as much as Madison's entire wardrobe. All of their hair was done perfectly and all in the same style, a textured but glossy look just below the shoulders. Hannah's was black, Carolyn's red and Jillian's blond.

"I hate this place already," moaned Jillian as she swiped her bangs out of her eyes. She pushed out her chin and pouted her lips like the good girl turned bad girl turned good girl that she'd always wanted to be. "This better look good on my transcript," she continued, her voice spiking sharply at the end of each sentence. "Not that it matters. Harvard can spot the best of the best without a stupid piece of paper."

Madison kept her head down, still looking at her feet. She listened to the crackling giggles of her classmates and to her own giddy heartbeat. The airport was a world of noise, from the flapping tongues to the grumbling jet engines. She closed her eyes out of habit. She'd trained herself to navigate using only sound to listen to the various noises, the buzzing of the lights or the footfalls ahead and to get a good idea of the shape of things. They teach assassins that technique so they can sneak up on their victims in the dark. Madison just thought it was fun.

She would often plug in her hairdryer, space heater, sound system and air conditioner at the same time just so that the circuit breaker would trip in the basement and she would have to make her way down in the dark to flip the switch. It was pitch black down there and the electrical panel was buried behind a million layers of boxes they still hadn't unpacked since their last move. Madison would navigate past the wardrobes and old dressers. She'd only broken two bones, which was good compared with most of her stunts.

But it was different to navigate that way in a giant room filled with hundreds of anxious people. Had she thought about it first she might have realized that using the sound in this room to see was like staring straight into a spotlight. It was sensory overload. No matter how good she was, she'd bit off more than she could chew.

So it didn't surprise her when she ran headlong into a jelly-like substance with a moist covering of polyester. When she opened her eyes she realized it was Señor Dipson. He turned his whole body, potbelly and all, to level a square look at her. From his head to his toes he was mismatched. His balding head didn't match his bull nose which in turn didn't match his muscular jaw. Likewise, his flimsy, sweat-drenched Hawaiian shirt would have better accompanied khaki shorts but instead he wore baggy running pants and old sneakers. As always he was frustrated, not least because he now had the circular outline of Madison's forehead as a giant sweat mark on the front of his shirt. Everyone else in the group stared. Señor Dipson tried to regain command by issuing an order, but everyone already knew he was a pushover so they stopped listening before he even uttered a word. "Be careful. We're counting on you to help us blend in," he bellowed at Madison. "I don't want to look like a bunch of tourists. You've got the best accent of any of us." He adjusted his shirt and pulled his white socks up to his knees under the baggy pants. "Speak up for once."

Madison glanced down and nodded. She tried not to let her eyes wander to her classmates.

The group, all twenty of them, slowly came together in the middle of the airport terminal and walked toward the security gate. Madison followed from a distance, walking slowly and watching the group get farther and farther away.

A man's voice spoke in her ear as she walked. "I need your help," he said. He had a gravelly rock star grumble and a thin British accent. He sounded like he'd been yelling all night and could barely get the words out.

Madison turned to look at him but kept walking. He was tall, built like a prize fighter with lean twitching muscles in his neck and arms. But he looked familiar. Maybe he was in the movies or on some reality show she'd only seen once. His nose fit perfectly between his carved cheeks and above his square jaw. A smirk danced at the edges of his mouth. He wore an unzipped red leather jacket and sunglasses. His short hair came to a point at his forehead. He was old though. Forty at least.

"Do you know where the NSA is?" he asked.

Madison regarded him cockeyed. "What?" she asked.

"The National Security Agency," he answered blandly. "The headquarters of which is the fifth most secure site in the world. Do you know where it is?"

She looked away from him and walked faster to catch up with the group. She said nothing, pretending she hadn't heard him.

He laughed and a wry smile cut across his face. "Two weeks from now I'll need you to break into the NSA and delete a file for me." He said it like it was the most normal thing in the world. Madison walked faster. He kept talking as he picked up his pace to keep just ahead of her. "I'm not threatening you when I say this next bit but I know it sounds like I am. There's going to be an earthquake in one minute. If you don't do exactly as I tell you, you're going to die."

Madison rolled her eyes. "You can't predict earthquakes," she told him with a bright snip in her voice.

"You're right," he said. "And I can't predict that Jillian Jacobs is going to grab Patrick Sutton's bum in five seconds but you're about to see it happen."

Madison believed beyond all hope that she'd have the chance to have a real conversation with Patrick on this trip. Her heart sunk as she realized she might not have the chance. Jillian's flaxen hair whipped across her shoulder as she snuck a crude glimpse at Patrick's behind as he walked next to her. It was an awkward pairing. He was almost a foot taller than her and the broad vee of his back contrasted with Jillian's cultivated shapeliness. He had every vestige of exotic foreign exchange student down to his long, dark, silky hair and sweet, Irish accent. Jillian's hand moved slowly. It was as if there were a magnet in Patrick's back pocket. She suddenly gave his butt a weird pat.

The man next to Madison shoved his phone in front of her face. It showed a video of the airport right in front of them. "I'm called Graham by the way," he said.

"You can't predict earthquakes," Madison repeated.

Then she studied the video on Graham's phone. There was definitely an earthquake. The lights shook. The walls crumbled. She had to look past the screen to make sure the video wasn't real. The airport in front of her looked completely normal.

"This shows you exactly what will happen thirty seconds

from now," Graham told her. "If you stay with me I can guarantee you'll live." Madison stopped walking and turned to him. She huffed out a deep breath. It wasn't until she felt her hands shaking that she realized how scared she was. "Please don't kill me. Don't kidnap me. I… I can't help you."

"I want to save your life," Graham said. "All you need to do is stand…" He led her by the arm ten steps to the left. "All you need to do is stand in this spot. If I tell you to move then you need to move." He sighed and braced for the tremor to begin. "I know you can do this, Mads."

Madison braced herself.

Then it started.

At first it felt like a loud concert, something hitting her in the pit of her stomach but she couldn't tell where it came from. Then she felt the floor shift underneath her. People screamed. Madison closed her eyes and tensed every muscle in her body. A blast of wind blew past her as the airport glass shattered. She opened her eyes to see a giant steel truss bend and curl almost directly on top of her. If she'd been two feet to the right it would have fallen on her and she would've died.

The ground felt like a trampoline or a tight rope. Her feet barely held her up.

"Just stay with me," Graham said. He peeked out over his sunglasses and Madison caught the blue of his eyes. "Please."

Graham pulled her by the arm again. She dropped her luggage. They climbed up over the truss and ran through the airport terminal. Madison looked back and saw the floor collapse where they'd been standing. Her sandals twisted between her toes so as soon as she could she kicked them across the concourse so that she could get traction with her bare feet. They sprinted down the long corridor, jumping over luggage trolleys and past the light fixtures hanging from wires.

"Stop!" Graham yelled. Madison froze in place.

They'd almost reached the food court. A huge sculpture of an airplane hung in the middle. Madison's class was screaming on the far side. The tremor suddenly got worse, as if the whole world dropped out from under them. Steel creaked all around. The plane sculpture slipped off its hangers and swung dangerously close to her and Graham, finally falling just a few feet ahead. The wing rolled toward them but stopped just before it would have leveled Madison into the ground. More glass shattered. The floor bent inward in front of her. Half of the food court collapsed into the ground. The ceiling disintegrated into a powdery mix of concrete and stone but thankfully the wing of the plane kept the debris from falling on their heads.

And then the rumbling stopped. Everything went silent.

"Are you OK?" Graham asked her. He bent down and looked her in the eye.

Madison checked herself for wounds. Her arms were fine. She felt strong thanks to the endless cross country practices and the beginning of lacrosse training. A couple of dark spots showed up on her arms. They'd be bruises in no time. She checked her chest and back through her sundress but she didn't find anything. On her legs there were light cuts and scrapes from the rolling rubble.

Then she saw what would make most people faint. A big piece of glass stuck out from the side of her hip like a dagger. She was about to pull it out but Graham stopped her hand. He pulled out his phone and pointed the camera at the wound. He looked up at her. "This is going to hurt a lot but you'll be better off. Are you ready?"

She nodded.

Graham pulled the glass out of the wound. Madison's deafening scream echoed through the airport which had become surprisingly quiet after the quake. He ripped two bits of his shirt from under his jacket and ran over to the cracked entrance to the restroom. He sprayed some hand sanitizer on both of the strips of shirt cloth. When he came back he held one in front of Madison. "I'm just going to tie this around your hip," he instructed.

As he did it she howled. She'd never felt anything quite like it. Her adrenaline pumped.

Graham spoke before the pain had the chance to overcome her. "Your classmates are trapped," he said. "We're going to save their lives."

"Which ones?" Madison asked without thinking. Someone like Jillian Jacobs might not have been deserving of much respect but Madison knew even her life demanded vigilance. Madison took a deep breath and nodded. "Let's go."

Graham ran ahead, vaulting over rubble and twisted architecture. Madison followed feverishly. She overcame her limp but the pain stabbed her with every hop and scramble. She started to hear voices crying out for help under the wreckage. She could recognize Jillian Jacobs' frenzied shrieks over everyone else's. Madison thought about turning her back when she heard that but she couldn't do it.

It was like climbing a cliff face. The rubble shifted as Madison pushed herself to follow Graham. Like a gazelle, he bounded from rock to rock, flying through the air weightlessly. He suddenly stopped, grabbed a block of concrete and threw it to the side. It bounced down the rubble hill past her. She caught up to him and instinctively pulled some steel and drywall from the ground.

Jillian Jacobs screamed out from under Madison's feet. "Help us!" Madison brought her ear closer to the rock. Jillian continued. "One of us is hurt! He's got a broken leg or something! Please help us! I think mine might be broken too."

Madison glowered at Graham. He rolled his eyes and shook his head. "She's fine," he groaned. "Patrick Sutton's the one with the broken leg. He's bleeding badly." He handed her the second strip of t-shirt with the hand sanitizer on it. "Take this." Madison slowly reached out and clasped the cloth. Graham pulled out his phone. "You need to take my phone too. It'll tell you how to set the bone. Then you need to wrap this cloth around his wound."

Madison took the phone out of his hand. It looked expensive—one of those phones you could drop out of a plane without denting it. It had a square screen which was smaller than the one she had at home. Its weight surprised her too, like a river stone in her hand, smooth and cold to the touch.

"I'm really sorry I'm giving this to you," he said. "I'd like to tell you not to do anything stupid with it but I already know you will so…" He shrugged and got up. "I'll call you soon."

Madison gasped. "You can't leave."

Graham laughed. "Look, Mads, I really can't be here." He turned to go but he stopped and said over his shoulder, "You can't show that phone to anyone. Ever." He looked guilty like he'd just told her Santa Claus wasn't real. His face drooped. It reminded her of the last time someone had given her bad news. But she couldn't think about that. If she did she might be moved to tears. There was too much else happening to get distracted like that. "I don't mean that," he corrected. "You can do whatever you want but you've got more power at your fingertips than the president has with all the missiles and jets in the world. I'm really sorry about giving it to you. It will ruin your life. I wish it didn't have to be this way."

"No!" Madison yelled. But Graham was already off and running, bounding off of the walls, reaching down to give a bandage or make a splint and then moving on. Everything he did was effortless. He was a football player mixed with a movie star with a hint of struggling artist in his eyes.

Madison pulled with all her strength against the pile of rocks. The phone in her hand blinked at her. The screen still showed the video feed from the camera just like the rocks in front of her except that one of the rocks glowed green. Madison pulled at that rock almost instinctually. Other rocks fell back with it and opened up a small hole through the rubble.

Jillian Jacobs stuck her head out from the cramped cave behind the rubble. "Help me out!" She screamed.

Madison held out her hand. Jillian pulled herself out of the small hole and tumbled down the rubble to the ground below. A few more students crawled through. They looked so frightened. Madison checked the phone and saw a few more glowing rocks. She pulled them out as well. The hole opened up enough for her to see Patrick in the corner. She crawled into the dark cavern with the sanitized cloth around her neck. Students scurried out behind her. Even Señor Dipson left.

Madison saw Patrick screaming in the corner. His leg was bloody. Instead of examining it, she held the phone up to see what it would tell her. There were glowing green arrows that showed which way she should pull his leg in order to set the bone. It even showed her where to put her hands. Without saying a word she grabbed his leg and yanked.

The bone cracked into place much more easily than she thought it would. Patrick screamed, but not as loudly as she expected. She immediately wrapped up the open wound, trying in vain to wipe the dust and grime away.

"We'll get you out of here," she told him. She put the phone down and grabbed him by the shoulders to pull him out. "Just push with your good leg, Patrick," she said.

He winced. "I don't know if I can do it."

Madison looked him in the eye. "Patrick," she said. "I know for a fact that you're going to make it out of here."

"How do you know?" he asked.

She shook her head. "Just push!" she commanded.

As Patrick heaved backward he screamed in pain. Madison couldn't bear to watch as the tears flowed down his face. He looked so small suddenly. His lips quivered. She felt his heartbeat through the veins in his arms. Her own wound was barely held together by the rag of t-shirt. It was entirely red-brown with her blood. "Do it!" she screamed. "If you don't push then we'll both die. I'm not leaving you."

She pulled. He pushed. The pain cut deep on their faces. Madison's winces contorted hers into a lemon squinch. Patrick screamed incomprehensibly.

Then they reached daylight. It felt like a hundred hands pulled them through the little hole. Madison breathed deeply and loudly. The cave behind her rumbled as if it was about to collapse. She looked inside for more people. All she saw was the phone that Graham gave her, still glowing with soft blue light.

She dived back into the cave even though the hundred hands tried to hold her back. She fought them off and crawled back down toward the tiny rectangle of light. The cave rattled again. She grabbed the phone and turned around. One of the rocks at the entrance gave way. The cave buckled but stayed open. As she pushed she felt the wound in her hip shoot daggers through her entire body. She almost passed out from exhaustion. As she reached the surface the huge piece of concrete that had been the cave's roof began to fall. She felt hands on her shoulders pulling her to safety. She just barely made it out before the concrete crashed down to the ground.

It was Señor Dipson who pulled her out. He screamed, "What were you thinking?" Madison hugged him tightly and gasped for air. He held her. "Thank you Madison," he said humbly. "Thank you so much."

The whole Spanish class just stood there staring at her, their mouths open and their eyes wide. She looked around, wondering what they might be thinking, why they all seemed totally shocked. Patrick moaned on the ground. None of the others looked seriously hurt except Jillian Jacobs. She writhed around in pain. "Madison Riley pushed me down the rocks!" she cried. "I think I broke my leg."

Madison pulled out the phone and took a subtle look at it as she pointed it at Jillian. "No serious injuries," it reported. She wanted to walk over and set the record straight but she couldn't help but look at her classmates instead. She'd never seen anyone look at her that way before.

Señor Dipson was the most shocked. "We'd all be dead if it weren't for you."

Madison couldn't talk. She tried to catch her breath. Out of the corner of her eye she saw a blinking red light on the phone. It was the outline of a person trapped under the rocks on the other side of the food court. "There are more people to save!" she screamed, and she ran over to the spot she'd seen and began to dig. She wouldn't dare stop until there were no more blinking red outlines on the phone. She wouldn't dare.

Chapter 2

Dirt covered Madison's face in a patina of soft streaks which blended her skin from her high cheek bones into her eye-line better than any makeup she ever wore. Her face looked good, somehow, with dirt on it, unlike the spa treated faces of her classmates. The dappled skin tone of Madison's brow was a light coffee, not like the perfect, blemish free alabaster of Jillian Jacobs. But when dust filled the air in a choking fog, all the facials in the world become meaningless.

The class set to work pulling wounded people from the rubble, improvising an infirmary in the middle of the food court. Madison taught them Graham's trick of the hand sanitizer and the clean strips of cloth. One after another they treated the people they found. Once she could do no more, she walked over to the abandoned burger joint exhausted and bloodied. She started filling cups with water to give to her classmates. Señor Dipson came over as well. He grabbed a large order of fries from behind the counter and a handful of burgers. Madison pulled out a handful of fries and wolfed them down.

"You were amazing," he told her in a rush. "I've never seen anyone work like that before in my life. I've never seen anyone so cool in a crisis."

"I have," Madison retorted absently.

Señor Dipson went silent. Madison knew what he was thinking. People reacted this way a lot, but she'd gotten used to it. There was no point in continuing to talk to him about it. He'd just fumble his words and tell her he was sorry for being insensitive. Madison reached out and grabbed the burger from his hand. "Thanks for this," she said. She wiped her hands on her bloody, torn yellow sundress.

Police sirens cried out in the background but she didn't really care. She drank a cup of water so fast that it poured down over her cheeks and onto the front of her dress.

"Maddy," Patrick yelled from across the food court. He was still lying down, Jillian Jacobs fawning over him like he was her froo froo poodle.

Madison walked over to him. No one ever called her Maddy but she didn't care. He'd never really spoken to her before. Certainly he'd never said her name. She handed him some water.

There were medical personnel and police scrambling all around outside. She didn't have much time to talk to him before he'd be whisked away on a stretcher. The problem was she had nothing to say. "Hey," she said. "How's your leg?"

Patrick winced just thinking about it. "It hurts a lot," he answered. "This is worse than the time I got cleated by that Limey from Winchester." His dark brown eyes and olive skin glistened with sweat.

Patrick's accent was deep, once in a while pitching up

sharply to remind everyone that he too was just fifteen. His life had been similar to Madison's, full of world travel with his dad, an Irish diplomat. He'd spent a year in Istanbul where he lived a life almost entirely within the walls of the embassy, not because it was dangerous, but because his father was so steadfast in his insistence that Patrick get a perfect education. Patrick yearned to break through those walls but his father forced him to study anything and everything in order for him to become the next James Joyce. Patrick hated writing, though he was an undeniable talent. It was the solitude that he couldn't stand. To write was to be sequestered with a pen and paper. He'd had enough of sequester. In Istanbul he'd never even gone out to see the ruins on his own. He vowed never to let his studies get between him and the world again. So soccer became his top priority because it brought him into the outdoors with people he wouldn't have met otherwise, like the street kids and the teenagers who were amazed by his ball placement. Patrick couldn't stand to be alone. Madison had learned all of this through Patrick's essays in Spanish class, which were the best in class. It's hard not to fall for a smart, beautiful boy who has an equally adorable accent in both English and Spanish.

"You should leave him alone," Jillian interrupted. "He really needs to rest."

Madison glared at Jillian. "I didn't push you," she said. "I'm sorry you fell."

Jillian sneered. "I know what happened. I was there." She put a wet rag to Patrick's head and patted him as if he was a colicky baby.

Patrick smiled at Madison and every hair on her arms prickled with excitement. "You're a hero," he told her. "Thank you."

Madison shook her head. The last thing she wanted to be called was a hero. She bit her bottom lip to stop from crying. She turned away and just said, "Thank you." She couldn't stand to talk to him anymore because she couldn't stand for him to see her cry. She waved to one of the medics. "Please help!"

Jillian stepped in front of her to scream at the EMT, as if Madison wasn't doing it well enough. "Patrick's leg is broken."

The medic sprinted over with his kit and knelt down by Patrick. Madison stepped back. Jillian stepped back too, finally looking as confused as everyone else. Jillian was the kind of person who demanded things. She never asked. She never looked confused.

Madison tried to smile. "Are you OK?"

Jillian returned the glance and they stared at each other for a long second. Jillian smiled too before looking away. Madison knew that whatever she said, Jillian would have a clever comeback.

After waiting around, shifting her weight forward and back, Jillian closed her eyes and said, "Thank you."

Madison felt tongue tied. She wasn't sure if she should say 'no problem' or 'you're welcome' or something even nicer like, 'I'm so glad you're safe.'

While she was waiting to speak, Jillian burst in, her tongue moving like a jackhammer. "But why were you looking at your phone so much? Were you expecting a call or something? Do you have an app that tells you how to do first aid? My phone doesn't work in Costa Rica. How does yours? And why did you need to go back into the hole just to get your phone? It just doesn't make any sense."

Madison's heart sank. She didn't have any answers. She wasn't good at improvising. A frog croaked in her throat. She closed her eyes and tried to think. She said, "I just needed to look at it."

"Oh," Jillian huffed as if she'd just figured out the secret of the universe. "Does it have a picture of your dad on it? I would totally understand if that's what it is. You know we all think about him and what he did. He was a hero."

Why is Jillian being so nice? Madison wondered. It didn't feel right. She didn't trust it. But at the same time, Jillian had just given her a perfect excuse to be looking at her phone. "Yeah," she said. "That's it."

Jillian clapped her hands and squealed. "I need to interview you for the school paper. Or better yet I could get an article in the *News Post*. This is the most exciting thing that happened to anyone at Shackleton High in the past ten years."

Madison clutched her phone tightly. Panicked police and rescue workers rushed around the airport. It was clear it wasn't a good time to talk. Jillian seemed to get the message and she shut up.

A nice looking woman in a police outfit came up to Madison with a blanket. "Are you injured at all?" she asked.

Madison looked down at the wound on her hip. It was still dripping sweaty blood lines down her leg. She ripped open the hole in her dress so that the woman could get a closer look. Everything faded into a blur. It felt like mere moments before she was on a stretcher. A big bag filled with red blood pumped into her arm. The medic told her in Spanish that she was lucky to be alive. She supposed that she was.

She couldn't wait one more minute to find out who Graham was and why he'd chosen her. Even as they stitched up her hip in the ambulance the only thing on her mind was that phone and what it could do. And would she really go along with him? Would she really break into the NSA? That sounded like treason. It took her a moment to cope with that thought. Then she began to pass out, still clutching the phone. She vowed never to let it out of her sight again.

Chapter 3

The Costa Rican hospital smelled like the ocean. In fact, there was a perfect view of the Pacific out the window. This was the first time in five years Madison had seen the west coast of anything except the Chesapeake Bay. The breeze cooled her aching muscles and the bruises that ran up and down her arms. A needle was stuck into her arm hooked up to a bag with a bit of clear liquid in it. Other than that she felt good. She took the chance to listen to the waves crash on the shore. A nurse emptied a syringe into her arm. Not a very kind wake up. The nurse didn't even say goodbye as she left the room.

Madison felt foggy. Some people from the class came into the room and thanked her. She barely recognized them. Señor Dipson patted her on the shoulder. Even Jillian Jacobs was there. She came over and hugged Madison as her tight blond pony tail fell into Madison's eyes. "Thank you," Jillian said. "You were so brave."

Madison searched. Patrick wasn't there. She felt even more dizzy. She wanted to ask where he was and if he was OK but she couldn't get the words out.

She fell back to sleep and dreamt the same dream she always did. The same terrible dream of explosions and fire and screams.

When she awoke for real, Madison suddenly felt great. She stood up in her hospital gown and walked out into the hallway. She had to pull along the cart that had the bag and some weird machines attached to it.

Some nurses spoke to each other in feverish Spanish. "*Hola*," Madison said calmly.

They turned to her. "Oh honey," the larger one on the left said. She wore a set of scrubs with palm trees on it. "You have to get back in bed. You lost blood."

"How is everybody from my class?" Madison asked. "How's Patrick?" The ladies didn't seem to know what she was talking about. She wanted to explain but she was still a little groggy.

"Oh," said the squat nurse. "Honey, hundreds of people got hurt. They're all in different hospitals."

Madison contemplated for a moment. She tried to be cool. Her bare feet felt cold against the smooth floor. She asked, "I'd like to have my cell phone so I can call my mom."

The skinny nurse planted her foot and turned her hip impatiently. "Go back to your room, miss," she said in a very good American accent, "we have work."

"What about my friends…" Madison hesitated. She wanted to call them friends but the truth was that her two best friends, Mia and Danny, were back in Maryland. She was the quiet one in class. She liked it that way.

Shackleton High was an endless campus of eclectic buildings interconnected by covered walkways through lush court-yards. Three thousand students were enrolled, most of them over-achievers. It was impossible to know everyone. She was lucky to have made the advanced class and then get past that to this super-advanced class. It wasn't that Madison was a good student. She'd be the first to admit that she wasn't. She just happened to have grown up in Spain for her first few years of school on the US naval base. Her parents were stationed there when she was little. Spanish class was so far the only place she'd ever been noticed by anyone aside from her parents.

Madison stepped forward. She looked the nurse straight in the eye without blinking.

The skinny nurse rolled her eyes. She disappeared behind a small curtain for a moment and came out with the dusty, bloody phone in her hand.

Madison grabbed the phone and ran straight back to her room. She barely even noticed her hip wound. Before she had the chance to sit back down, the phone rang. The caller ID just said "Graham." Madison glanced at it for a second before she answered. Did he know she'd just picked the phone up? If he could see the future, could he see other things?

She answered. "Hello. This is Madison."

Graham chuckled. "Yeah," he said. "Don't be so nice to that Jillian Jacobs. She's trouble." He sounded light and happy over the phone. His voice was still barely more audible than a grumble but he sounded sharper than he had at the airport.

Madison normally wouldn't have spoken to a strange man over the phone. Relaxing slightly, she realized that she either needed to hang up immediately and alert the authorities or be honest with him, careful to protect herself along the way. That he'd saved her life was not a good enough reason to trust him. There was something else that set her at ease. It was his voice and the way that he spoke straightforwardly. He'd told her that she could do whatever she wanted regarding the phone. He wasn't trying to control what she did or didn't do. That had to count for something.

In fact, where she usually felt too timid to speak to adults, with Graham she felt the opposite. She felt an extreme need to scream at him and put him in his place. His almost petulant coolness was a glaring affront to the dire situation that he'd laid out for her.

"I know she's trouble," Madison said. "All those girls are like sharks. They just keep circling, changing directions constantly. They'll sometimes take nips but sometimes they'll come at you full speed ready to swallow you whole." For once in her life her mouth moved faster than her mind and she'd lost the conversational thread and had to pause to regroup.

The pause thickened until Graham asked in a musing voice, "Do you know what a fractal is?"

"Is it math?" Madison groaned. "Talk to my mom. Math is my worst subject."

"It's a type of equation. It makes this beautiful kind of picture where you can keep zooming in forever and it will always look similar. People get nervous when they hear a word like 'fractal' because it sounds smart but really it's not. You were talking about girls being sharks. Now sharks, like teenage girls, move with this specific type of motion called a Levy Flight. They bide their time for a while and then they strike at random, sometimes more than once. It's a type of fractal. It's math. Once you figure out the equation then you know everything."

Mads asked, "So you figured out the equation for the universe?"

"No," Graham answered. "But I figured out how to make a computer powerful enough to graph the equation. I'm still trying to get the equation right. Let me put it to you another way. Have you ever taken one of those color blind tests? The one where you can only see a number if you aren't color blind."

"Yeah."

"You passed, right? You saw a number?"

"Yeah."

"Well I'm colorblind," Graham explained. "When I look at one of those tests I just see a bunch of dots. No matter how hard I look I can't see it and I never will. If I could just see color I'd see it instantly like you...suddenly what was impossible becomes completely obvious." He sighed. "I figured out how to see in color in a world where everybody else sees in black and white."

Madison paced around the room. She felt dizzy. Maybe she got up too fast. "I suck at math."

"Everything is numbers, Mads." He sounded like he was frustrated. "Everything is language. Everything is music. You just have to pay attention. You're fine," Graham said. Then with a terrible American accent he added, "Chill out, dude. Sit down and catch your breath."

Madison looked around for a camera or some way he knew what she was doing. She tried to catch her breath. "How do you know..."

Graham interrupted with a sigh. "Stop," he said. "That's a much bigger question than I have time to answer. How do

I know anything? How did I know there would be an earthquake?"

Madison sat in the chair in the corner of the room and peered at the ocean. "But I have the phone," she said.

She still felt so weird talking to this stranger she'd only met for a few minutes in the middle of absolute chaos. She didn't trust him but somehow she felt close to him. He'd given her the key to the world and told her it would destroy her life.

He groaned like he was bored. "We really can't go back and forth about how you don't understand this or that. All you need to know is that you have a phone in your hand that can tell you anything. Any information that exists in the universe, it has the capability to tell you. It's like Wikipedia except it's actually right about everything, past, present, and for the most part, future. The hard part is knowing what question to ask."

Madison pulled the phone from her ear. She juggled it between her hands feeling its weight. No matter how advanced that phone was it couldn't possibly hold all of the information in the world. "So it's on the Internet," she said. "The phone just logs into the all-knowing computer that you're talking about."

"Sort of," Graham answered. "And the only people who know about it are you and me." His tone wasn't lecturing in the same way most adults spoke. He was really trying to talk to her about this, working through it as he spoke.

Madison got back up. Even though she was dizzy, she paced around the room trying to collect her thoughts. "You're asking me to commit treason," she said.

"No I'm not," Graham said. "If I were a government then this would be treason. This is more like felonious tampering. I just need you to stop your mom from breaking a code that would allow her to read something that will get both her and me in trouble. I'm not asking you to learn state secrets. In fact, I'm intentionally hiding the secrets from you." He sounded so calm that it was funny. "You're not going to hear from me for a while but you need to start doing your homework on this. You need to understand this situation better. Try to figure out why you need to break into the NSA." He sounded unlike himself, at least unlike he'd sounded at the airport. He almost pleaded with her to get this done. Madison was wary. "Do you know what the NSA does?" he asked.

"Of course I do," she answered. "My mom works there. They break codes. They hack into computers. They do all the stuff you see in movies except they never leave the building."

"Good," he said. Then he paused for a moment. Madison let it sink in. Her mom worked for the NSA. Wouldn't this betray her mom somehow? She'd have to lie to her own mother. Graham continued. "I'm really sorry, Madison. I can't ask you to do any more. I shouldn't have even talked to you in the first place." He started muttering to himself but she couldn't make out the words.

"I'm not going to force you to do anything," he continued. "I want to make that very clear. Everything you do from here until eternity is your choice. But you're in danger. There are people in the world who want very badly to have the technology that phone represents. They'd kill for it. In fact, the safest thing you could possibly do is smash that phone right now and never talk about this to anyone ever again. That's your choice. But if you say anything to anyone, it puts you in danger and it puts them in danger. It puts me in danger too."

"For now just…" He suddenly sounded impatient, like he

had an important appointment and he was running late. "You have the phone," he said. "Just look it up!" He started breathing heavily into the phone. There were loud voices near him. A gun shot. Madison listened. She feared for him. She nearly screamed out in terror. "I have to go," he said. Then he hung up on her. She fell back into the chair and passed out.

Chapter 4

For the next three days of her eight day trip, Madison was stuck in the hospital. She craved the sights and experience of Costa Rica, the first Spanish speaking country she'd seen since she was little. She felt like she'd fit in better here than in Maryland or on any of the dozen military bases she'd lived on before that.

The phone remained in her sight at all times but she couldn't bring herself to actually look up the things Graham asked her to. She wanted badly to save her mom from whoever was targeting her, but what if the answer was "Iran" or "China?" How could she possibly help? Instead she asked a very simple question, one that she thought would satisfy both her anxiety and her tendency to procrastinate.

She tried hard to make her questions clear and concise. She typed, "Can I wait a week before investigating the NSA without making matters worse?"

The green cursor blinked for a second and then answered, "Yes." She decided that was good enough and she let the matter leave her mind for the time being, which was a relief. Before she asked any of the big questions the first order of business was to understand what kind of answers the phone would give. She needed to check to make sure it worked so she asked it a question that she knew no one could answer. "What boy did I have a crush on when I was ten?"

The phone answered in an instant. "Miguel De Lugo." That was proof enough for her.

"Is Graham a secret agent?" she wrote.

"No," it answered.

"Does Graham work for the government?"

"No."

"Is Graham trying to save my mom's life?"

"Yes."

Then she just looked out into space, not sure what to say or what to do. She mused to herself, "Should I learn more about this Graham guy?"

The phone spoke to her for the first time. It had the delicate voice of a woman in her thirties who liked to read long books about the countryside. Her accent was similar to Graham's, but a little bit more heavily English. It had the halting cadence of a computer voice but it spoke with the heart of a real person. She said, "Not yet. Wait about two weeks."

Madison was stunned. The green letters still blinked at her. She hadn't meant to say it out loud. Was this a real woman or was it just a computer voice? She assumed it was the latter. But it sounded more honest and real than any other computer voice she'd ever heard. A hundred times better than the GPS on her old phone.

Having been told twice that she shouldn't think about

Graham or the phone or her mother, she decided to take the advice and try not to think about any of them. Madison assumed for her entire life that her mother was being chased by bad guys every day, given that she worked for a spy agency. Madison wasn't surprised to hear it for sure. She felt surprisingly peaceful about it. If an all-knowing phone told her not to worry, it was probably best not to worry. The comfort she felt at the thought of being absolutely assured came suddenly and powerfully. She hadn't felt so relaxed in a long time, since even before the earthquake.

When she was finally allowed to get up and move, Madison walked on the white sand beach outside of the hospital. They'd given her a crutch but it didn't work well in the sand so she just left it on the patio and limped toward the water. It was a beautiful day, the sun bright above her.

People came from the distance in bathing suits and sunglasses. First she saw Carolyn Kaplan, the second most notorious back stabber at Shackleton High School. She had a coy smile like an airline stewardess. It was as if she was always being just polite enough to keep everyone quiet. Her red hair wasn't suited well for the intense sun, and she looked like she was incapable of tanning, but the freckles on her shoulders had gotten darker. Next to her, Hannah Chanel stood tall in her bikini. Just like her name suggests, Hannah was a fashion mogul at Shackleton. She always went to New York or LA and bought the latest and greatest from the top designers even if they were incredibly ugly. Some other people from the class followed them but Madison couldn't tell who they were. Hannah's trademark was her eye makeup, always brightly colored to contrast her dark cheeks.

Hannah shouted "Madison!" as if she was just so happy to see her. Hannah had never said anything to Madison before that moment.

"Hi," Madison said back. She cringed, waiting for them to hate her.

"I can't believe you're up and walking," Carolyn said with a wide, white smile. "You're just so strong." She gazed at the ocean as if she saw something meaningful in the distance. "Can you believe how much of a wimp Jillian was? I'm not inviting her to my welcome home party next week. It's at seven-thirty on the Saturday after we get back."

Hannah added, "All the soccer boys will be there." Her lips curled up as she talked as if she wanted the words to form on the outside of her mouth in the space between them. She wore an orange tinted lipstick and white eyeliner. Because of the shortage of hair products due to the earthquake, she'd taken to braiding her hair, which Madison thought was a good look for her. But she knew it wouldn't last. Hannah required no less than the most fashionable styles for everything and braided hair just wasn't expensive enough. "Plus half the swimmers are coming. Already got their confirmations online."

Madison smiled but didn't know what to say. She didn't care about their stupid party. Why were they telling her about it?

"The swimmers will probably stick to the pool but everybody else will want a seat in the hot tub. I'll save one for you," Carolyn said. "I usually save it for Jillian but I'm done with her. I can't wait to tell everyone about what happened." And she casually left, bobbing up and down toward the water. Half of the class was there. They all said thanks to her with huge smiles beaming under their hundred dollar sunglasses.

Madison looked down at her phone in disbelief. She typed in, "Did I just get invited to Carolyn Kaplan's party?"

In tidy green letters on a black background it responded simply, "Yes."

She stayed on the beach until dusk. The moon glowed in the sky like a thin crescent as the sun tucked under the horizon. Madison wondered if she'd get a day or even an hour to explore Costa Rica with its forests filled with monkeys howling into the night and insects the size of her head. She assumed that this would be the crowning memory of the place, standing on a darkened beach watching the stars pop into existence as the light meandered lazily away. It was a clear night though the moon crowded out its neighboring stars. She knew this was the memory she'd keep closest. It matched her fantasies of her father, sitting up at the edge of the Caspian Sea sipping goat's milk and missing her back.

Chapter 5

Madison barely got to enjoy Costa Rica before she was on a plane back to Maryland. She wanted to help with the earthquake relief efforts but the doctors wouldn't let her out of the hospital long enough to do it, even though her leg felt fine. Well, not fine, she had to admit, but good enough that she didn't need crutches to walk. Her mom preferred her back in the US as soon as possible even though the rest of the class got to stay and play in the sand.

Her flight landed on a dreary spring afternoon in the midst of a thunder storm. The turbulence was brutal, tossing her around in her seat, making her feel weightless and then crashing down with a thud. She'd been through worse when she was ten as a passenger on a C-23 cargo plane which felt as though it would fall from the sky at any moment. The soldiers had given everyone parachutes and a crash course on using them just in case. There was only a very small chance that they would have to ditch the plane but they were still worried about it. They didn't have a parachute in Madison's size so she was strapped to the front of one of the rangers for the duration of the flight with two ton ratchet straps.

This time, her mom picked her up from the airport right away. They didn't even have to wait at baggage claim because Madison's baggage was long gone, lost in the Costa Rican airport. Mrs. Riley was a short woman with keen eyes that always seemed to be flitting about the horizon, noticing something that no one else noticed. She wore her hair in a frizzy ball on top of her head, held up by bobby pins and pencils.

"I was so worried about you," her mom said in the bellicose nasal tone she used only when Madison had really screwed up. "When I heard about the earthquake and realized it happened right when your plane landed I called everyone I know." She sounded exasperated, completely out of breath. "I called my friends at the Pentagon, at NORAD. The OSD doesn't have great intelligence compared with my office but it didn't hurt trying."

They drove in the cold rain along the Washington DC beltway. The traffic lumbered along the wet road. Dim red tail lights from the cars ahead dotted the horizon, not moving an inch. They would be stuck in that car for a while.

"Mom, I can take care of myself," Madison said. "I was fine."

Her mom shook her head. "Madison Riley, I don't want you to take care of yourself. Mr. Dipson told me about how you ran around with that hole in your leg. You could've bled to death. Do you realize that? I just took a weekend class at the CIA and they said that the first thing you do when you've treated an injury is to find shelter and water."

Madison didn't say anything. She wouldn't have done it

if Graham hadn't been there. She trusted him. How could she afford not to?

"Can I take a class at the CIA?" Madison asked.

Her mom shrugged. "I don't know, Madison. I'll look into it." She wiped some condensation from the windshield. "Are you supposed to turn on the heat or the air conditioning when it gets foggy inside the car?" she asked.

"Turn on both, Mom," Madison answered.

Her mom did it and the windshield magically cleared up. "You may be a genius, Madison," she said, "but you have to exercise some common sense. Do you think I would have gotten this job at the NSA, the most advanced agency in this nation's government, if I didn't have any common sense?" She laughed. "And I still had things to learn. They teach us what to do if we're kidnapped, if we're drugged. Maybe I should get you into one of those classes. Maybe you need some survival training."

Madison took a deep breath and turned off the air conditioning. "I'm not a genius, Mom," she said.

"You're just like your father," her mom said, halting abruptly after she'd said it like a news anchor who'd just cussed on live TV. "Even when I ask you not to be, you're still a hero."

Madison sat up in her seat even though her wound ignited with pain when she did it. She spoke louder than she meant to. "It's easy to tell me not to be a hero but when it actually happened to me I couldn't help it. Maybe I finally understand what Dad was thinking now that I've been in that situation."

"Madison!" her mother yelled. "You were not in that situation!" Her eyes were red like she was about to cry.

They made it home without saying anything more. Madison went up to her room and got on her computer to check if any of her friends were online. They weren't. Of course not. They were always too busy playing video games or making art to be online.

She grabbed the phone that Graham had given her and wondered if she could actually call out. She dialed her friend Mia.

Mia picked up. "*Hola*. Who is this?" she asked. She had a fantastic lisp that turned all her *esses* into long, beautiful hissing sounds.

"Mads," Madison answered. "I got a new phone. Save this number."

Mia screamed out loud. "Mads!" She was barely understandable. "You got home! What happened over there? You have to tell me everything. Don't leave out a single detail. Send me pictures." Her accent had gotten better but she still rolled her *r*'s and pronounced her *i*'s like double *e*'s.

"Come over and I'll tell you about it," Madison said. "We can have a sleepover."

"It's Wednesday," Mia said. "But if I could I'd sleep over with you every night, Mads. I wish we were sisters and we could braid each other's hair and make omelets together. But I bet it's better that we don't hang out on weekdays because my sisters get on my nerves—"

Madison laughed at that. As if Mia ever had any trouble holding up her end of any conversation, even if she was accidentally insulting someone. Madison hadn't even realized it was only Wednesday. It had only been five days since the earthquake. It felt like months.

"Just come over," she told Mia. "Bring Danny. I need to

see you guys."

It felt like forever before Mia came to the door. She burst through in a bright yellow top and plaid skirt and yelled, "Mads!" She scurried up the stairs. Her olive skin shone brightly with a sheen of sweat. She'd run full speed to Madison's house. "I love you, Mads!" she screamed before she hit Madison's door. "Danny's coming but he said he had to finish some homework first!"

She jumped right onto Madison's bed like there was a hockey player to cross check against. "I'm so sorry about your leg!" she screamed. Her hair had been held back in a tight pony tail but she'd run so fast that hairs pulled out and frizzed out into a halo over her head. She was a ball of energy in every way, from the quickness with which she spoke to the roundness of every one of her features. She was even shorter than Mrs. Riley but twice as wide and three times as excitable. Her fingers were covered with charcoal, like always, from her constant sketching. She covered Madison's sheets with grey but neither of them cared.

Madison hugged her close. "I missed you, Mia," she said. "It was such a strange trip."

Mia undid her pony tail and her hair fell down over her shoulders. "So the other day I was at the library and Arlo Henderson was there with UFC shorts and a full-sized steel chain around his neck. Where do the nerds have left?" She giggled. "I heard you saved Patrick Sutton's life. You know that means he owes you his life. I think that's an Irish thing. Or maybe that's a pot of gold."

"He's not a leprechaun," Madison laughed.

"He came home too, you know," Mia said. "Josh Ratzinger saw him last night. His leg was really broken. He said that Patrick said that you pulled the bone back into his leg. One of the doctors told him if you didn't do that…" She came in really close and looked Madison square in the eye. "They might have amputated his leg," she whispered.

"Wow," said Madison. "That's crazy."

"He's so cute."

"I know," Madison laughed.

Mia kept talking. "I heard his lips caused a pile up on the beltway. There was a lady who they thought was texting while driving but really she took a picture of him. I'm not kidding. I'll send you the link. Someone brought the picture to court as evidence. It was on the news. I mean, if you saw him for the first time, could you look away?"

Madison laughed, and Mia continued on, pulling her sketchbook from her bag. She talked about how lucky Madison was to have gotten to know Patrick as she poked at a drawing. She muttered to herself from time to time in Portuguese. She was the only one in the school who spoke it save for the few phrases that Madison had picked up. The native Spanish speakers made fun of her. They pretended like she was trying to speak Spanish, and didn't know her own language. Madison wanted to tell them how stupid they were to say things like that, but she hadn't. Had there been one more Brazilian at the school they could've stuck together, but not every country could be perfectly represented at Shackleton.

There was a knock. They both heard the front door open and assumed it was Danny. Mrs. Riley yelled up the stairs. "Madison, there's a boy here to see you."

"Mom," Madison said, "just because Danny's a boy it

doesn't mean that he's not allowed up here."

"It's not Dan," yelled Mrs. Riley. "His name's Patrick. He's on crutches."

Madison and Mia stared at each other with big puppy eyes. "This is happening," Mia said. "You saved his life, Mads! It's like that nurse all the patients loved. You're Florence Nightingale."

They ran down the stairs but stopped midway to try to look cool. Patrick smiled up at them.

"Hey Maddy," he said shyly, looking frail on his crutches though he still had a thick frame and obvious power in his arms.

"Hey Patrick," said Madison. "How are you feeling?"

Patrick avoided her eye. "I don't know. They gave me a bunch of painkillers but it still hurts. It's not bad though. The doctor said it could've been a lot worse." He pulled out his phone. "I've been playing a lot of video games on my phone. I can't do much else. Although the cast they gave me is brilliant. They 3D printed it to fit my leg exactly. I can wear it in the shower and to your friend Carolyn's pool party on Saturday."

Firstly, she barely knew Carolyn but apparently everybody thought they were friends. Second, the cast was pretty impressive, a plastic mesh over his legs with holes in it to let air move through but still sturdy enough to keep his leg stiff. Madison laughed anxiously then got mad at herself for laughing. She couldn't think of anything to say so she asked, "What games are you playing?"

"*StarX*," he answered. Madison just shook her head. He handed her the phone. "It's the best game out there." Then he launched into a stumbling explanation of a game that was obviously far too complicated to explain in a single conversation.

"You talk to the phone and it turns you into a plebe, which is basically a computerized version of you, except it doesn't look like you. If you want it can look like you but it doesn't have to. It takes video of you and it records your voice. Then other people can see you and talk to you in their games even though you're not there. They talk to the recording. Except it's not a recording. It's like a 3D character that does stuff. Plebe is the lowest level. If enough people like your work you become an extra and then a C-lister and eventually a star."

Madison was confused but she pretended to understand. She studied the screen. It was like a cross between a video game and a Hollywood movie. Mia pulled out her phone and showed Madison.

"I have it too," Mia said proudly. "I've done a lot of work on my plebe. I've recorded over thirty hours of audio and she has over two hundred emotional states." She turned to Patrick and exploded with glee. "Will you be friends with me so I can see your plebe in my game?"

He smiled. "Sure," he said. "I really want people to see my work. I'm working on my in-camera performances. I already have two thousand fans."

Mia's mouth opened wide. "Oh my god!" she shouted. "I can't believe that! You must be so talented." She turned her phone around so that Patrick could see it. "I only have thirty-three fans."

Madison handed Patrick his phone and he swiped his finger across it quickly. "Thirty-four," he said with a smile.

It took all of Mia's self control to keep from screaming out loud. "Thank you," she said.

Patrick nodded at Madison and asked, "Let me see your

phone. I'll download it for you."

Madison's real phone was upstairs in a drawer in her room. She hadn't touched it since she got the new phone from Graham. She looked down in horror because the phone that Graham had given her was sitting there in her hand. She couldn't tell him no. She couldn't help it but she handed it over.

He scanned it for a second before he turned it on. The square screen was unique, the rounded back thicker than most. If someone didn't know better they'd think it was just an old relic. "I've never seen this phone before," he said. "What kind is it?"

Madison shrugged. "I don't know," she said.

Patrick poked at the phone, not quite sure what to make of it. He just kept looking for something that he'd recognize from other phones but he drew a blank. "Where's the store?" he asked. "I mean, this looks like a regular mobile but there's no place to download apps."

Again, Madison looked for some way to make this make sense. "My mom works for the National Security Agency," she said, trying hard to come up with some clever cover. "We need extra security."

"Do you mean that someone might be watching you?" Patrick looked stunned. "Blimey," he said. "You just blew my mind."

Just then Danny ran through the door but stopped dead as soon as he saw Patrick there. Danny's floppy hair was soaking wet and it fell over his eyes. Though he wasn't quite at the point where he was willing to wear eye shadow, he wore almost exclusively black. His outfit consisted of black shoes, a black hoodie over a black t-shirt and a pair of the most ill-fitting jeans on the planet. He said something under his breath. Madison couldn't quite hear but she thought for sure he said the Japanese word for "Oh no." He looked stunned, barely balanced on his skinny legs. "Hi," he said timidly, like he was late to class.

Danny always looked both confused and insightful at the same time. Like a dog that wants a treat and can't understand why he hasn't been given one, Danny's head would tilt to the side occasionally and his mouth would open as if ready to taste any latent information in the air. Madison often related Danny to a sponge, every bit of him always ready to soak up the world wholesale, even the bits no one else wanted. That might have been how he'd learned English so quickly although he'd retained some habits of speech from his Japanese upbringing. His most consistent error was to call people friend. Madison liked that about him. Too many people at Shackleton seemed to think that they were too good even to admit to having any friends at all lest they be pinned down to belonging to one social group over another. Instead, it all seemed to boil down to a constant process of mingling without anyone ever admitting to being lonely. They were all friends online, but that was the only context where it was appropriate to refer to people as such. Danny never seemed to realize that and Madison hoped he never would.

They were all silent for a second. Then Mia out of nowhere said, "Patrick has two thousand fans on *StarX*."

Dan nodded coldly. "Of course he does," he said.

"Your name's Dan, right?" Patrick said. "Dan Kai?"

"That's right. We've had English together for the last six months." Then he put his hand out to shake Patrick's. Patrick stared at it for a second and shook it. Danny stood awkwardly in front of Patrick, looking up at the ceiling. Finally he said, "Your hair looks…expensive."

Patrick laughed. "Thanks," he said wryly.

"I heard you almost died," Dan continued. "Way to stay alive."

Patrick looked back to Madison. "It was Maddy. She saved my life."

Both Madison's and Dan's faces went beet red but it was obvious they had very different things on their minds. Danny turned to walk out of the door. He smiled at Patrick and said, "I've seen you in school a lot but I'm glad we finally got to talk." He stood there rocking back and forth for a second and said under his breath, "I've got to let you go. I'm sure you have a lot of mirrors that need your attention," and he walked off, down to the street.

Chapter 6

The road to Carolyn Kaplan's house meandered through forests and a river crossing from the eighteenth century where you actually had to drive through the three-inch deep stream. The road narrowed into a tree lined gorge with perfect lawns etched into the hillside amidst the rhododendrons. The houses shot up once in a while like Roman temples. Each driveway had a gate. The gates popped up out of the brush without signs or mail boxes as if they didn't wish to be seen. Madison had to use her phone just to figure out which house was Carolyn's.

Her mom drove her. None of her friends were invited so she sat in the car looking vacantly out the window. She wore another of her bright floral sun dresses with her bathing suit underneath it. Her eyes lit up under her eye liner and her lips shimmered underneath them. She liked for her makeup to be tasteful, but also worthy of notice. A little shimmer, tastefully executed, was the best accent that Madison had to offer.

"Be careful tonight," her mom told her.

Madison nodded. "I'll call you if there's any problem."

And she got out to ring the buzzer at the gate.

Carolyn's voice came over the intercom. "Yes? Do you know the password?"

Madison panicked. She thought maybe this was all just a prank. Maybe she wasn't actually invited. She thought of pulling out Graham's phone to ask it for the password but instead she just said, "It's Madison."

"That's the password!" Carolyn shouted. The intercom clicked off and the gate opened before her. She walked slowly up the winding driveway toward the warm yellow lights ahead.

Madison wasn't sure whether or not to call it a mansion. It was definitely big and impressive but it felt weird to think that someone she knew lived in a mansion. But there were pillars in front of the house and a stained glass window above that. As she got closer it just seemed to get bigger. The door was extra-large and the windows taller than she expected. She could hear laughter and splashes echoing off the hills.

She rang the doorbell. Nothing happened. As she waited her stomach tightened. After a while she felt like she'd just shown up for a pop quiz and forgot to read the book. Maybe there was another secret code she needed to know before she could go inside. Maybe they were still just messing with her. Why was the code word 'Madison?' She almost felt sick.

She'd been good about ignoring the phone. It felt like a gremlin in her purse. It taunted her. Maybe she could just ask it how she should go in and it would tell her. Maybe she could ask it if Carolyn Kaplan would make fun of her. She considered ringing the doorbell again but instead she rifled through her purse for her phone.

Then she heard the door creak. It opened slowly like the

door to a bank vault. Madison half expected a butler behind it but instead it was a sweet-looking woman around her mom's age. Her wet hair fell on her slender shoulders and even down to her bikini top.

"Mrs. Kaplan?" Madison said unsurely. She almost stuck out her hand to greet her but then felt stupid for thinking it.

Mrs. Kaplan nodded with a wide, warm smile. She motioned to the pool. "They're out back," she said. "You can use the bathroom here or the one in the pool house to change." Mrs. Kaplan had a sweet voice. She didn't ask Madison her name. She acted like she recognized her. "You better get out there quick," she said. "They're waiting for you."

Madison said her thanks and went to the bathroom. She felt silly though. She was wearing her swimsuit underneath her dress so she could have just as easily taken her sundress off anywhere, but it embarrassed her to undress like that.

A mirror covered one entire wall of the bathroom. She couldn't help but look at her outfit. She liked her haircut, just past her shoulders and neatly textured. She liked her jaw bones and her tiny mouth. Her eyes always needed work to improve the slightly squinted look she naturally wore. Her one piece swimsuit fit her well without showing off her midriff. It was a good day to take on the popular kids like Carolyn Kaplan. At least she looked the part.

Madison walked slowly out to the pool. The party was smaller than she expected it would be, but she expected girls like Carolyn to throw massive parties where people swung from chandeliers, not quiet outdoor hangouts like this. She was relieved. Madison wasn't the partying type. Steam rose up from the hot tub. The water glowed light blue under the dark sky. She heard Patrick Sutton say something about the muscles in his leg and about next year's soccer season. Madison couldn't tell if he was saying he'd be able to play or he'd never play again. Her heart sank to think that she'd maimed him for life when she set the bone. Jillian Jacobs was noticeably absent.

Hannah Chanel saw her first. "Madison!" she screamed as she jumped out of the hot tub. She ran over full speed and gave her a hug. Soon the rest of the partiers crowded around her so tightly she felt like she couldn't get any air. They all screamed her name and hugged her like she'd just won the Super Bowl.

"I have to follow you on *StarX*," Carolyn said. "When I first met you I figured you'd just have a sweet little nothing plebe. Either that or you'd be like one of those theater nerds who overacts the whole time. But now that I know you I see how intense you are. You know that's how Hollywood actors are. They're quiet on the outside too. I heard Hollywood is re-cruiting people based on their plebes these days. It's the newest thing."

Madison surveyed them with her quiet eyes. "I don't have a plebe," she said.

"What?" asked Arlo Henderson, a six foot tall bundle of blonde testosterone with a perpetually open jaw and a baseball cap. "You must be the last person on Earth who doesn't play."

"It's OK," Carolyn said. She took Madison by the arm and led her to the hot tub. They entered the hot water together. Madison tried not to look like the scalding water hurt. "You're so funny." Carolyn laughed as she took a sip from her lemon-ade. "You're quiet and calm but you pulled our whole class out of that cave." She looked Madison up and down. "And you're so strong."

Patrick waded into the water. His waterproof cast looked robotic but also manly and fierce. "It's like when moms pull their kids out from under a car," he said. "You get super human strength when there's a disaster."

Hannah came close to Madison's other side. "I think Madison's just super," she said quietly with a sibilant ess.

Madison felt like she should say something but had no idea what it would be. She felt uncomfortable speaking English and instead just burst out with, "*Esta es una increíble piscina.*" She got up out of the hot tub uncomfortably and walked across the patio to the pool itself, dipping her toe into its astringent cold.

"*Echale ganas!*" Patrick screamed. He dove right into the pool, cast, bandages and all.

They all laughed and started jumping in, half of them speaking in Spanish. Madison wasn't sure if they were making fun of her linguistic ability. Maybe she sounded stuck up. This could all be a put-on to make her look stupid. Everyone at school knew that Carolyn was a back stabber. In eighth grade she told everyone that Todd Simpson had asked her to the semi-formal but she ended up going with Aaron Burger instead. No girl spoke to Todd Simpson for a year after that. She once told everyone that her then best friend Donna Epstein had webbed feet. Donna cried when Jimmy Dougherty pulled her socks off during gym class and showed the world that she really did. Carolyn did that to her best friend.

Someone started a game of Marco Polo in the pool. At first it moved a little too quickly. The 'Marco' with their eyes closed would say "Marco" and then as soon as anyone said "Polo" the 'Marco' would lunge and tag them out. Each game lasted all of two minutes.

Madison hid in the corner of the pool the entire time. Staying quiet and out of the way was her specialty. It was fifteen rounds before anyone even got close.

The game ramped up quickly. People started ducking under the water to avoid saying 'polo' as much as possible. They started mimicking Madison's techniques. After one particularly difficult round, Hannah clicked her tongue and huffed. She said, "Maddy Riley, you are a shark!" This time she emphasized the *k* in shark. Her voice just sounded sarcastic all the time, regardless of who she spoke to. She then groaned with a flamboyant, throaty groan, rolled her eyes and flopped her head back in the water. Madison figured she was just looking for attention. It seemed to work. Arlo Henderson swam over to her to make sure she was alright.

It was Carolyn's turn. She counted to ten while everybody scattered. It seemed to Madison that everyone was hiding behind her. Wherever she went there was someone in the way. She wasn't sure if they were all conspiring together or if they'd just stolen her technique, but she didn't like it. Carolyn inched closer.

"Marco," she said.

Madison responded quietly, "Polo."

Just then, Patrick surfaced next to her. He gasped for breath. Carolyn lunged at them full speed with both arms outstretched.

Madison was tagged out. She saw Carolyn's hand lingering on Patrick's strong chest. He always looked so sure of himself.

"I guess we're both it," he said.

"Back to back!" someone shouted.

"I don't know about that," Patrick said. "How can we lunge at people if we're back to back? We'd just push away from each other."

Carolyn Kaplan's eyes lit up. "Front to front then," she said. "Madison, face Patrick and put your arms underneath his."

Everybody laughed. Again, were they taunting her or were they just having fun?

Patrick nodded. "OK," he said. He turned to Madison and smiled. He tilted his head down and whispered in her ear. "Just hold on to me." He held up his arms. She slowly hugged onto him, careful not to get too close to his chest. It was like they were dancing, her chin on his shoulder. He pulled her in closer. "You gotta stay close to me," he warned. "Otherwise we won't know which way the other is moving."

She felt his heartbeat through her chest. Suddenly he started counting. Madison quickly closed her eyes and shivered with excitement. He held her up as they swam together, their legs bumping up against one another from time to time. She worried that his broken leg might not be able to swim but he didn't seem to mind. His good leg must have been so strong from all of those days on the field.

Patrick reached ten. He lunged forward toward Madison and she pulled backward. Her own wound hurt a bit, but not so much that she couldn't swim. They split the duty of saying "Marco" between them. Madison tried hard not to yell too loudly in his ear.

She'd never been so close to any boy in her life, let alone the hottest in school. Just feeling his breath against her neck was enough to send her into the stratosphere. They listened together for the subtle splashes nearby. Every so often Patrick lunged this way or that. Madison felt like she was just along for the ride.

Then Madison heard the huffy breathing of Hannah Chanel just in front of her. She pushed against Patrick subtly with her chest. He must have heard it too because he pushed backward with all of his might. Madison felt her hand graze past someone. It must have been Hannah. All three of their bodies, Madison's, Patrick's and Hannah's, collided with each other and tumbled backwards, crashing together against the hard concrete around the edge of the pool. Madison's arm was scratched from her wrist to her elbow. Patrick had the wind knocked out of him.

Madison opened her eyes. Hannah was there, bleeding from the head. Already there was a rush of people swimming toward her. Arlo Henderson was out of the pool, pulling Hannah up onto the patio in one quick motion. Madison and Patrick just watched, slowly making their way out of the pool with their respective gimpy legs slowing them down.

Everyone immediately went to their phones to call for an ambulance. Madison grabbed hers as well but wasn't sure what to do. She just asked it the most obvious question. "What should I do?" she typed.

She never expected the answer it gave her.

Hannah bled profusely on the patio. Everyone gasped and crowded around her. On Madison's phone the following instructions were written:

1. Go inside to the bathroom and grab the bottle of hydrogen peroxide from under the sink. Grab two

white towels from the towel rack. Run to the freezer and grab the two black ice packs. Bring them outside.

2. Pour the hydrogen peroxide over one white towel and over the wound on Hannah's head located just over her left ear. Place that towel on Hannah's wound and apply pressure. Place the other towel beneath her head. Place the ice packs on her forehead.

3. Tell Carolyn to talk to Hannah and ask her questions to make sure she doesn't fall asleep.

4. Stand up and step between Arlo and Patrick. When Arlo tries to push you out of the way, step back. He will stumble. Stomp on his foot and push him into the pool.

5. Kiss Patrick.

At first Madison couldn't believe what she was seeing. She expected it to give her a few instructions but the list just kept on going. There were numbers six, seven, eight and nine, seemingly on into infinity but she couldn't even think of anything past "Kiss Patrick." She looked up. Hannah's head dripped red blood.

Madison raced inside. She grabbed the hydrogen peroxide and the towels. She grabbed the ice packs. She ran back and attended to Hannah's wounds. Normally she'd be intimidated to speak to Carolyn but in this crisis she forgot about her inhibitions and almost bowled her over with unexpected power. "Carolyn!" She yelled. Carolyn stared at Hannah blankly. "Carolyn," Madison said again, more forcefully. "I think Hannah has a concussion. You need to keep asking her questions so that she doesn't fall asleep. The ice packs will help make sure her brain doesn't swell up. Just keep her awake."

Carolyn set to work immediately doing what she did best. She started talking as fast as she could. She started asking questions faster than Hannah could answer. Madison finished dressing the wound just as the phone had instructed. When Carolyn put her hand over the towel to apply pressure, Madison got up and looked back toward Patrick.

Arlo stomped furiously toward Patrick. "You gimp idiot!" He lunged forward. Patrick didn't flinch in the least.

Madison ran between them just like the phone had told her. She screamed out, "Don't fight!"

Arlo lunged at her to push her out of the way. She stepped back, more out of reflex than out of anything the phone had told her to do. Then she realized what was happening. She realized that she was doing exactly what it said. Arlo was off balance, so she took the opportunity to stomp on his foot. He screamed out in pain and stooped down to massage it. It just seemed like the most obvious thing in the world that she should push him into the pool.

Arlo flailed his arms as he fell. Everybody stared in awe at what just happened. Little Madison Riley beat rough neck Arlo Henderson in a fight. And she'd done it right after she saved Hannah's life for a second time.

Step number five came without her even having to think about it. Patrick came up from behind her and grabbed her in his arms. He turned her around to face him, pulled her up to his chest, closed his eyes and kissed her gently. The feeling of saving lives in the airport was nothing compared to this.

Chapter 7

The sprawling campus of Shackleton High looked even more manicured and pristine than Madison remembered with its bright white buildings, each in its own architectural style, its blooming azaleas in all different shades of pinks and reds, and its green grass lawns. Madison sat in the back of the bus glaring at the school out of the corner of her eye. Monday morning came all too soon after Saturday's party. Sunday passed by in a blur.

On the bus, she had listened to the rhythm of the wheels beneath her as they hummed and drummed in what sounded like a random assortment of noises. But as she listened closer and remembered Graham's advice, the sounds became something very different. First, there was the beat. If the front tires hit a bump then the back tires would hit the same bump a moment after. It gave the bus an irregular pulse like a monster still acclimating to its freshly implanted heart. Then there was the hum. It changed in pitch depending on the speed of the bus and the surface it drove on. The gravelly cinders of Hackamore Street were a different song entirely from the concrete bridges of I-95. It wasn't a music you could dance to or even one you'd choose to listen to over the willowy vocals of whatever indie band that the hipsters were into, but if you listened closely enough and for long enough you would know every stretch of pavement by the sound it made and you'd never be lost along the way. Like sharks swimming, it was a language she'd never heard before and the better she listened, the better she understood.

The party had ended with an ambulance in the driveway and a lot of silence. Patrick held her close while it all happened. Then her mom came and yanked her away.

But did Patrick actually like her? She wasn't sure. It seemed like all bets were off when the school day started. The entire world changed once predators like Carolyn Kaplan and Jillian Jacobs collided. They had been good friends, or at least everyone assumed they were good friends. Nobody quite knew if they were just waiting until the upcoming semiformal to pull the rug out from the other.

More important, probably, was the phone in her pocket. Graham had said people wanted it. What would they do to get it? Was she safe, even at school? She could ask it any question, but could she trust it to give the right answer?

Madison grabbed her backpack from under the seat and heaved it over her head and onto her shoulders before skulking off of the bus towards the school. She walked slowly up the tall set of stairs into the main foyer trying not to make eye contact with anyone for fear that it might be Jillian. Everyone knew Jillian had her eye out for Patrick and now they all knew Mads kissed him two nights before.

There were three sets of glazed double doors in the main

building, white with dark wood. A row of high windows poured light into the tall, dark wooden foyer. The doors to the auditorium were on the right. The band kids and the theater kids hung out there in the mornings. It was where she felt the most secure, mostly because it was where Mia and Dan would invariably be huddled together in the corner looking at their phones.

Madison came up to them slowly. They only noticed her when she was on top of them. "I need to talk to you two," she declared anxiously. "So much has happened."

"Hold on," Dan said, not looking up from his phone. He made funny faces at it, his lips contorted into an awkward curve. Madison again watched as he played. The digital people on the screen looked like Hollywood actors in that they were too beautiful to be real. Often, they would converse directly with Danny like a video chat, although Madison couldn't hear what they said through the headphones. Danny would answer them with more emotion than he usually had in his slightly demure voice. Once in a while he'd fight what appeared to be a zombie, although it seemed that Danny was the sort who would mostly run away from them, miming being out of breath. Sometimes, when he had enough room to stretch his legs he'd quite literally turn and run, still with the screen in front of him. He looked ridiculous and Madison was sure that one of these days he'd trip and his precious phone would shatter into a million pieces on the pavement, but that hadn't happened yet. He'd tripped a few times but he somehow always landed upright and ready, like a circus performer. He always looked like he'd meant to do it all along.

He pressed a button on his phone. "Sorry," he said. "I've got three more fans on *StarX*."

Mia laughed. "Does that make four?"

Dan pushed her with his shoulder.

Madison had never looked so serious in her life. Both Mia's and Dan's eyes grew wide, Dan's covered by his curving bangs and Mia's nearly bulging out of their sockets. Madison put her finger to her lips for them to quiet. "You can't tell anybody anything that I'm about to tell you."

They glanced at each other. "Mads," Dan began, "everybody already knows you kissed Patrick. The picture got a hundred comments already. It's on Carolyn Kaplan's page."

Madison eyed his phone. He let it slip out of his hands into hers. There she was for the whole world to see, on her toes with Patrick Sutton's arm around her back. It felt more real seeing it online than it did while she was there. Then she thought about it for a second. Carolyn Kaplan took the time to snap a picture while her best friend was bleeding from the head.

"How was it?" Mia asked. Dan snatched his phone back and started playing his game again.

Madison looked around to make sure that no one was watching. "I can't even describe it," she answered. She shook her head slowly. "The whole night was so strange," she went on. "First of all, Carolyn's house is enormous. I don't know what her parents do but they must be some of the richest people around."

"They're lobbyists," Dan said, not even looking up from his phone.

"Well her mom was really nice," Madison continued. "Everybody was nice. Except Arlo Henderson. He's the reason Patrick kissed me." She leaned in and lowered her voice even further. "I beat him up."

Mia stomped her foot into the ground. "What's gotten into you?" she huffed. "We left you at the airport and everything was normal. Now you're risking your life almost every day. You hate risks. You don't stay out late. You don't listen to loud music. You don't ride the Metro. What made you suddenly turn into a rock star and a jujitsu master rolled into one?"

Madison had to step back. Her face went red and her eyes swelled up. What had she done to make Mia so upset? Dan even looked up from his game to see what was going on.

"She's got a point," Dan said. "When you came here in the beginning of the year you didn't even talk to anyone. You just stayed in the corner and tried not to let anyone see you." He shook his head. "Now you're popular all of the sudden and it's like you're a different person."

Madison rifled through the bottom of her school bag for Graham's phone. It was time to explain. "I know I can trust both of you," she said. "But I just need you to keep this to yourselves no matter what."

Before she could explain everything, the phone rang. She didn't answer it at first. She just saw that the screen said, "Graham" again. She wondered if she should just tell them anyway, even though this was obviously Graham's way of showing her he knew everything about her no matter what she did.

Madison finally answered the phone after letting it ring a few times. She mouthed "Sorry" to Dan and Mia. She tried to sound casual even though part of her was scared to death. "Hey," she said. "How you doing?"

"I'm alright," Graham answered. He sounded more together than he had before. He actually sounded kind of normal. "I'm sorry I had to duck out on our last phone call. I'm a pretty popular guy."

Madison tried to think of some way to ask him about the gunshots without actually mentioning guns. She settled on saying, "It seemed like there was a lot going on when we last talked."

Graham laughed. "Yeah," he said. "About ten or fifteen drug kingpins were trying to kill me for ruining about a half a billion dollars worth of cocaine." He laughed again. "All in a day's work, Mads."

Madison tried to wrap her head around what he was saying. Not only did he save people in the airport, but he also ruined cocaine shipments and got shot at by thugs. Was he a good guy or a bad guy? Why hadn't she turned him in?

"Are you OK?" she asked, trying to hide her anxiety.

He said, "Sure," with a swagger in his voice like a rapper. "That was easy. All variables were accounted for." He cleared his throat and then got terribly serious. "I can't believe you haven't even begun to investigate. Your mom's in danger!"

Madison took a deep breath. She closed her eyes and tried to stay calm. "I have a lot going on in my life," she said.

"Put it on hold," he retorted. "I don't want to have to tell you again."

"I should talk to my mom about this," Madison said.

"If you think that's best," Graham agreed. "But do just a little bit of homework first. One warning—don't ask it anything about what you're going to do. Don't ask it if you'll get hurt. Don't ask it if you'll win the lottery. Don't ask whether your friends and family will die. That's a hundred percent definite no."

"Why?"

"What if you knew you were going to die tomorrow?" Graham asked. "How would you feel?" He waited for an answer but she didn't say anything. "You have to leave room in your life for chance, otherwise you've taken away all the meaning."

Madison spoke through gritted teeth. "OK," she said. "I'll do my homework." She trembled. "I should go. School is starting in a minute."

"Sure," acknowledged Graham. "Be safe and be well. Don't let this interfere with your personal life."

Madison didn't even know where to begin regarding that advice. What planet was he from? How could this not interfere? "Goodbye," she said coldly.

"Bye," Graham said.

Madison hung up the phone. She quickly typed a question into the phone. "Can I trust Graham?" The little green cursor said, "Always." Madison wasn't sure if she could trust that. Graham was the one who'd given her the phone. He could have programmed it to say that.

Mia groaned in Madison's ear. "Here she comes. Why does she always wear her pants so tight? It makes her butt look like a squirrel in a plastic bag. It would be cute if it wasn't trying so bad to bust out."

Madison looked up to see Jillian Jacobs standing in front of her. The tall, blond haired and blue eyed menace of Shackleton, Jillian stood with her legs parted and her hands on her hips. "Where did you come from?" Jillian asked. "I mean, you were nobody. You were nothing. I pitied you enough to write a story for the school paper for you. And now you call me a coward and post a picture of yourself kissing Patrick Sutton online for everybody to see. You were on that trip with me. You saw how much of a connection we had."

Everyone in the foyer stared. She didn't know what to say. "I didn't post the picture," she said.

Jillian took a step closer. "You still kissed Patrick!" she fumed.

Madison stepped forward too. This was the first time she'd ever stepped up to anyone in her life. "He kissed me," she said forcefully. She couldn't believe that such a loud voice came out of her mouth.

"And then you told people I was a coward," she shouted. "You pushed me down to the ground at the airport and told everyone you saved me. What kind of coward does that make you, talking behind my back?"

Madison couldn't think of a comeback. She knew she didn't push her but no one would believe her if she said so. Then she quickly changed the subject. "I don't talk about you behind your back. I've never talked about you at all."

Jillian shot the meanest eyes at Madison. Something like a growl or a purr came from her flared nostrils. They stood there face to face. Mia and Dan watched in amazement. Jillian looked over to them and smiled. "I like how your friends are coming to your rescue," she said coldly. "I guess it's the same for you as it is for me. You just can't trust anyone. Not even the people who say they care."

Jillian huffed and spun around. She knew everyone was watching so she smiled proudly. "Madison Riley just made history," she told no one in particular. "She beat me in an argument." Everyone was stunned by how loudly Jillian spoke. Morning light poured through the foyer doors onto Jillian's blond hair. She was so practiced at this she'd even figured out how to find the right lighting. She stared ahead and stuck out her chin. "And to think, a week ago no one even knew she existed. We've got a new baller in town, everyone. Meet Madison Riley. The most popular girl no one's ever heard of. You'll all read about her in my column tomorrow. Don't miss it."

Chapter 8

Enchiridion de la Chica
Madison Riley – Hero
By Jillian H. Jacobs

By now all of you've all heard about our resident hero, Madison Riley but you probably only know three things about her. You know she saved Hannah Chanel's life at a party this Saturday night. You know she saved our class from certain death in Costa Rica. And most of you know that five years ago her father died defending our country in Afghanistan. That's probably it. She's the hero daughter of the greatest hero Culver, Maryland has ever seen. But what else do you know?

Even her best friends feel like she holds back. A post written by her best friend, Freshman Mia Castillo says, "Mads made cake. I dnt no y. ynk."[sic] It's because that's the anniversary of her father's death.

Likewise her friend Dan Kai writes, "I've never heard her talk about her other friends but I know she's got more in her life than just me and Mia. I figure she's got a boyfriend from her old school she keeps in touch with. I asked her where she went on Monday nights and she said, 'It's personal.'"

Just what personal business Ms. Riley tends to on Monday nights is a secret that no one knows but Madison. One thing we do know is that there's quite a lot of her life that she considers "personal." When asked for an interview Riley gave scant information. She only divulged that she constantly looks at a picture of her deceased father in moments of strife. She said she needs to in order to do the heroic things she does.

Of Lieutenant Samuel Riley, Madison's father and a Culver native, news reports show a man of honor and distinction. A veteran of two tours in Afghanistan, Lt. Riley is credited for saving an entire town from an insurgent attack in December 2009. During that skirmish he suffered multiple grazing gunshot wounds but continued to fight to save the innocent women and children of the village, all of whom survived with only minor injuries. Lt. Riley's full military record is not a matter of public record, however. The naval archive office said the file was not available, but did not give a reason.

The title "Navy Seal" has never been used to describe Lt. Riley in any documents regarding his service, but his service may still be classified. The photo above, discovered on an online photo sharing site, shows Lt. Riley just weeks before his death in August 2013. A patch on his arm clearly shows the insignia for the United States Naval Special Warfare Development Group (NSWDG), a highly selective wing of the US Navy.

We do know that Lt. Riley's death was both tragic and heroic. According to an article about his service published in the

Washington Post, Lt. Riley died during an insurgent offensive that included heavy mortar and small arms fire near Kandahar, Afghanistan. Insurgents attacked a small American and British encampment without warning. A car bomb exploded nearby, injuring several officers. Lt. Riley was the first to the scene. He pulled eight soldiers to safety within the compound before getting trapped in a small guard post near the insurgents. He suffered shrapnel wounds and a broken arm but fought against the insurgents for several hours, isolated from the rest of the troops. Lt. Riley is credited with stopping the insurgents single handedly until reinforcements arrived.

That story is more than heroic. It's awe inspiring. No one I have ever met in my life is more of a hero than Lt. Sam Riley. Madison has had to deal with the death of her father every day. Without giving it a second thought, she risked her life to crawl into a hole in the ground the same way her father risked his life to save his fellow officers.

Then, as soon as she made it back to the US she had to contend with another life and death situation at a party at Carolyn Kaplan's house. A freak accident left Hannah Chanel with a concussion and blood pouring from her head. While everyone else stared at Hannah, Madison administered expert first aid. Dr. Henry Jacobs, the emergency room physician who treated Hannah's injuries said of her concussion, "She could have died or suffered brain damage from the swelling if Madison hadn't thought fast enough to grab ice packs from the freezer and place them on Hannah's head." According to Dr. Jacobs, concussions of this sort are one of the most common causes of neurological issues in the lives of American teens. Hannah was lucky to have someone so cool under pressure in her presence that night.

Did you know that Madison speaks five languages? Did you know that she's lived in twelve different countries on three different continents? Did you know she was the fastest freshman cross country runner we've had in the last seven years? Did you know that she was the captain of her state champion lacrosse team at her middle school in Mississippi?

You didn't know that because you didn't ask.

Madison posted the following comment regarding a picture she posted on her first day at Shackleton. It was a picture of the front steps of our school, American flag in the foreground proudly waving. She wrote, "My new school. I guess this is where I belong but I don't know how to blend in. Everybody looks like a movie star. Not another Navy brat in sight. I've got nothing to say to them. How did you always make it look so easy? I wish I could hear your voice again. People just listened to you even when you didn't talk." That was written on August 28th, the fifth anniversary of Lt. Riley's death.

Ever since Madison came to Shackleton this fall we chose to ignore her instead of reaching out to her. I for one feel ashamed of that. It took Madison Riley saving my life before I realized how cynical we all are. Why can't we get over our petty differences and actually make friends with people who may be a little quieter? Maybe being quiet is the truest strength.

Madison Riley is a hero. She saved my life. She saved my whole class. She deserves to be the most popular girl at this school. Get to know her. Listen even when she isn't talking.

Jacobs, Jillian H. "Enchiridion de la Chica: Madison Riley - Hero." <u>The Shackleton Post</u> [Culver, MD] 8/28/2018, 3+.

Chapter 9

Madison picked up her copy of *The Shackleton Post* on the Thursday morning it was published. She knew the article would be in there but she didn't realize just how huge it would be on the page. And she didn't realize there would be a giant picture of her dad dead center. As she sat in a quiet corner of the foyer and read, her hands shivered. She'd been angry at people for doing something mean before but she'd never been so angry at someone for doing something so incredibly nice. It was a tremendous article. Jillian wasn't kidding when she said she was headed for Harvard. In a week she'd already done enough research about Madison's dad to know he was a Navy Seal even though the navy had never published the fact. Jillian sounded so compassionate.

It sickened Madison to her stomach.

She didn't want that kind of attention. She just wanted to fit in but not because people felt sorry for her about her dad. And even more importantly, it wasn't her bravery that saved the class in that airport, it was a cell phone given to her by a stranger. She felt so fake.

Then she reflected on it some more. That post she wrote about her dad on her first day of school was a private post. How did Jillian read it? How did she know so much? For a second, Madison wondered if Jillian had a phone just like hers.

She didn't want to confront Jillian about it, but she felt like she had no choice. She just imagined Jillian's wide smile as she brushed aside her long golden hair. Madison wouldn't know what to say. Jillian's words in the article were so kind. She seemed so honest and heartfelt. How could Madison get mad at her about that?

Jillian stood among a group of admirers in the lobby. When they saw Madison coming they parted in half, staring her in the face as she walked right up to Jillian's nose. Madison's face was numb with anticipation. When her mouth opened she was surprised by how mousy and cold her voice sounded. "Jillian," she said.

Jillian smiled and wrapped her arms around Madison. "You jewel!" she gushed. "I'm so glad you've forgiven me for being so awful to you the other day. I really did some soul searching."

Madison sort of hugged back but before long she pushed away. She stepped back and looked around at all the fawning boys, some of them sophomores and juniors and she motioned with her head for Jillian to follow her. "Can I talk to you alone?" she asked meekly.

Jillian nodded silently and pulled her by the arm into the girls' bathroom down the hall. Inside the bathroom there was a tall, lanky girl fixing her hair in the mirror. Jillian tapped her on the shoulder and said, "Get out. We've got business and we need to be alone." The lanky girl just gawked at her at first but when Jillian didn't flinch she walked off in a silent huff.

"Go ahead," Jillian told Madison impatiently.

Madison had no idea what to think. Jillian had been so nice in the hall and now she was mean again. Madison was dumbfounded. "It was a really nice article," she said quietly. She tried to build up her nerve. "But I don't like to be the center of attention, Jillian."

"Are you kidding?" Jillian cackled. "I just made you famous. I just made a green light flash over your head that says 'Like me.'" Jillian grabbed Madison by the shoulders. "Patrick Sutton is chump change compared to some of the boys who were asking me about you. Do you know how lucky you are to be so interesting?"

Madison shook her head. She spoke in a barely audible whisper. "My dad died," she said.

"You know what I mean," Jillian scoffed. She grabbed some makeup from her bag and turned toward the mirror for a touch-up. "I don't know what you're hiding, Maddy, but I know you're hiding something. I just showed you how good I am at investigative reporting. Tell me now and we can save a lot of time."

Madison looked in the mirror too. She compared her slightly bony, slightly neglected face to Jillian's smooth tan. "Why were you so nice to me in the hallway and now you're so mean?"

Jillian seemed absolutely hurt. "I'm matter of fact, Madison. I'm not mean. Deal with it." She tossed her hair to the side. "It's too late for us to be sis and sis but that doesn't mean we can't be hi-bye friends. I'll say hi to you in the hallway and some of my popularity will rub off on you. How does that sound?"

Madison studied Jillian and wondered how she could say two completely contradictory things. Jillian just said she'd gotten the green light to popularity, yet now she was saying that maybe her popularity might rub off on Madison.

They turned and faced each other, sizing each other up. Jillian lunged forward. "How did you know how to set Patrick's bone? Are you a spy? I know your mom works for the NSA and your dad was a Navy Seal. Did the government recruit you to be a super soldier?"

That was probably the most insane thing Madison had ever heard, but then she realized that the truth was even stranger.

Madison wondered how Jillian read her personal post from the first day of school. She was a ratfink. Graham had told her as much.

"One more thing," Jillian said. "You need a plebe on *StarX* and you need to become a fan of mine. Her name's Heather Myers and she's got a score of ninety-one. That's better than anybody at this school." She went back to fixing her makeup. "You're popular now. People have expectations. "

Just then Madison's phone buzzed. It was a text from Graham that said, "I just made you a plebe and made you friends with Jillian. Her name is Belle Camillo-Chang and she has a score of ninety-two. You might as well tell Jillian."

Madison looked up with a polite smile. "Actually," she whispered, "I haven't told anyone, but I do have a plebe." Jillian's eyes darted toward her but she didn't turn her head. Madison continued. "Her name is Belle Camillo-Chang and she has a score of ninety-two." She watched as disgust spread across Jillian's face. "I just added you to my list."

Jillian sneered. "I'll be sure to become a fan," she said. "But if you're going to lie, you should at least be more clever about it. Add more than one point to my score next time. 92 sounds a little too good to be true, doesn't it?"

Madison nodded. "You'll start noticing that about me," she said with a confidence that made her chest tingle. She bounced her phone up and down in her hand. It was just as oddly heavy as it had always been, but also light as a feather.

Chapter 10

Madison sat in her room staring at the phone, wondering whether she should talk to it, type on it or just wait for her life to split apart again so she'd have no choice but to use it. It was time to learn why her mom was in danger.

She knew she was a coward for waiting so long. Her mom's life was on the line and she procrastinated. Even though the phone had told her it wouldn't help to work any faster, she felt guilty.

Her room was sparse. There were a few posters on the walls. A painting of a cat that her best friend in Spain made for her when they were eight. It still looked good. That kid, Raul was his name, had talent. Madison swore he was related to Picasso. The book case in the corner was the resting place for six different languages worth of learn-to-read books, all thrown haphazardly on top of one another. Madison figured there was no way to alphabetize them so she might as well not try. Her Japanese was rusty though, so those books tended to stay on the bottom of the shelf.

Madison's laptop sat on her desk in the corner of her room. She hadn't used it since she'd been back. The actual internet had less appeal now. It felt sad to reach out to people over a computer screen. She wasn't sure why, but having that phone changed her, even though she didn't use it. It made the world seem so much less important.

She felt like going for a run to get ready for lacrosse tryouts Sunday but her leg still hurt. So instead she sat and typed the question over and over again. She knew it was bad to get too much information. She didn't want to ask if her mom would die. She couldn't bear it if it said yes.

She just wrote, "Who wants to hurt my mom?"

It spit out a list at least a hundred long. A hundred people sought to hurt her. Madison didn't recognize any of the names. What if she had? What if it was the next door neighbor or the plumber? What could she have done to help?

She tried again. "Graham is concerned that mom is in trouble. Who does he think is going to hurt her?"

Two names blinked on the screen. It said, "Connor Pike and Orson Crawley."

She didn't recognize those names. She checked back. Those names didn't show up on the previous list of people who wanted to hurt her mom. Madison thought about it for a second and realized that this Pike person must not have known about her mom. He was probably looking for her but hadn't figured out her identity yet. That must be what she was supposed to stop.

Her head hurt. She was scared to death of asking too many questions. Graham had told her again and again that it was a horrible thing to know the future.

"Why does Graham think that Connor Pike will hurt her?" she wrote. This was the only thing she could think to ask.

The square screen zoomed along, text filling the page all the way down. It just kept spitting more green letters on the screen. When it was finished, Madison tried to scroll back up to find the beginning. She kept scrolling. The thing was full of dates and times. It was full of places and names she didn't recognize. The bit that she read was so boring. One line went, "On the 13th of January the Bank Suisse account 8633-89-112229 transferred $89 Million to the Deutsche Bank account 72917-44161-13-166. That same night a check for the same amount was written from the same Deutsche Bank account to the Bank of America account 137-101-235-663593. That account later transferred the same amount to the Fubon Bank account 8383-97-89-79-6887."

How was that significant? Eighty-nine million dollars seemed like a lot of money but Madison couldn't imagine what that had to do with her mom. They certainly weren't that rich. Graham said her mom knew too much. Maybe this Connor Pike stole some money and her mom was hot on the trail.

But she had no idea. This wasn't helping.

"What does Graham want me to do next week at the NSA and how will it save Mom?"

The letters raced across the screen again but this time it said much less.

"Thursday April 27th is 'Take Your Daughter to Work Day.' Graham wants you to go to your mother's office with her. Though you will not be permitted past the visitor's area of the building for most of the visit, you will be given limited access later in the day. Graham wants you to pretend to trip and fall.

He wants you to knock your mother's computer off of her desk and step on it. All of this should look like an accident. Then he would like it if you pick up the broken computer as if trying to fix it. The computer screen will be broken but it will still be functional. Very quickly, as if you're punching random keys, type the following sequence in on the keyboard:

[tab] stockmadisonquenchinvegle [enter] [alt+tab] [alt+f4] [tab] Pike, Connor [enter] [tab] [tab] [dn arrow] [dn arrow] [enter] [shift+tab] x77 [enter] [enter] [enter] [ctrl+alt+del] [rt arrow] [rt arrow] [enter] [enter]

You will need the following items:
HX1-7271 superconducting electromagnet
17-AFF-1899 RFID spoofer capable of 128 bit encryption
Three hollowed out pens
Spring semi-formal outfit

You will need to acquire the following skills:
Counter-interrogation techniques
Lock picking
Map reading

That all looked like jibberish. Too many steps to remember. Too many things she could screw up.

She stood up and paced around the room bobbing her head as she went, mumbling to herself, stomping her feet. She watched her feet move underneath her, the carpet under her feet had barely been worn in. She'd only moved in six months before so the new carpet still sprang back with every step. She took up a fighting stance and punched the air in front of her, imagining this Connor Pike as a punching bag whose face she could ruin. She didn't actually know what he looked like, but she could imagine. She imagined her fist smashing through the monitor of the computer on her mother's desk after she'd screwed up that code for the fiftieth time and the security guards were bearing down on her with handcuffs.

She caught her reflection in the mirror on her door among the US Navy stickers she'd collected over the years, her face flushed and damp with sweat. On the top of the mirror there was a bumper sticker written in white letters across a black background with one of her dad's favorite slogans—one he'd overused with her to the point where it had lost its meaning. It said, "There's no place like home." But this house didn't feel like her home. She didn't know any place that did anymore.

There was a single photo of her family shoved into the left-hand side of the mirror. She was sitting on an old anchor between her dad and her mom with half of the fleet in the background. Her dad stood next to her in his dress uniform, a proud white suit gleaming with medals. His wide smile was Madison's surest memory of him. But also, she always thought of the caring in his eyes. He always looked as though he knew what she was feeling, even when she tried to hide it. The straight line of his hair, cut tight as always, was almost the same color as the skin beneath. Madison always suspected that he could have grown it out into long wavy locks like her Uncle Ben, but he never did.

Her mom was looking into the distance, past the camera as if there was something nefarious happening a mile away and she had to get all of the details. She was wearing a bright coral colored A-line dress with a matching bow in her hair. She looked beautiful, with just enough intensity to seem focused but not enough to look like she was about to kill someone.

Madison sat between them in the photo. She was seven at the time, in beaded braids, blue dress and saddle shoes. That was the day after her father returned home from his first deployment, after she'd believed for a long time that she'd never see him again. That navy yard half-way across the world was her home. Anywhere they were together, even though it was only for a few months at a time, was home. Her family was the only home she ever had.

She looked over at the phone on the bed. Whatever it was that she needed to do, instead of punching the air she realized that she should start doing it. It was worth it. It was for her family.

Once she got back into investigating the code she puzzled out that the things in [ ] brackets were keys that she needed to push, but it seemed like such an odd code. There was a line about 'Pike, Connor' in there. Maybe this was the code to delete his file, like Graham had said in the airport. The computer had to be broken so that she wouldn't be suspected. It all made sense. The problem was that she didn't know why she had to do it and she didn't want to just ask a question that would give her a five hundred page answer.

She asked the first question that popped into her head. "How does Connor Pike know Daddy?"

The screen blinked its green letters at her again. The letters ran across the screen in another long run of text that didn't say anything interesting. It would have taken her hours to understand it. Instead of reading it all she tried to be more specific. "Did Connor Pike ever meet Daddy?"

"No," it answered.

That was it. For a computer that knew everything it was really unhelpful. The only thing that seemed to work was asking it what Graham wanted her to do. That and yes or no questions, but even those weren't easy.

The doorbell rang. Madison ran down and answered. Her mom wasn't home yet so she was alone in the house. She thought for a moment before she answered. Was she in danger? Could someone be coming for her? She tiptoed down the stairs and tried to judge how big the shadow of the person was against the curtain. Her mom had a gun but it was locked up tight. She could look up the combination to the gun safe on the phone if worst came to worst. She closed her eyes. It was probably no one.

She peeked out past the curtain.

It was Dan, the goofy little guy she'd known for so long. Like always, he wore his headphones around his neck. His eyes were glued to his phone, playing *StarX* for sure. But he looked funny. He squinted and gritted his teeth.

Madison opened the door. He didn't look up. "Are you OK?" she asked.

He blinked for a second and put up his finger to silence her. "I'm working," he said. "This is intense."

"You look like you're in pain," Madison said.

He nodded. "Sometimes you just can't stop yourself when your plebe is on a roll, Mads. Even if it hurts."

She smacked him lightly on his shoulder and he finally put the phone down. She gave him an angry look and he laughed to himself. "Sorry Mads. I know you like eye contact and everything. Your eyes are probably the only ones I've looked at enough to know what color they are."

She laughed, relieved that she didn't need to think about guns anymore. "Stop being weird," she said.

He barged in past her and ran up the stairs. "I saw you have a plebe," he yelled over his shoulder. "Did you cheat?" He was already in her bedroom before she knew what he was talking about. "I thought you would have told me about her."

Madison stood in her own doorway looking at the thin-limbed boy sitting on her bed staring at his phone, rubbing his left temple. "Are you sure you're OK?" she asked again.

He blinked a few times. "I don't know. Sometimes I look at the screen so long it makes my eyes go cross but right now I feel like my head's about to crack open. Maybe it's just allergies. I haven't been playing for that long."

Madison came over and looked down at his screen. "Everyone just got addicted to this game over night."

Danny shrugged. "It's just that good," he said. "It's like acting without the lights and the director. You just look at your phone and pour all your feelings out."

Madison couldn't help but feel sad for that. "I have to tell you something," she said, cautiously. "But you can't tell anyone in the world. Not even Mia."

Danny nodded furiously. She wasn't sure where to start so she just began to blurt. "I know things," she said. "I didn't really make a plebe. I cheated. I'm a cheater. Everybody thinks I'm a hero, Danny, but I'm not." She sat down on the bed next to him with a thud. "They just think that I'm brave because my Dad was brave. I'm not."

She tossed a pillow across the room. It crashed against her book shelf and threw a few old paperbacks to the floor. Danny got up instinctively to put the books back. He picked one up. He ran his finger over the spine. "*Tokage*," he said. It was written both in Japanese and English.

Madison rolled her eyes at him. "I haven't read that in a long time. I don't even know if I could understand it anymore. My Kanji is pretty rusty at this point."

"Mine too," Danny said. "It's amazing how quickly you forget."

"*Obasan*," Madison said. "My grandma gave that book to me to help teach me Japanese." She shrugged. "They say I'm so good at languages but sometimes I can barely speak English. It's all just stories people make up about me because I'm too quiet to tell them to shut up."

Danny came back with the pillow in hand. He stood in front of Madison. He offered his hand in peace, like a cowboy would in a Western. He slowly put it on her shoulder and gave an awkward pat. "You are a hero, Madison," he sounded so sincere. "And a genius."

She shook her head. "What did you want, Danny?"

He took out his phone and held it in front of her limply. "I just thought you could give me some pointers at *StarX*," he said. "You're the best I know."

She winced. She wanted to tell him everything. She wanted to have someone to talk to about all of this but she just couldn't bring herself to do it.

Danny just held the phone out there in front of her, his other hand still on her shoulder. They stayed that way far too long for either of them to feel comfortable. Madison bit her bottom lip. "Not now Danny," she said. "I'll tell you later."

She walked him out the door quietly. She tried not to let

him hear her cry as he walked down the driveway to find the bike he'd left laying on the lawn.

Chapter 11

It was Friday night, a week and a half since Madison made it back from Costa Rica. Less than a week before she had to break into the NSA.

Mia called, just like she always did, with the latest movie they should go see. Madison said, "No Mia." She surprised herself. Even with Mia she usually didn't say no. It was just so much easier to go along with the crowd to see where they took her. This time she felt different. She didn't know what she wanted to do that night but it was important that they do something different.

"We're going out," she said. She tapped her fingers against her desk. Her room felt so small. She had to get outside into the night. She needed a change of pace. "Meet me at the Metro stop," she said. "We're going into the city."

Mia shuddered audibly. "What?" she asked. "My Mom doesn't want me to go into the city, Madison. If we leave now we still won't get back before midnight. This is such a bad idea. I don't even know what we're doing but I know it's a bad idea and I don't want to do it. What are we doing? Are we breaking any laws? Are we staying out past midnight?" Mia spoke faster than her tongue could really move so the words jumbled up. Somehow you could still understand what she said. It was a talent. "What bug crawled in your ear, laid eggs in your brain and started controlling your mind? You're acting crazy."

Madison ignored her. "Call Danny and let him know."

She hung up and sat on her bed looking at her phone. She never could think of anything to do. She could ask the phone. But at the same time she couldn't handle the thought of relying on her phone for something so stupid. But maybe that was the perfect way to use it. Maybe it's better to use it for stupid things like figuring out the most fun Saturday night she could have. It could ruin her life to know her future, but how could it hurt to make it a friend? Madison almost started to think of the phone as a companion, as another person working alongside her. She considered what she could call it. It was more than a phone. It was a thing of immense power. She almost didn't want to do it but she had to. She asked, "What is your name?"

The phone wrote back with a single word answer. "Charlotte."

That was enough for Madison. "Hi Charlotte," Madison whispered. "Nice to meet you."

She picked up the phone and tapped the screen that let her ask it questions. She spoke to it quietly. "Charlotte, what's the most fun thing my friends and I can do in DC tonight?"

Charlotte, the slight computer voice answered in her posh British accent. "Night at the Museum." Madison knew exactly what that meant. It was perfect.

She practically flew out of the door. The Metro train station was only a few blocks from her house. It was a short trip into DC from there, mostly underground. She loved how she entered the train in the suburbs but by the end would be in a bustling city with more to do than could be done.

She got there before either Danny or Mia arrived and stood by the turnstile waiting for them to show up. Madison closed her eyes to invite the music of the place to seep into her, as she had with the airport, feeling the sounds pile atop one another, waiting for them to all come together in chorus with each other. Trains shook the station beneath her feet. The ticket machines sputtered as they spit out change. She could see in her mind's eye the brown and yellow entrance gates open with a swish for each passenger as they slid their ticket through. Slowly the contours of the room began to take shape. The footfalls against the concrete grew louder and more distinct. Madison was ready to take the walk, eyes closed, and see how well she could navigate in the dark. She walked with pride over to the ticket machine, never so excited to take the train in her life. She smoothed out her ten dollar bill and the machine slurped it up. She finally opened her eyes to see how much the trip would cost. She'd have enough to get downtown and enough to get back.

"Oh Mads!" screeched Mia. It echoed against the concrete walls. "Where we going tonight? You never have ideas about where to go. How did you come up with this one? Who we gonna see? Is there food there?" She danced on her toes in excitement.

Madison put her hand on Mia's shoulder to stop her from jumping so much. "Do you have enough money on your Metro card to get to Judiciary Square?" she asked, trying to calm Mia down as much as she could. It was hard though. This was the most excited she'd been in a long time.

Mia ogled her. "Judiciary Square? Why not just go to Gallery Place? Mads, I know this great place that serves these frittatas—"

"Mia!" Madison yelled. "We're going to Judiciary Square and we're not getting frittatas." She smiled widely. "I have something so much better than frittatas planned." Against Madison's better nature, she hugged Mia and they danced around the Metro station in excitement. Mia shrieked with laughter and Madison giggled quietly.

Danny stood by the entrance, staring at them.

"Danny!" Madison screamed. She ran over and grabbed his arm, trying to get him to dance. He limped along with her, his eyes darting to see if anyone watched.

"Judiciary Square!" Mia yelled. "Mads has a plan!"

They heard the train coming so they bolted toward the entrance gates, each with their ticket ready to go. They ran down the stairs to the platform dodging important looking people who wore suits and frowned like it was their job. Mia, Danny and Madison had to work to stay together. Madison ran far ahead, quick enough to walk right through the train doors. They were already closing when Mia came through. Danny just barely squeezed in.

"We made it!" Madison screamed. All of the commuters around her on the train just stared up at her, angry that she'd distracted them from whatever screens they were looking at.

"What's at Judiciary Square?" Danny asked. "I mean, it's too late to see anything on the national mall."

Madison winked. "You'll see, Danny." She giggled again. She never got this excited. She surprised herself with the giddiness of her laugh. She smiled so widely it almost hurt. "Just trust me, Danny. This will be the best night of your life."

There wasn't much to talk about on the crowded subway car. Madison wanted to keep the secret of where they were going. Her eyes wandered across the eyes of the other passengers. A couple of older kids in sparkly dresses spoke to each other. Their obnoxiously loud voices filled the entire subway car. They were talking about sneaking into clubs to dance with college boys.

Madison was sure that, if she had asked, Charlotte could find a way for them to get into the VIP of the most exclusive clubs, be the center of attention for a celebrity's posse. She could beat those girls at their own game, suddenly exploding, not only onto the popular spotlight of Shackleton High but becoming a fixture of DC nightlife. If she wanted to, she could ask Charlotte to help make absolutely certain that she wouldn't get caught. She was already breaking into the NSA. She could probably sneak into a bar, go to an R-rated movie, or even rob a bank.

But she'd have to do it perfectly. Just because Charlotte told her to do something, it didn't mean she'd be able to do it right. This night was a test. It was the perfect first step into the world of absolute freedom.

They arrived at Judiciary Square Station. A kindly voice spoke over the intercom. "Please stand clear of the doors." Madison pushed through the crowd. She grabbed Mia's and Danny's hands. When the doors opened, Madison burst through. She pulled them both along behind her, desperate to make it there on time. "Hurry," she yelled behind her. Both Mia and Danny struggled to keep up.

They ran up the escalator to 4th Street, took a right on D then hooked left at the court of appeals. They skidded through slow moving remnants of the District government. A group of reporters crowded around a fat man.

"Wait!" Danny shouted. He pulled his hand away from Madison's. "Senator Childress is saying something about the Supreme Court. He's from Wisconsin, which is the state where they're trying to outlaw *StarX* for anyone under eighteen—like with retinal scans. He's against it but it's a state law, so the only thing the federal government can do is try to overturn it in the courts."

"Are you kidding me?" Madison gasped. She knew the difference between state and federal government, and she knew that a retinal scan was like a fingerprint, in that everyone's retina was unique, but she hadn't heard anything about Wisconsin passing a law. This was a distraction, and they had to get to where they were going before it closed. Madison grabbed Danny's hand to pull him along. "I can't believe you're more interested in the stupid senator than you are in having the greatest night of your life."

"Yeah…" Mia agreed. "Senators are boring. I'd rather be governor than a senator or a mayor or president because governing sounds more badass than senating and presiding and maying." She giggled to herself. "Representing ain't bad."

"It's about *StarX*!" he shouted. "There's a decision Monday. It's the most important thing to happen to free speech in twenty years!" He groaned and ran back to where the senator was standing.

Mia screamed out after him, *"Eres un chico babosa!"*

Madison laughed. *"Babosa!"* She jogged toward him and

whispered in his ear. "That means slimy." Danny rolled his eyes. He motioned that they should listen to the senator.

Senator Childress spoke with authority in a deep, gravelly voice. "This park commemorates John Marshall, one of the greatest Supreme Court justices in American History. I want to send a message that we must follow his lead. We must all stand up as citizens in our support of free speech." He was a tall man with a triple chin and a perfectly tailored suit that gave him the broad shoulders of a football player. "Now I hate *StarX*," he continued. "But my two little girls can't seem to get enough of it. I've tried to pry it out of their hands and they just keep playing. But that doesn't mean that we should take away the rights of our citizens to say and do what they have the right to say and do."

Danny clapped his hands. No one else did. One of the cameras turned to him, its lights flashing in his face. The reporter shoved her microphone in his face. "What's your name, young man?"

Danny stared at her, squinting from the harsh light. "Dan," he said. "Dan Kai...I mean my real name is Denji but people call me Dan."

The reporter smiled at him. "Sally Gershon, Channel Twelve News." She spoke really fast. "Dan, do you think the Wisconsin law is fair? Do you think it should be possible for people your age to play *StarX*, even if it's against the law?"

Madison could see Danny's mind race. There was always something behind his eyes churning toward a smart, delicate answer but most of the time what came out of his mouth was just silly nonsense. She hoped this wouldn't be one of those times.

"Yes," he said finally.

The reporter waited for more. Danny gave her a big "er," and then his mouth made all sorts of shapes before he spoke again. Finally he said, "I think that *StarX* is beautiful and honest. I don't know why anyone would want to take that away from us." Then he went back to his ums and ers.

The reporter said a quick thanks before spinning around to find some congressman or another. Madison grabbed Danny's hand and yanked him away, almost pulling his arm out of its socket. "Let's go!" she yelled again.

Danny was in shock. "I'm gonna be on TV," he said. "I can't believe I'm gonna be on TV."

"Greatest night of your life!" Madison exclaimed. "I'm telling you, Danny!"

They ran across Pennsylvania Avenue, hung a right and arrived. Madison gestured ahead of her with a wide wave of her hand. "We're here," she proclaimed.

The building was wide and white with tall columns and austere doors with no sign to tell you where you were, like many buildings in Washington. There was just a big blue banner that hung between the giant pillars that said, "Klimt."

"Where are we?" Danny asked.

"The National Gallery," Mia answered, she'd been there a million times. She shook her head at Madison. "But they're closing, Mads. We'll barely get in. And the Klimt exhibit isn't even open yet."

"I know," Madison winked. "That's the idea."

Chapter 12

They ran inside. The museum was free but Madison was careful to put a dollar into the donation bin, just to feel good about herself for a moment. Mia did as well. Danny didn't. It was as if he'd never been in a museum before.

She pulled them both into a corner.

"Look," she said, her voice stern, serious and excited all at once. "I have a plan but you have to trust me." They pulled in tight for a huddle. "I was able to get the passcodes to get into the basement of this building." She almost couldn't contain her excitement. "In the basement there are tunnels to each of the Smithsonian Museums. We're going to sneak into the basement to see the Klimt painting because it's Mia's favorite in the whole world." Mia squeezed Madison's hand in thanks. "Then Danny's going to choose his favorite museum and we'll head there, underground, after hours and under cover."

They all stayed silent for a moment. Madison's smile almost reached the corners of her eyes.

"That's so dangerous," Danny said. "I can't believe you'd

even think about doing that. It's wrong."

Madison gave him a playful sneer. "You're the one who just talked about our rights to see things that are beautiful. That's what we're doing. We're using our right to see beautiful things and we're sneaking around to do it."

Madison pulled out her phone, finally ready to show it to them. "I have this," she said. Mia and Danny weren't sure what to make of it. Madison held it as if it was a bomb ready to blow, just to show how important it was. "This looks like an ordinary phone but actually it's the absolute state of the art in spy equipment." She turned it on and fiddled with it for a second. She hid the screen from them and typed, "Show me what's around this wall." It showed her a video of people looking at art around the corner.

They walked through the foyer and turned the first corner. There in front of them were the same people that had been on the video. Mia and Danny were stunned. "Are you kidding me?" Danny said. "Did you steal this from your Mom?"

Madison shook her head. "Maybe," she told him. "I will guarantee you that we won't get caught if we use this."

Danny and Mia looked at each other, breathing through their mouths. "Are you kidding me?" Danny repeated.

Mia asked, "How does it see around corners, Mads?"

Madison shrugged. "I don't know," she answered. She checked the time quickly. The museum really was about to close and the docents were already looking eager to kick people out. "We have to go now," she said.

She started typing into the phone again. She asked it, "How do I get to Klimt's *The Kiss* without being seen?"

Like always, it spit out a huge paragraph of instructions. It was all too complicated for her to follow. She had to think of a better way. She wrote, "Show me arrows on the floor that point to where I need to go to get to the Klimt painting *The Kiss*. Show me text on the screen that says what to do to get there." She figured that was good enough direction for it but she could never be sure with that thing. It so often took her either too literally or gave her too much information.

This time though, it worked. Just like it had at the airport, it showed her the view from the phone's camera except super-imposed on the screen were arrows showing her where to go. She pointed to Mia and Danny. "This way."

They crept along the corridor. Then Madison put up her finger to stop them. "Look," she said. "We're not cartoons. We can just walk normally. Pretend you're supposed to be here. Remember, we haven't broken any rules yet."

Madison pointed to the right, following the arrows on her phone. It was a narrow hallway to the bathrooms. The lights were already dimmed to tell people it was time to leave. At the end of the hall, past the women's room, there was a door with a keypad next to it. Madison held the phone up to the key-pad and it showed a sequence of numbers above it, "53260." Madison typed the numbers in and like magic the door opened. Mia squealed but Madison shushed her. "Come on, Mia," she scolded. "This is serious."

They walked through the door. It was a stairwell with cold fluorescent lighting and steel railings. Madison walked cautiously, careful to point the phone up the stairs and down before she went any further. She worried that she hadn't asked Charlotte to alert her if someone might see, or if there was a camera, or if there was a motion sensor. There were so many things that could go wrong with this plan yet she trusted in the phone enough that they didn't bother her. She let Danny and Mia go ahead down the stairs. She pulled Charlotte out and typed, "If there's any chance that we might get caught, flash a message on the screen to tell me how to get out of it."

Nothing changed on the video she was watching so she assumed that Charlotte understood.

They descended the stairs. A thick metal door stood before them at the bottom of the stairwell. Neither Danny nor Mia would pull it open. They stood there, almost frozen in their confusion. Madison consulted her phone. There was no one on the other side. "Here we go," she said. "I just want to make this perfectly clear. We're all in on this, right? I don't want to force anybody into breaking the rules."

Then she went into the speech that her father had given her once before. "Yes is the most important word in the English language. Never use it lightly. It means that you're taking responsibility for whatever stupid thing you're about to do. If you shrug or nod or say 'yeah' then you'll probably blame someone else for your mistakes instead of learning from them. Experiences are worthless unless you decide to either say yes or no."

Mia immediately said, "Yes. I'm in."

Danny just looked straight ahead. He breathed out slowly. His throat muscles twitched. The dim, strobing stairwell light flickered in his eye. "That's not fair."

Madison felt her heart beating like she'd just run a mile. She felt her fingers tingle and her toes twist. She couldn't wait for Danny. If he wasn't in, he wasn't in. "OK," she said without hesitation. "I understand." She turned to the door and pulled the handle. She was ready to run through. Then she turned back to Danny. "You're a good guy." She smiled. "I'll see you on Monday."

She burst through the door and checked her phone. It showed an arrow pointing to her right telling her to hide behind a row of lockers there. She pulled Mia along with her beside the lockers. Danny must not have come. He must have been hiding somewhere else. She held Mia against the wall, waiting to see what she was supposed to be hiding from. She pointed the phone down the hallway. There was a line of text floating further down the hallway. She zoomed in to see the text. It just counted down from eighteen. Madison showed it to Mia. "I think we should go when it hits zero."

They watched the seconds tick down, not sure what might be coming. It could be a security guard. It could be a museum curator. The numbers ticked down to seven, then to six. Madison couldn't hear any footsteps. She couldn't see anything at all. But she trusted in the phone.

The numbers counted down to zero. Then it said, "Run here."

Madison grabbed Mia's hand and pulled her down the hallway. She heard the squeak of a door behind her and she hid behind the corner, her heart beating out of her chest. Footsteps tapped against the concrete floor. Whoever it was ran toward them at full speed. Madison held close to Mia. They tried not to breathe.

They jumped back and screamed. It was Danny. Madison smacked him in the shoulder. "You!" she screamed. "I almost had a heart attack." She pulled him into the hallway. Charlotte didn't have any more alarms. They were free and clear.

Mia hit him on the shoulder too. "*Bromista!* What's your

problem?" Danny just shrugged.

The arrow pointed down the hallway, through the big metal door at the end. Madison walked with confidence with Mia and Danny cowering behind. She opened the door. It led to a huge warehouse style room with lights dangling from the ceiling. Mia gasped. In all directions were priceless works of art waiting on ceiling high metal shelves like at the hardware store. People scurried around, carefully moving the pieces inches at a time.

Someone saw them but didn't seem to care who they were or what they were doing. Madison decided they should just act like they belonged. There was no alert on Madison's phone. There was no text telling her what to do. She decided just to walk along the arrow's path like it was the most normal thing. She turned back to Mia and said with a wink, "I'm so excited to see it," she said. "I'm so glad my mom got us in here to see this painting."

Mia tried to play along. "Me too," she said, as they walked past workers in coveralls next to men in expensive suits.

"I don't know much about Klimt," Madison continued. She was just trying to seem normal. "He was a painter, right? I know he's your favorite."

Mia nodded. "He used real gold in his paintings," she said. "I tried to copy *The Kiss* in art class. It's made of circles and lines and it's really complicated. It took so long to try to paint it." She tried to sound more confident. "It's a picture of a man and a woman. He's standing, she's kneeling. She's in his arms and they're both covered by this gold blanket. You can't even see the man's face, just the top of his head. And he's kissing her on the cheek. It's sweet and bright and beautiful."

"One of his paintings sold for a hundred thirty-five million dollars," Danny said. "And it wasn't as popular as this one."

And then Madison stopped. They'd reached the end of the arrow. Right in front of them, fifteen feet up, this giant square, bright gold canvas was being pulled out of an even bigger crate. Ten people surrounded it. A small crane strapped around the bottom and held it in midair. The beeps of a truck backing up ripped through the air as the painting descended right before their eyes onto a push cart. The people slowly grabbed hold as the painting lowered. They guided it gently onto the push cart. The gold leaf glittered in the dim light of the underground warehouse.

Madison realized her mouth was open. She looked to Mia, then to Danny, and she grabbed them both by the hand. They drank it in. Just the fact that people were touching it made it feel more real than something stuck on a wall.

"*Oro...*" mused Mia. She extended her arm like she was going to touch it but it was at least ten feet away. "I feel like I should play *StarX* so I can save the look on my face," Mia said, her mouth agape. "I'm never going to feel this way again."

Someone came over to them. Madison knew they were in trouble so she grabbed Charlotte like a security blanket. Her phone gave her a little script of what to say next. She quickly memorized it and the words just came out of her mouth. She looked up at the tall man in the suit and she said, "Hi. You must be Roger."

The man smiled. He looked down to see if he had a nametag. He wasn't wearing one. "Who are you with?" he asked.

Madison smiled again, feeling incredibly calm. So far, the phone had never steered her wrong. "Heidi Schlegel."

Someone yelled to him and he was distracted. He nodded, satisfied, and walked away. Mia squeezed Madison's hand
again, complete terror on her face. Madison just smiled and
motioned with her head for them to follow.

Chapter 13

They found themselves in another corridor and ran along the arrow's path. "Where are we going?" Danny asked.

"What do you want to see most?" Madison asked back.

As always, he waited to answer. "I don't know…" Just like Madison, Danny usually deferred to Mia when they were deciding what to do. Mia usually knew right away what she wanted to do and was excited to share.

As they ran, Madison noticed the phone's screen flashing. Someone was coming. The arrow told them to take a quick right. They ran full speed without holding back a bit. Madison sprinted, her cross country and lacrosse training propelling her forward. She ran up the stairs as fast as she could, following the arrows, snaking through the deepest bowels of the museum, through store rooms and offices to laboratories and computer rooms. She hit the door at the end of another long hallway and stopped. She didn't even see Danny and Mia behind her. Her heart thumped so hard she could feel it in her ears. Had they been caught?

It was almost thirty seconds before she saw them emerge from around the corner. Madison threw open the door so that it slammed against the wall on the far side, echoing down the hallway. They stopped before stepping through the door.

The room was a dusty, cramped space with lights hanging from chains above long metal tables. There were mounds of electronics piled haphazardly on each of the tables as if to be sorted one at a time, separating the old junk from the priceless electronic artifacts. At the far side was a locked door that wouldn't open. The lock was the kind where you just wave a keycard in front of it to get through. The phone didn't say anything about how to get past it. Madison wondered if there might be some magic piece of technology in that room that could open the door, but finding it would probably be impossible without the phone telling her where it was. She tried to turn the knob but nothing happened. She pushed against it. "What do you think is back there?" Mia asked.

Madison checked the phone again. She looked around for some kind of note about how to open the door but she couldn't find anything. "Look for a vent," Madison told them. The alarm on her phone went off again. Someone was coming. They all hid under one of the tables. They didn't know where the footsteps were coming from and in a way it didn't matter. They just needed to stay quiet and out of the way until the intruder left.

This time it was a security guard, or at least his shoes and creased pant cuffs looked like those of a security guard. He came through the door on the far side of the office and walked casually along. His loud footsteps rang through the room until they hit the carpet and became soft as a lamb's. He pattered along slowly. Was he looking for them? Did he see the camera feeds? Madison didn't know but she was absolutely sure she couldn't move a muscle.

They clung to each other under the table. Mia laid her head on Madison's chest. The security guard walked past them, not even slowing down. When he got to the door, Danny pushed away from Madison. He crawled behind the guard and, absolutely silently, stuck his wallet into the bottom of the door jamb. Madison was surprised by the pride she felt in him for doing it. Sometimes doing things the low-tech way is the best policy. She appreciated that Danny, a born tech head, could see that.

The guard's footsteps kept clicking through the next room. They didn't say a thing until they heard another door open and close. After a few minutes they got up from behind the table and went through the door that Danny had propped open. The room they entered was pitch black and cavernous with an unbearably resonant echo. Madison turned on the lights.

Bright fluorescent tubes covered the entire surface of the ceiling making the room almost as bright as day. The walls had big black star charts on them, yellowed like the pages of a forgotten magazine. There were old style TVs in every corner in absurdly large boxes, some of which towered ten feet tall. Hundreds of metal switches dotted the work stations. Indecipherable text above each switch explained what it was. It was a surprisingly homey room with comfortable furniture next to the hulking computers. Cracked leather rolling chairs were stuffed under each one of the desks. It felt like Madison's great grandma's sewing room, which her grandma hadn't been in since she'd gotten arthritis years ago, and probably hadn't redecorated for twenty years before that.

Everything pointed to what looked like a bizarre twenty

foot tall sculpture like a jagged plastic box, all sorts of angles jutting out of it randomly. There were huge black cables snaking across the awkward shape of the structure. Danny ran right up to a hatch on the side of the thing. He opened it and climbed in, seeming to know exactly what he was doing. Suddenly the whole room came to life. Machines started whirring. Lights started flashing. He howled with excitement, his voice muffled by the walls of the weird little room he'd crawled into.

"What did he do?" Mia asked.

Madison ran up to the blocky sculpture and stuck her head through the hatch into the little room where Danny poked at old style dials and lighted buttons. She was staring at his feet while he towered over her, barely able to see his face from her angle. It was a tiny room with switches and gizmos everywhere. Danny crouched inside, looking through a tiny triangular window. It looked like the stars were behind it. The stars looked real.

"It's the lunar excursion module training simulator," Mia read from a plaque in the corner of the room. "It's the only one in the world."

"OK," Madison said after she pulled herself back out of the hatch and walked over to Mia. "Whatever that is it sounds like fun."

Mia was in awe. "It's an exact replica of the space ship that brought Neil Armstrong to the moon." She covered her mouth with her hand.

Danny jumped out of the simulator and ran over to where Mia and Madison were reading. "Your phone has a million times more power than the computer they used to control this thing," Danny told Madison, picking up reading where Mia had left off. "They were able to go all that way to the moon just by being smart people who planned for ten years to do it." He touched the joystick in front of him. His eyes turned to saucers. "This might be the first video game ever made," he said.

Mia stuck her head up through the hatch. "How do we use it? I bet all those switches work. Can I touch that? It could be infected with a moon virus and if we touch it, it will infect all of humanity and we'll be responsible for the end of life on Earth…" She laughed. "I know there aren't any moon viruses, Danny. Don't roll your eyes at me. It looks like fun."

Madison nodded. "Yeah," she said. "We're landing on the moon."

She fired up her phone. It told her point for point what buttons she had to press and in what order she needed to press them. The old machines shuddered to life. An old computer with a twelve inch circular tape hanging behind glass began to pull data. Like an ancient device found in a tomb that felt their presence and responded with welcome, this thing breathed for them. It became real again.

"You and Mia pilot," Madison told them. "I'll tell you how to steer."

"I got shotgun!" Mia screamed as she pulled herself through the tiny hole.

Danny held Madison by the shoulder and regarded her tightly. She'd never really noticed his eyes before. They were deep and dark. She'd never held his gaze for so long because he'd never asked her a question like this before. "Is this the right thing to do?"

The fact that she had to think about it made Madison pause. They'd snuck into the Smithsonian, gotten through a locked door, hid from security officers and restarted a nearly fifty year old computer that they could easily break. She looked him in the eye and didn't stop looking. Danny was stunned, the hair in his eyes seemed to hang lower than usual. His cheeks fell. His mouth opened. "But it's so much fun, Danny."

"There's a button that says 'Engine Thrust Cont'," Mia yelled from inside of the simulator. "Do you think we'd all blow up if I press it? I think I should press it. There could be jet fuel around here or liquid helium…old computers had mercury in them. There are about a million ways this thing could kill us." She shrugged. "Awesome!"

Danny left Madison at the control booth and climbed into the module. They got set. Madison started the simulation from zero, as if the lunar module had just started descending to the surface of the moon. There was an intercom that went directly into the simulator. It all still worked. "Houston to Lunar Module. You need to descend at one hundred and fifty feet per second." She was just making it up.

"I see it," Danny said. "It actually looks like we're in space!"

Danny never got excited like that. From where Madison stood it was just a giant weird box in the middle of a big room. It had wires sticking out of it and a cramped ladder leading inside. For Danny it was a beautiful object. He'd never experienced anything so magical. This was NASA history. She heard it in his voice.

Madison could see the two of them through a TV screen in front of her. Mia's hand moved deftly over the controls. She gripped the silver switches like paint brushes, her movements echoing the ease with which she marked ink across a page. Madison worried that the paint stains on her hands would in turn stain the instruments but she reconsidered when she re-membered the way Mia constantly braided and rebraided her own hair, never discoloring it in the least from its jet black shine.

Madison kept listening over the intercom as Danny and Mia bickered about controls. "Could you check the glycol lev-els please?" Mia asked him. "Also, do you think jalapeño pep-pers and habanero peppers get into fights about how spicy the letters *j* and *h* are?" She asked in a daze.

"Mia," Danny snapped. "I don't know what glycol is so I can't tell you the temperature."

"There's a gauge right there," Mia grumbled. "What num-ber does it say?"

"There's two numbers there," Danny complained, his voice reaching higher and higher in pitch. "And there's two other numbers next to it. And they're hard to read. One says sixty degrees," Danny argued. "What does that mean?"

"Is it going up or going down?" Mia screamed.

"Up!"

Exhausted, Mia poked at buttons. "We might be screwed!"

Madison was glad she wasn't inside of the tiny capsule as their bickering increased in volume to an almost deafening shrillness. She said, "Settle down you two," and she surveyed all of the tiny numbers on the screen in front of her. "It says a bunch of numbers here. Most of them are going down. I think that's good."

"I'm trying to land on the moon, Mads," Danny shouted. "This is literally rocket science. Give me more information than that. I'm trying to land a sixteen ton spider here."

Mia just laughed at him. "But how big is the moon?

You're trying to land a sixteen ton spider on a three thousand mile wide web. It can't be that hard."

Madison wanted to check her email. This felt like it was going to take hours. She inspected the room for something interesting. Everywhere there were insane gizmos and gadgets. It all looked so technological, all chrome and silver, beautiful technology from a time when they still made things out of metal. Then she saw it: a sign that said "HX1-7271 superconducting electromagnet," the same electromagnet that Charlotte had told her to pick up. That didn't seem right. It felt like a setup, as if Charlotte knew she'd be at the Air and Space Museum in that very room. She walked over and looked into the display case. It was a strange looking device, very small and very delicate. It was like a robot hand with only three fingers. She picked it up and fiddled with it for a moment.

Then a red light started blinking at the control panel. Madison turned to see what it was. She grabbed the magnet. It seemed to fall apart into three pieces in her hand. She wasn't sure if it was broken or if it was supposed to look like that. She decided just to shove the three pieces into her pocket and pray that she didn't break the only device that could possibly save her mom. She ran over to the control panel and pressed the intercom button. "Guys, there's a little light that says 'Descent Rate'. It's blinking red. What does that mean?"

"It means we're going too fast," Mia answered.

Danny asked, "How do you know we're not going too slow?"

"Danny," Mia groaned, "Nobody ever gets upset if you're going too slow. We need to hit these thrusters here." A loud noise echoed through the room. Nothing happened, it was just from a speaker but it sure was loud.

"You're gonna kill us," Danny said.

"I am not," Mia groaned. "I watched *Apollo 13* with you like a million times. We have to make sure the little lines stay in the center and you gotta make sure the little altitude thingy goes slower till it gets to zero. It's not hard, Danny."

"Mia," Danny groaned. "They never got to the moon in *Apollo 13*."

"Do you think I'm an idiot? I just said I watched that movie a million times. I know what happened. Tom Hanks used the lunar excursion module, the thing we're sitting in right now, to change the course of the Aquarius capsule in order to get back to Earth. They fired the descent engines just like I'm doing now. I saw him do it. The button's right here."

The sound got quieter. "See," Mia continued. "Now you've got to mess with that controller by your knee and make sure the lines all stay in the center." Mia groaned again. "Quit being a baby and just land the thing. I need more thruster. Worst that could happen is that we don't give it enough thrust and we crash into the moon and die. That or we give it too much thrust, run out of fuel and then crash into the moon and die."

"Guys," Madison said. "The little light is still blinking red."

"More thruster!" Danny shouted.

"I know!" Mia shouted.

Madison stared at the blinking red light. "Slower!"

"We're only fifty feet off the ground. We're gonna crash!"

"More thrust!" Mia yelled.

"Forty feet!"

"The light's still blinking," Madison gasped.

"It's OK," Mia said calmly. "We're fine."

Another red light began to blink. Madison yelled into the microphone. "The pitch rate light started to blink."

Danny sprang into action. "I'm on it!" he yelled. "Fifteen feet!"

Then suddenly both of the red lights stopped blinking on Madison's console. Suddenly a bunch of the numbers said zero. Nothing happened. There was no game over music. There was no ding to say they'd done it right. Nothing.

"What happened?" Danny asked.

"I think you guys landed on the moon," Madison answered.

Mia started talking with the same gusto as usual. "So amazing! There were a million ways we could've ended up in a crater the size of a house, our organs pulverized into little mounds of—"

"We landed a spaceship!" Danny screamed so loudly that Madison had to turn the intercom off.

Chapter 14

It was Madison's turn and she knew exactly where she was headed. She didn't even need to think about it. Even though it was dumb, really dumb, she had to do it. She'd dreamt about it. It was the last good dream she could remember.

"Where are we going?" Mia asked incessantly as they trudged along.

"You'll know when we get there," Madison told her over and over again, mostly because she was embarrassed to tell the truth.

They came up a flight of stairs and stopped on a landing at a plain white door with no window. Madison reviewed the map on her phone. The metal and concrete stairs around them echoed enough that she only whispered as loudly as a breath. "On the other side of this door is the actual museum again, not a back hallway. There are motion detectors and surveillance cameras so if we're not careful we'll alert all the security guards and our faces will be on camera. Everything bad that could happen to us will happen to us unless you do exactly what I tell you. This is going to be nearly impossible but we can do it."

Danny nodded like a cat watching a fly buzzing. He wasn't really looking at Madison. Mia's nod was so fierce that all of the paint stains on her shirt flickered in the light with the motion of her shaking body.

Madison asked the phone how to get what she came for. She never expected that it would be so complicated. As she read she felt heavy, like she was wearing a backpack filled with stones. Not only did she need to make sure that the plan went perfectly but she needed to make sure that Mia and Danny still thought Charlotte was a CIA thingamabob, not an all-knowing phone. It took her fully ten minutes to read through the directions while Mia and Danny bickered over who it was who really landed on the moon. Danny swore it was his last minute save and Mia said she did all the hard thruster work and he was just there to look pretty. To Madison it sounded like Mia won.

"So," Madison said proudly. "I have a plan." She looked straight into Danny's eyes, just like he'd looked into hers earlier. "Danny, do you have anything in your pockets?" She already knew that he had what she needed. Her phone told her so. But she didn't want to tell him that.

He turned out his pockets. At first all he showed her was his phone, his keys, his wallet and his headphones. "Anything else?" she asked impatiently. He went through the pockets of his hoodie. He had a pack of gum. She took a piece of gum and started chewing. But the thing she really needed he hadn't shown her yet. "Come on, Danny. We can't go back the way we came. We either go forward or we get caught. It's as simple as that."

So Danny pulled out what he'd been hiding. It was a

knife, a sharp one, the kind that folds into the handle. This was not the kind of knife that they give you at scout camp when you pass knot tying. This was a rip-the-skin-from-a-deer kind of knife. Small but serious.

"Where did you get this, Danny," asked Mia.

Madison was so preoccupied with what they were doing that she hadn't even considered asking a question like that. Then she turned to Danny and looked him deep in the eye for a third time. "Why did you get this, Danny?"

He trembled, not able to respond. He put the knife back into the place he kept it, on the inside of his jeans between his underwear and his pocket.

"No," Madison said. "We need it."

"We need a knife?" Mia asked. "Why?"

Madison waved her hand to dismiss the question. There wasn't time. "Also, we need your undershirt," she said to Mia. "Don't worry. We'll both look the other way while you're taking it off. We need to make masks so they can't identify us on the video."

"What are we stealing?" Mia asked with the apprehension of a slaughterhouse calf.

"We're not stealing anything," Madison answered.

Danny looked down at his feet. "This is so illegal," he said.

Madison shook her head. "We have no choice. This is the only way out. If we don't go through this door then we'll get caught." She didn't feel like she'd convinced them yet. She needed to keep talking so that they wouldn't have a chance to think. "One last thing," she said. "Do you remember when we took CPR class?" They both nodded. "When we learned how to do chest compressions they taught us to sing 'Another One Bites the Dust' by Queen to get the timing right. One compression every beat. Do you both remember that song?"

Mia groaned. "Every word of it. I had to listen to it every time I practiced pounding on that dummy's chest. I must have heard it twenty times. I hate that song. It makes me think of those creepy dead eyes." As always when she said something morbid she sounded completely cheerful.

"Hey," Danny said. "You practiced on me!"

Mia laughed. "Dead Eye Danny."

"She meant the mannequin," Madison assured him.

"I got the joke," Danny said. "Don't condescend." He looked like a fourth grader who was just told the same knock-knock joke for the tenth time. "But I feel the same way. That song is probably the thing I hate the second worst of anything in the world."

"What do you hate the worst?" Madison asked.

"Arlo Henderson," Danny answered.

"Me too," Madison said, not really surprised by his answer. "Even though we hate it, it's probably the only song we all know note for note." Both Mia and Danny just stared. The phone had told Madison to use that song so that they could stay synchronized. She'd have chosen a different one because she hated the song too. Hearing any song twenty times in a row will do that to you. "We'll all listen while everything goes down," Madison said.

Mia and Danny had the wide eyed confusion that Madison had seen before sailors are shipped off to war for the first time. She had to pull them together to calm them down. "You look like you have questions," she said.

"How do we get past the motion sensors?" Danny asked.

Madison shrugged. "My phone," she answered.

Danny looked so uncomfortable that he almost sneered. "But how does it work, Mads?"

"It's complicated," she answered, trying to sound as if she knew exactly how it worked and he was the dumb one.

"I need to know how it works before I trust it," Danny said. "I can't trust what I don't understand."

Madison poked the question into Charlotte, "How are we going to fool the motion sensors?" For once, the answer that came back wasn't as long as she thought it would be, but it was still too complicated. Madison read it out loud to Danny, whose mouth slowly fell open as she spoke. "There are two motion sensors in the room. Each one uses a piezo electric transducer that resonates at a specific ultrasonic frequency. That's a sound that's so high pitched that humans can't hear it, but I can..." Madison realized she was just reading what Charlotte said verbatim and that Charlotte sometimes spoke in the first person. "I mean the phone can hear it..." She chuckled uncomfortably, still trying to act like she understood what she was saying. She decided to replace every instance of the word 'I' that Charlotte said with 'the phone.'

"The phone will triangulate the locations of the motion sensors in 3D space. It will then mimic the frequencies using pulse width modulation, adjusting for Doppler distortion as I... as the phone moves, by varying the pulse width to compensate."

Danny nodded as though he understood, but his gaping mouth said otherwise. Mia looked less confused, which troubled Madison because it looked like she had a real question, and Madison didn't have any answers.

"How does the phone know what frequencies to use?" Mia asked, her head tilted to one side introspectively.

For once, Madison did know the answer because it was the same for every question regarding what Charlotte knew and didn't know. She knew everything. It was as simple as that. But Madison couldn't just go ahead and say that, as much as she wanted to. She had to think something up, on her feet, with enough of a technobabble knowingness to make it sound as if she knew what she was talking about. "The phone has a CIA ultra-sensitive microphone," she answered. "It can hear the frequencies." Of course, compared to Charlotte's answer this sounded lame, and probably wrong. Did Charlotte even need a microphone? If she knew everything, did she even need to hear at all or would she just know what you said before you said it?

Madison just kept talking to make sure she said everything before it was time to start. "You have to move really slowly so that the motion sensors don't pick you up." Knowing that Danny was about to ask why, Madison looked down at the phone and asked, just to preemptively shut him up. She read exactly what Charlotte told her. "There's a natural sonic resonance to the room that peaks every two point four seconds, which is once every four beats." That had to be enough explanation. She continued. "Keep your hands at your sides, don't move anything but your legs. It's like a dance. If you count out four beats—one, two, three, four—only put your foot down exactly when you count four. You got that?"

Danny looked Madison in the eye and asked, absolutely seriously, "Mads, are you or are you not actually a super soldier who was genetically engineered by the government to be the ultimate killing machine?"

"No," Madison answered. "I'm just a girl who knows how to ask the right questions."

"I don't believe you," Danny said. "You're my friend, but I just don't believe you."

Madison's heart sank. He was right not to believe. She was lying to him and she respected him for noticing.

Her speech was over. They were ready to start moving. "Danny, download the song and play it through your phone's speakers. Mia, swap out your undershirt while Danny and I look away."

As Danny started downloading the song, Madison pulled him into the corner of the stairwell and pushed him against the wall. "Why do you have the knife, Danny?" she asked.

"Arlo," he answered without taking a breath so his voice was thin and wispy.

Madison's heart sank. "Danny," she said. She hugged his head into her chest. He latched onto her. "You didn't bring this knife into school with you, did you?" He didn't answer. Of course he did. He didn't have time to change after they got home. "You're never bringing this to school again, Danny." She was livid, the muscles by her jaw vibrated. "You're never bringing this to school again."

He shook his head. "You don't know what it's like. Girls are mean but they don't threaten to use you for batting practice."

Madison's rage came into full force as she felt the knife in her hand. Not only had Arlo attacked Patrick, he'd also attacked Danny, at least verbally. It was so wrong. But she was just as mad at Danny for taking the bait. She wanted to yell at him but there wasn't time. It was time to fulfill a childhood dream, and also get home. "We are going to talk about this later, Danny. Remind me that we need to talk about this later. Promise."

Danny nodded. "I promise."

That wasn't quite good enough for Madison but she felt she had no choice but to move on. She couldn't get into a personal debate with Danny about knife safety and bullies. Mia had finished changing her shirt so Madison pulled Danny back across the room so that they were all in a tight little circle on the cramped landing.

Madison looked them each in the eye before starting, making sure she had their full attention. "What I'm trying to see is in the next room. It's where they keep Hollywood stuff in the Smithsonian. There are a bunch of display cases with old costumes and props from movies. You two need to climb on top of the display cases. Danny, you have to help Mia onto the one in the left corner. After she's up there go to the far right corner. You're strong enough to climb onto the display case there. When you're up there, you'll each see a security camera right above you. It'll look like a little black bubble coming out of the ceiling. What you have to do is take a picture of the room with your phone from your position on top of the display case. Then you need to hold your phone about three inches in front of that camera so that that your phone's screen is facing the camera. Hold it as steadily as possible. From the security guard's point of view he'll be seeing the picture you just took. It will look like an empty room."

"Danny, turn your speaker up to full volume before we go in. You need to take one step for every beat of the song. When Freddy Mercury first starts to sing, lift Mia up onto the first display case and she'll hold her phone in front of the first camera. Don't go too fast because it'll throw the timing off.

"Then Danny, you'll move to the far left corner. When he says the line 'Another one bites the dust,' do the same thing with your phone in front of the second camera. You have to hold your phones there perfectly still until the end of the really long guitar solo. You got that?"

Danny fumed but Madison didn't know why. Thirty seconds left. She didn't have time to ask. Madison and Danny would both press play and then it was time to go. They each tied the pieces of fabric around their mouths to cover their faces. They looked like thugs or like they were trying to survive a sand storm in the desert. Madison was surprised by how different the masks made them look.

"Ready?" Madison asked. They both shrugged. She asked again, louder this time. "Ready?"

"Yeah!" Mia said.

Then Danny groaned. "Yeah."

"And…go."

Madison pressed play on Charlotte's screen but she couldn't hear any sound coming out. Then she remembered that Charlotte had said that humans couldn't hear the ultrasonic frequency, so she just had to take it on faith. Danny pressed play on his phone and the song began to hum out of his tinny speakers. It sounded hollow. For someone who cared as much about music as Danny, his phone speakers were really bad. Madison guessed he didn't care because he only listened to music through those giant headphones he always wore. She wished that the song were louder so that they could all be sure to hear it, but she had no choice.

Mia and Danny slowly made their way along the left hand wall to get to the first camera. It was only four feet from the door to the display case but it took forever for them to get there with those slow steps. Madison watched through a sliver in the doorway as Danny boosted Mia up onto the big glass display case which lit his straining face in pale blue light. Soon, Mia was standing eight feet above the room above a tuxedo and some other random James Bond memorabilia. When Madison saw that Mia was holding her phone in front of the camera, she slowly took her first slow step through the door, arms locked at her sides holding her breath.

The room was an octagon. The ceilings sloped upward making the room feel like a circus tent, coming to a point in the center. The space was dimly lit by the lights of the display cases which covered every side of the room. Behind the glass all around her were remnants of the most important movies ever made, plus some that weren't nearly as important. There was the umbrella that Gene Kelley danced with in *Singing in the Rain* and Scarlett's dress from *Gone with the Wind*. There were the boxing gloves that Rocky wore and a sword from *The Hobbit*. Madison had watched a lot of these movies with her dad. She could name almost everything she saw.

The room was cut in half by one long case that stood like a crown jewel centerpiece on which everything else was focused. Madison was looking at the back side of the central display case so she couldn't get a good view, but her fingers already itched with anticipation. She was almost there, sneaking across the floor, keeping in mind the next important lyric to the song as she crept. The cases were made of brass with thick fingerprint marked glass. When she'd finally reached it, Madison knelt before the two foot by two foot door that locked up her target. She didn't even look to see what Danny was doing. She had too much to think about on her own. The directions told her to plunge Danny's knife into the gap between the door and the jamb right next to the lock. Then she had to twist to the right as hard as she could exactly when the song started making weird laser noises. She just had to go on faith that it would work.

The next part was much more complicated. Charlotte had told her to use the HX1-7271 superconducting electromagnet she'd just stolen to break the lock. She fiddled with the thing for a second trying to figure out how it worked, which she realized she should have done while they were in the stairwell. The three metal pieces screwed together with audible clicks when they were properly configured. She took pains to move slowly, working as closely as she could to the song's rhythm. When she'd gotten it assembled it looked like the claw of a robot bird, three fingers sticking out from the thin, syringe-like protrusion at the end. It looked like a peace sign without the circle around it. She held it to the keyhole. There was a tiny round knob on the top of the peace sign marked "Liquid Helium" in tiny letters. Charlotte had told her to twist the knob a half turn and then press the button at the top. She took a deep breath and turned the knob. The electromagnet hissed, spraying a thin stream of white gas out of the end of the big middle toe of the peace sign.

It was only after holding the magnet in her hand for a few seconds, getting ready to push the button, that she realized how cold it was, but not where her fingers touched, on the inside of her palm. The whole big toe started to frost over. It must have been cold enough to give her frost bite and probably worse if she touched it in the wrong place. Even the way she was holding it probably wasn't correct. She screamed out in pain and let go, but it stayed there, probably frozen in place. The next step was to push the tip of the big toe of the peace sign to the key-hole and to press the button at the top. The metal crackled like popcorn popping. The magnet dropped to the ground. Madison realized that the tips of her fingers felt completely numb, which was nice because it meant that they didn't hurt.

Next, she had to carefully disengage the sensor that would set off the alarm if the little door opened. Using the end of the knife, she pushed the piece of gum she'd been chewing into the little space between the door and the sensor. Then she nudged the knife toward the tiny door jamb. It opened. There was no alarm.

Inside, still lit by the display lights, glimmering in pink and purple shimmers, preserved perfectly behind glass, were the original ruby slippers from *The Wizard of Oz*.

Madison slowly reached through and lifted them lovingly from the case. The shoes felt jagged and firm. She didn't know what she expected but they were lighter than she thought they'd be. They didn't really have rubies on them but sequins. They looked more like a cheap cocktail dress except for the dark red bows on top. Yet they were perfect. She'd never imagined actually having something like that in her hands.

She pulled them out of the case then pulled her own shoes off. She delicately slid the left slipper on her foot. It fit. Size 6 ½.

Mia half whispered and half yelled from her perch above the display case. "Is that what you wanted?" she asked. "Just to try on some shoes? Mads, we could've just gone to the mall for that and not gotten arrested and thrown in jail for fifty years. We're going to get stabbed together in the bathroom." Mia pondered for a second. "But Mads, I wouldn't want to get stabbed with anybody but you."

Madison didn't pay Mia any attention. Instead she looked down at her feet as she slid the right slipper on. They didn't even look like her own feet. In the sparkling light of the display case they shimmered dark red like the wine at a midnight party with dancing and bow ties.

She'd only been to one party like that, on the base in Spain. It was gorgeous. She sat and watched as the elegant ladies danced the tango with roses in their hair. Her mom and dad looked like they were floating. Their legs moved fast but calmly. They gazed into each other's eyes without looking away for a second. It almost felt like a black and white movie but with pops of red peeking out from the corners and from behind curtains. The old world flushed through their faces, the respect of tradition and timing. It was pure. It was gentlemanly. It was perfect.

Danny shouted, "Hey," from where he stood, still clutching his phone. He looked confused but also excited. He finally noticed her shoes. "Those look incredible. Where did you get those?"

"They're from *The Wizard of Oz*." Madison told them. "Didn't you ever see *The Wizard of Oz*? It's this old movie where this girl gets pulled into a tornado and ends up in this magical land and she wears these slippers the whole time."

Danny just shrugged. "You risked everything to wear shoes from a movie?"

"They're nice shoes," Mia said. "You could wear those to the club and get tons of guys who want your number."

"You don't understand," Madison said. Before she could

explain, Charlotte's alarm went off again, telling them that there was a guard in the area. They panicked. Both Danny and Mia jumped down from their display cases. They ran right out of the door to the outside, which set off a loud alarm as soon as they opened it. They ripped off their masks and sprinted straight to the Metro stop they'd come from just in time to board the train before the doors closed.

They made it halfway home before Madison realized she was still wearing the ruby slippers. She was too worried about the numbness in her hands, as well as the numbness of having just accidentally pulled off a major heist, to notice. Slowly, the feeling came back, and with it a feeling of dread. They were going to get caught.

In the corner of the subway car was a camera looking directly at her. There was one in the opposite corner as well. In fact, everywhere she looked there were cameras. This was a bad idea. She'd drawn too much attention to herself. Any shadowy figure could be a government agent ready to snatch her up and interrogate her about Graham. It was the worst thing she could have done, stealing something so significant. If anything could have jeopardized her mom, this was it.

"I just committed grand theft," she said. "I deserve to go to jail."

"But you'll return them, right?" Mia asked. "I mean, you don't really need sparkly red shoes, do you?"

Madison felt her toes wiggle. "I guess I have to," she said. "But not tonight. Tonight they're still mine."

And then she went home. She didn't break curfew. She didn't drink. She didn't do drugs. She'd just stolen a pair of shoes worth at least $100,000. That was all. It could have been worse.

Chapter 15

When Madison got home her mom was still working. Madison went up to the attic where her mom kept her study. "Mom?" she said sheepishly as Mrs. Riley typed away at the computer.

Mrs. Riley looked up and raised her eyebrows. Nothing bothered her more than being interrupted mid-sentence, but she waived that rule for her daughter. "What happened?" she asked. "What's wrong? The muscles at the corners of your mouth are tense: your zygomaticus major." She stood up. Her chair rocked back and rolled across the floor.

Madison's heart sank. Those classes her mom attended at the CIA taught her a lot of things. One of the most annoying was the ability to read a person's face and tell when someone is lying. Madison wasn't sure what to do. She rolled her eyes. "Mom," she moaned. "I have to ask you something but I already know the answer is no so it doesn't even matter."

Mrs. Riley stepped closer and tried to eye her daughter's face one more time. She was good at reading these things but she wasn't perfect. Madison had lied to her before and not gotten caught but not about anything more important than eating the last bit of ice cream.

Madison shrugged and continued with the script she'd planned for herself. "You were saying that I need to take better care of myself," she said it exactly like she'd meant to. "So I was thinking I want to learn more from you." She couldn't quite look her mom in the eye but she decided she had to. She had to make eye contact, but only for a second. No more than she ever did. "I know I'm a little old but it's Take Your Daughter to Work Day on Thursday."

Mrs. Riley read her face again. She knew something was going on. She could tell Madison was acting strangely but she couldn't be sure why. There were a million reasons Madison might have asked to come to work with her and the least likely was espionage. "Come sit with me," she said. Madison sat right down on the wood floor.

Mrs. Riley's study was filled with books about math and history. Papers littered every horizontal surface. Madison sat pretzel legged in front of her mom, waiting for something to happen. They both smiled but neither knew what to say.

"I know a lot happened to you recently," she said. She patted Madison on the knee. "I'm sure it was emotional." She looked off into the distance, frowning. "I thought about him when I heard you weren't safe."

Madison nodded. She hadn't anticipated how her mom would feel having almost lost her to an earthquake. She hadn't expected her own feelings either.

"When we lost your dad," Mrs. Riley continued in a calm tenor, a soothing alacrity, "I wasn't exactly surprised. He signed up for dangerous missions all the time. I knew he'd give his life to save those boys he served with. He never said that to me but I knew it." She wiped a tear from her eye. "Do you still have nightmares about the video?" she asked.

Just hearing the word video sent a chill down Madison's spine. Of course she still had nightmares about the video. It plagued her. It was all she dreamt about and when she closed her eyes she worried she'd relive it, if only for just one second. "People keep calling me a hero, Mom," she said. "Everyone always told Daddy not to be a hero. Every day. I took that to heart. I tried for years not to be a hero. And then there's an earthquake and the first thing I do is risk my life."

Mrs. Riley sat down on the floor next to Madison and pulled her close. She rocked her back and forth. Madison's pretzel legs kicked out violently but then settled down. She hugged her mom back. "Your father just couldn't help it," Mrs. Riley said. "It wasn't his fault. He was addicted." Then she stopped petting Madison on the head. "Or else I thought he was addicted. I always told myself that." She sounded sad beyond belief. "But here you are. You're a hero even though you tried as hard as you could not to be one. Maybe some people are just born to be heroes."

"I'm not a hero," Madison said. She wanted so badly to tell her mom the truth about everything but she just couldn't bring herself to do it. She cried into her mom's shoulder. "I don't want to talk about Daddy."

Mrs. Riley nodded. They both cried. The first time they'd cried together since the funeral.

Chapter 16

Sunday morning. Four days until Take Your Daughter to Work Day. Four days until Madison's date with the NSA. But first, lacrosse practice. It wasn't every week that they had Sunday lacrosse, but Coach Dipson forced them into it whenever he could. One o'clock. Madison rode her bike. She met Mia there. She wanted to talk to her about the Smithsonian but she was afraid that other people would overhear. She made Mia swear not to bring it up.

This was freshman trials day. It was rumored to be grueling but according to Hamida Jones it wasn't anything Madison hadn't experienced during cross country season. The only difference was that this time she'd be up against the triumvirate of Jillian, Hannah and Carolyn. Madison had seen them during winter practice. They were swarthy, angry and vicious. They went after the ball with abandon, ready to crash into whoever stepped in their way. Rumor had it that Hannah had doled out three separate concussions during her junior league career. She led with her shoulder and her head. She whipped her lacrosse stick in wide arcs that swept backwards across her body, blind to whoever's face might be in the way.

Coach Dipson stood in the middle of the field, clipboard in hand. He'd recovered from the Spanish class field trip and returned to his duties as lacrosse coach, and to a lesser extent, guidance counselor. His puffy black nylon pants made him look like a maharaja or a rapper from the early nineties. In his cold brow Madison noticed deep creases above his nose as if he perpetually snarled and whined at the same time. He loved it when the girls got aggressive. He preferred them to be warriors even though lacrosse wasn't supposed to be a contact sport. Back when he still had workable knees he'd been a professional player but the constant contact destroyed his body. He wore those parachute style pants in order to hide the thick braces that locked his legs into near vertical robot limbs. He was younger than most of the other head coaches but he'd already started to work on his paunch.

Most of the girls crowded around in a big group. They talked about boys and parties and things that Madison cared nothing about. Mia came up to Madison from behind. "They're the worst." She fiddled with her lacrosse stick which was about as tall as she was. "It's one thing to judge people. I judge them. But that's all they do. They talk about what boys are better. They talk about who has the ugliest outfit. They talk about how so and so got drunk and is never getting into an Ivy League school."

"I had fun at their party," Madison admitted. "Carolyn's mom was really nice."

Mia slapped her stick against the ground. "And later today she'll cross check you to the ground without thinking twice about it. I bet you she will."

Jillian looked over at them. Her eyebrows shot up into her hairline and her mouth split open with an impossibly gigantic smile. "Madison!" she shouted. "I love your hair!" Thankfully that was the only thing Jillian could note about her appearance. In the unflattering uniform of a lacrosse player there isn't much to compliment, but there's no hiding hair.

In fact, Madison had spent a lot of time tying her hair up that morning. She threw at least three bobby pins in and a small but carefully selected smattering of product. It hadn't exactly gone to her head that she was now popular, nor had it really struck that she possessed the ruby slippers, one of the most iconic fashion emblems of the twentieth century in her closet. What really made her do it was fear. Now that the popular girls noticed her, she was afraid they'd start judging her even more if she didn't keep up her appearances. It was easier being a background player.

Jillian threw her arm around Madison and paraded her back to the popular set. Mia stood where she was, uninvited. Madison was too overwhelmed to notice. Everyone looked at her, even the team captains. They were senior girls who never ever took interest in the dealings of their freshman colleagues. It seemed to Madison that writing that article really had gotten Jillian back into the elite social circle because it showed that she had inside knowledge on Madison, even though they didn't actually know each other. She felt used by Jillian but also kind of exhilarated to see behind the curtain into the top tier.

"This is the toughest girl on this team, ladies," Jillian announced. "She's here to set us straight. This is going to be our best freshman class in ten years, I guarantee."

The senior girls smiled. They started in on the girl's lacrosse cheer which Madison hadn't learned yet. She tried to follow along but couldn't quite keep up.

Four, Three, Two, One,
We're here to battle, not for fun!
Cut, slide, check, run,
We eat the grass, we drink the sun!
Win! Win! Win! Won!
We ice you 'cause we're Shackleton!

The first thing that Madison thought was that the team needed a better cheer but she wouldn't dare say anything. It took someone with much more nerve to do something like that.

Mia's voice picked the perfect moment to slice through any lingering cheers with a mixture of excitement, squeal and confusion. "That's a stupid cheer," she said. She had absolutely no filter, no ability to lay down her opinions for a moment and just enjoy the camaraderie of the team. Everyone looked over at her now, suddenly not interested in Madison. Mia didn't seem to mind. "It's too sing-songy," she continued. "And why would we ice them 'cause we're Shackleton? Why wouldn't we just get lost some place and almost die?"

It wasn't a fair fight. Mia was so short and defenseless with dimples and tiny legs. She'd only signed up because she wanted to follow Madison. It had become a theme. When Madison told her she was joining the cross country team on the first day they'd met, Mia decided it was a great idea and showed up alongside of her, never having run a hundred yards in her life. Yet she persevered. She finished every race. The fact that she was dead last each time didn't stop Madison from admiring her. Not many people continue with something even though they're the worst at it. It was brave.

Carolyn Kaplan stormed across the field, her nostrils flared. "Ernest Shackleton was a hero! He was the first man to cross Antarctica and even though his ship got stuck in the ice he persevered without a single one of his men dying. He's one of the great heroes of Ireland."

Mia scoffed. "What do we care about this guy? How did a school in Maryland get named after him?"

A crowd began to form with Mia and Carolyn in the center. Madison wanted very much to get between them but she didn't know where to start. She felt like Mia could hold her own. She felt like there was room for both viewpoints without her picking a side. Then, within the same instant, she felt like a coward. She stepped forward, feigning confusion. "That's a good point," she said, trying to pull the focus away from Mia. "Does anybody know why we're called Shackleton? I mean, our mascot is the Ice, which is an awesome mascot, but Shackleton didn't found our school. He never even came to America."

It was Coach Dipson's voice that answered, his high pitched, slightly southern voice with the tiny wheeze at the end. "Ernest Shackleton is the bravest man who ever lived. His story is about endurance and respect. Those are the most American values in the world." Coach Dipson stared her down. His eyes turned into fine slits, white then black then white. "I've changed my mind about today's practice. Instead of the regularly scheduled freshman trials we're doing something different. To commemorate Shackleton we're running an endurance competition, ladies. Every one of you must run at least thirty-six laps. That's nine full miles. None of you can stop running until the last girl finishes. You better all work together as a team on this one. That's the lesson of Shackleton. You all have to work together, no matter what. Whichever freshman girl runs the farthest before the last girl finishes will be guaranteed a spot on the travel team this year. So, if it takes the slowest girl three hours to finish the nine miles and the fastest girl runs ten minute miles, she will have run eighteen miles by the end of the night. That's almost three quarters of a marathon, ladies. Do the math, it works.

"This is a special privilege. Our team is big enough and we travel far enough for tournaments that even being on varsity doesn't guarantee that you get to go to every game. Travel is a step above varsity. It's for the best of the best. Run smart, encourage each other, but do battle."

Every eye was on Mia except Madison's. She held her head in her hands. This was no way to begin a season, forcing every single girl on the lacrosse team to run nine miles. Even with all of Mia's cross country training she'd still never managed to run more than three miles. Madison knew she'd be the last to cross the finish line. She knew that every single girl on the team would want to kill Mia after a practice like that, and they would do everything in their power to make her life a living hell for the rest of the season.

Mia smiled from ear to ear, jogging in place, oblivious to the fact that she'd just invited a world of hurt upon herself. "Where do we start, coach?" she asked eagerly. "I'm ready for anything."

Madison doubted that very much.

Chapter 17

Luckily for Madison, she knew better than anyone how fast Mia could run. They'd gone on so many runs together. Mia would try to talk at first but after the first half mile she'd be sucking so much gas she could barely even breathe. For Madison it was barely a workout yet, but she enjoyed it all the same. It was one of the few situations where she talked about herself. She wanted to encourage Mia as much as she could and Mia seemed to appreciate listening to Madison talk about her feelings, so she obliged. During one of these runs was the first time that Madison confided in anyone about her crush on Patrick Sutton. It was also the first time she'd ever talked to anyone about the times she'd had with her dad in Spain. It's not often that someone will listen to you without trying to talk back, least of all Mia. Madison was surprised how much she enjoyed those runs.

She could tell exactly how tired Mia was by listening to her breathe. It was an unfair advantage in a way, but it was one that Madison had come to honestly, without ever really thinking about it.

Madison took Mia aside while the other girls plotted to find a way to get through this with the least amount of work possible. She put her hand on Mia's back as she always did when they talked race strategy. "Listen, Mia. You have to start slow. Remember, this is three times as far as you've ever run before. Don't try to keep up with the other girls. Just keep your pace and make sure you stop for water every mile. OK?"

Mia nodded. "This is gonna be fun," she said, even though Madison knew very well that this would be torture. Self delusion was one of Mia's strong suits.

Madison smiled too. "I'll encourage you when I pass. I know you can do it."

"Thanks, Mads," Mia said. "You really are a great friend."

Everyone started lining up at the starting line. She coveted that spot on the traveling team. She'd already done the math in her head. She could run three six and a half minute miles back to back. If she was going to run eighteen miles or so, she had to run more slowly from the beginning, probably closer to seven and a half minutes per mile. She decided that was her pace, seven minutes and thirty seconds. It was insanely fast, but she had faith that she could do it. She set her watch.

Coach yelled in his bellicose, blustery squawk, "Ready…" He paused a little longer than anyone expected. "Get set…Go!"

Many of the girls had no idea how far they were going to be running so they set off full pace. Madison stayed back toward the middle of the pack even though she could have run much faster. She had to conserve her energy. This would be a long run. She thought for a second that she should have consulted the phone for her perfect pace but this was her race to win. She didn't need to see the future to do it.

She'd calculated that Mia should run fifteen minute miles in order to finish. That meant she was running twice as fast as Mia. It wasn't long before she'd run two laps but Mia was still ahead of her. That meant that Mia was going too fast. Madison sped up slightly to catch up to her for the first time. She slowed down for a moment to talk to Mia who was already breathing heavily. "Hey Mia," Madison said. "You're gonna do great."

Mia nodded. "Thanks," she said, barely able to get the word out of her throat.

"You have to slow down, though," Madison said. "Just slow down a little bit so you can make it the whole way, OK?"

"OK," Mia said. She nodded and immediately slowed.

"Way to go!" Madison shouted. Then she picked up her pace and ran ahead.

The other girls cheered Mia on as well, once they'd decided she was the slowest of the herd. Mia seemed spurred by their yelling. She kept speeding up. Every time Madison passed she encouraged Mia but at the same time asked her to slow down.

It had only been a week and a half since Madison's hip had been wounded in the earthquake. It wasn't a hundred percent healed but she could easily make her way around the track. It hurt a bit though, more like a sting. She kept pushing ahead as if it was nothing.

After about three miles a few of the girls had started to get winded. A few others realized there was no way they wanted to run more than nine miles so they slowed down significantly in order to conserve energy. Some of them were running almost as slowly as Mia. That included some of the older girls who had been through things like this before and knew how to game the system.

After about four miles Madison realized that most of the girls were holding it together at about eight minute miles so she kept her pace at the 7:30 mark. A few girls were out ahead of her including Hannah Chanel and Jillian Jacobs. Madison tried not to worry about them. She just kept her pace and made sure to drink water every few miles. She cheered Mia on when she passed and tried not to think about her hip.

The miles ticked off, slowly at first but after a while they just flowed into each other. She would have lost count had she not been checking the time every mile. It was soul crushing running the same circle over and over again without any end in sight, without any assurance that she'd make it across the line.

After Madison's seventh mile it became very clear to her that Mia was crashing badly. Mia had just run three and a half miles, farther than she'd ever run before. Her brow beaded with sweat and her feet stomped the ground with each step.

"Way to go, Mia!" Madison would yell as she passed. "You're doing great!"

Mia smiled. Her breath heaved in and out. She was moving just faster than walking pace but she was still trying. She pushed with all of her might to get across the finish line but Madison wasn't completely convinced she could do it. She wondered if she should forget about making the travel team and instead stay with her friend encouraging and supporting her. She'd never abandoned a friend before. But at the same time she knew she should push herself. This was a competition and she was supposed to compete.

The beat of Madison's heart echoed that of her feet except that its lub-dub rhythm added syncopation to the methodical plod of her shoes against the track. As the laps clicked away their repetition sounded a low harmony against the plaintive sound of the wind.

When she headed east toward the school the wind was at her head. Its whistle sounded an ugly alarm and she realized that when she heard it, every forty-five seconds or so, her heart rate would jump up in preparation for the fight against the wind.

Her body had mapped the course without her and was making decisions in its own haphazard way. If she could have controlled it, Madison would have made her body build up to the higher heart rate but she couldn't just command her circulatory system to beat at will. So she compromised. Every lap when she began to round the home straightaway, she would turn her head so that the air wouldn't whistle in her ears. Then she'd slowly swing around to warm up to her eventual rise in heartbeat. It was a way of telling her involuntary muscles what to do without really being able to speak their language.

Madison passed the nine mile mark. The older girls who finished with her just jogged it out at that point. Madison kept pushing along with only a few other runners. The track slowly started to fill up with people not really pushing themselves. Madison hurt at that point. She'd run that far for cross country but never any farther. She realized she felt just like Mia. This was her point of no return, the wall she needed to break through in order to make it to the end. She knew she wasn't in first place among the freshmen but she was close. There was a lot more race to go and there was a lot more she had within her.

She walked for a few seconds every few miles when she stopped for water. She slowed down slightly when she passed Mia to give her encouragement, but for the most part she just kept up the same pace. She kept her eye on Hannah and Jillian who stayed together, fighting tooth and nail for a few extra footfalls along the course.

At mile ten they'd actually lapped her which put them a full quarter mile ahead. Madison decided to run with them for a while, keeping their pace. She knew she had a lot of steam left in her despite the huge distance she'd already run and she suspected that they were already running out.

"How you doing, girls?" Madison asked, breathing heavily but not quite out of breath.

"Fine," Jillian answered.

"Yeah," Hannah seconded. "Totally great."

"Mia's a little more than halfway done," Madison informed them. "So that means we're about half-way too."

Jillian and Hannah both had sour looks on their faces when she told them that. They probably hadn't quite banked on how slow Mia was when they calculated their paces and started too fast. It wasn't Madison's intention to break their spirits but at the same time she couldn't help but feel excited to have done it.

As they passed Coach Dipson he yelled, "It's down to you three! All the other freshman girls gave up. Are you gonna give up or are you gonna keep this up and get on that travel team?"

"Yes, Coach," they all shouted as they passed, almost screaming just to get the words out.

They kept pace, almost step for step even as more and more girls decided it was better for them to walk the rest of the practice instead of kill themselves. It was probably the smart move on their part. A group of them congregated around Mia, yelling encouragement and even grabbing water for her. It was obvious that she was the slowest and so she was the most in need of help. To Madison it felt like a double edged sword. On the one hand it meant that the girls gave their attention to Mia and it looked outwardly as though they cared, but Madison wondered what would happen the second that practice was finished. Would they instantly hate Mia for making them stay so late? Would they remember this moment until the end of time?

But the people most likely to resent Mia weren't the ladies who accompanied her around the track shouting encouragement, it was Jillian and Hannah, who had been forced to run more than ten miles already and who might have to run ten more.

Madison considered offering a détente. She could bargain with Jillian and Hannah to run a few slow laps. If they all agreed to walk for a while then they could start up again at an agreed upon time and there would still be a race. Then she remembered, she was still a lap behind. That was a lap she had to make up over the last few miles, probably the hardest miles of the race.

She decided on a different strategy. Since she still had some wind in her lungs, she picked up the pace slightly. Instead of running her fairly comfortable 7:30 pace she decided to run 7:10 miles. Hannah and Jillian barely realized the change in pace but she could hear their breaths hasten and their heels dig deeper into the track with every step they took. Madison still felt light on her feet, though she wasn't sure how much longer she could keep that up.

Madison decided at mile thirteen that she should pick up the pace again, if only for one straight away. She had to break away from Jillian and Hannah. She had to make her move to regain the quarter mile she'd lost to them.

She began almost to sprint, absolutely sure that she was leaving Hannah and Jillian behind. Her hip began to shoot spikes through her nervous system that reverberated in every muscle and in every joint. She winced after she finished the straight away and slowed back down to her normal pace. She didn't dare look back to see how much room she'd opened up. It may have only been a few steps or it may have been more. She couldn't be sure. But she had to keep pushing no matter what. Her feet were numb, as if below her knees there was just a wobbly cloud upon which she bounced. It was both euphoric and slightly scary. She felt as though she might topple over at any second.

All of the girls had stopped running save for Madison, Hannah, Jillian and Mia, although Mia's run was about as fast as everyone else's walk. The group had grown restless. They'd stopped encouraging Mia for a while and instead just talked among themselves about whatever gossip they had on their minds. She still had two miles to go, which at her rate meant they'd still be there for another half hour. She looked as though she was dying. Her arms bounced with every step. She wasn't even able to keep them up and at her sides.

Everyone was tired, of course. Everyone dragged. But then people started to notice the rivalry between Madison, Hannah and Jillian. Word spread that Madison was making a comeback and before long the team began to cheer whenever the girls passed them. It all came down to Mia's last mile. The cheers became uproarious. Madison estimated that she still had two more miles to run. She'd almost lost count of how many she'd run so far but after looking at her watch and doing some quick math she realized that she'd already gone over sixteen miles. That would make her total distance a staggering eighteen plus.

That's when the pain really hit her. Fire ran through her veins. Her stomach filled with acid and her heart felt like a sputtering wound. She could just feel the blood struggling to pass through her ever more polluted veins. She felt as though her legs would seize beneath her, almost like Coach Dipson's robot legs. She felt woozy, confused, tight. Sinew crackled under the stress of the run. But she wouldn't dare stop.

As she passed Mia again she patted her on the back and gave a tired cheer. The other girls cheered back, a scene so full of energy it could make you believe in the power of the team. But then there was Jillian Jacobs to contend with. Then there was Hannah Chanel. She saw them out of the corner of her eye, only a quarter lap ahead of her now, still driving their own pace. She picked up her speed even though fire burned through her legs and into her brain. She wanted so badly to stop. She nearly cried from the pain of it but she just had to get a little farther and keep up enough juice to pass them at the end. They were slipping, she knew. They'd set out a pace that they couldn't sustain and now she reaped the benefits. But it would be close. If Mia really picked it up and ran with her whole heart then Madison couldn't possibly catch up, but if Mia stayed slow it would give enough time for Madison to pass them. It was one of those math problems they give you on a standardized test. If four girls run around the track, Girl A at X speed, Girl B at Y speed and two girls at Z speed, and the race ends when Girl A has gone X miles, who wins? It made Madison's head hurt just thinking about it.

Then she saw him. Patrick Sutton, standing at the fence by the soccer field, watching her intently. She felt his eyes on her, his quiet assurance that she could make it. Other boys had come to the fence as well. Someone must have told them about the crazy lacrosse players running almost a marathon. Someone must have let the news spread to all the other teams. Madison once again felt all eyes on her. She felt the old admonishment she'd been given over and over again, "Don't be a hero." She thought about that for a moment, head full of steam and jelly in her legs. She'd overcome it when she saved her class and she could overcome it now. Then she told herself again, "Don't be a hero."

She'd closed the gap to Hannah and Jillian. The two of them were neck and neck but one of them must have had more left than the other. Only one mile left. Cheers surrounded her, both from the boys and the girls, more people than she'd ever expected. She felt as though she was sprinting even though it couldn't have been that fast. She came around for another lap and saw Patrick's face once again. She reached Mia again and tried to say "Don't rush," but the words came out muddled.

Then it happened. She came alongside Jillian and Hannah. It only lasted a second though, because she wasn't about to let go of her phantasmagoric pace and Hannah couldn't keep up. It was a race between herself and Jillian, full speed for the last half mile until the finish line. Madison felt Jillian's strength but she knew she could pull out the win. She knew she could push past in the final straightaway. She knew it.

Then the voice echoed in her head once again. "Don't be a hero." The tension came into her belly again. Her muscles tightened. That second wind she felt when she first saw Patrick was gone. It was all pain once again. The finish line might as well have been a hundred miles away. She couldn't make it. It wasn't worth destroying herself over a spot on the travel team. It wasn't worth it.

She saw Mia ahead of her one last time. She saw Mia heading down her own final stretch. The last hundred meters. This really was it. This really was the final few paces until the end.

She told herself one more time, "Don't be a hero." Tears rolled down her cheeks. "Don't be a hero." The words had never felt more intense than at that moment. She'd gone far enough. She didn't need to go any farther.

And so she fell.

Chapter 18

The trainer came to the bleachers by the side of the field with a five gallon water cooler full of ice for Madison to soak her aching legs in and a blanket to make sure that the rest of her stayed warm. The girls all huddled around anxiously to see what was wrong. There are always rumors about distance runners, that if they run too hard they won't be able to control their bodily functions because they'd exerted themselves so hard. Madison read on some of the faces around her that they hoped she'd pooped her pants. It would become legend at Shackleton High for years to come if she'd done it. But she couldn't even tell. Her legs were so numb and her body so far flung from its normal routines that her bowel functions were the lowest on her list. She'd almost welcome the moniker of the girl who pooed on herself if it meant being finished with that moment.

And then came the disappointment. Having been called a hero so recently, she couldn't help but hate herself for having given up. She wondered if she'd sabotaged herself, if the thoughts inside her head were on purpose. Part of her just didn't want to win. As cowardly as that sounded in her brain it was absolutely true. She just didn't want to win.

Jillian Jacobs came over, still standing on her own two feet and gave her a big, gracious hug. "Photo finish," she said. Madison was so exhausted and confused that she hugged back with all of her might, happy just to have some human contact. The ice water shot daggers through her legs and the feel of another person warmed her heart, regardless of who it was. The rest of the girls came in close as well in a sort of group hug that felt as though it lasted for days.

"The two bravest girls on this team!" shouted Mia. "Mads Riley and Jillian Jacobs!"

"And Mia Espindola!" someone else shouted. "We all made it across the line together!"

It was all very sweet. Sweet enough to make a sane person gag. Madison heard a tinny, hollow sound in her ears like a radio with a half broken speaker. She didn't care if she was brave. It didn't matter. She'd given up on running. She let her legs fall out from underneath her. Maybe she'd even pooed on herself, she didn't know. She checked and was happy beyond words that she'd kept her bowels in check.

Then came more people. It was like a grand crowd descending after an Olympic event. At the front of the pack was Patrick, his long dark hair noticeably more magnificent than anything else on the field or even in the world.

"Are you OK, Maddy?" he asked.

Madison shivered and tried to smile. She pulled her legs out of the ice water. "I guess," she said. "I fell." She wished she could have said something more interesting or witty than that but she could barely think so it had to be good enough.

"I saw it. You're incredible." He stepped closer. Everyone watched intently. A rapt silence fell over the crowd. Even Coach Dipson listened in on what was happening. "So," Patrick continued, "I want you to come with me to the spring semiformal next Thursday. I'm planning to make one of those big entrances. Bigger than anything anybody's ever done before. I want you to be a part of it."

Madison nodded. She received a hug from Patrick but could barely wrap her sweat covered arms around him to hug back. She didn't stop shivering.

Jillian stepped into the ice bath and squealed loudly. Everyone looked at her, but only for a second. It was once again Madison's show even though she hadn't meant for it to be.

"The limo will pick you up at your house at seven on Thursday," he said. "Dress to impress."

Madison never expected Patrick to say something as corny as "Dress to impress," but then again it was a moment where he was in the spotlight. Just like her, he probably didn't really know what he was doing and was just making up everything as he went.

When the crowd dispersed, Jillian and Madison both needed help from the trainer. They'd pushed far beyond their limits and just the blisters on the soles of their feet required a good ten minutes of attention apiece. Jillian winced as the trainer applied fake skin to her heel.

"Patrick Sutton," Jillian said as they sat across from each other on the field, both nearly doubled over in pain. "Way to land the big one."

Madison nodded. She wasn't sure if this was nice Jillian or fake nice Jillian. Luckily she didn't have to make conversation for very long. Her mother ran up to her, nearly in tears. "I heard what they did to you," she said. "I'll have that coach fired—"

"No!" Madison shouted. "Don't worry about me."

Mrs. Riley shook her head. "We're not just taking Krav Maga anymore. It's settled. We're going to those classes at the CIA. This is going to be serious. Real situational awareness, real self-defense. You need to know how to stand up for yourself and not to get into races that you can't finish." She was pacing back and forth like an army soldier, her feet picking up and stomping down with every step. "And I'm taking you to work on Thursday. I didn't know about it but the NSA does have a program for Take Your Daughter to Work Day. You won't be able to see my work station but that doesn't matter."

Madison didn't even care. She'd almost forgotten about that stupid phone and about all of the responsibility that she supposedly had to the world and to Graham. She had a date with Patrick Sutton, and most importantly, she had a bed to crawl into after all of this was over. The only thing she could really think about was sleep.

Jillian jumped out of her ice bath and walked straight up to Mrs. Riley on wobbly legs. "Hi Mrs. Riley, I'm Jillian. It's nice to meet you."

Mrs. Riley smiled, instantly charmed. "It's nice to meet you too. I'm really impressed by you girls but I can't believe you couldn't just agree to stop before you killed yourselves today."

Jillian laughed cordially and said, "I thought about it." She was a pure picture of suck-up. "Mrs. Riley," she continued, "I didn't realize that you work at the NSA. One of my great passions is math and computation and I only know stories about what happens at your office. It's one of the most exciting places in the world for a mathematician. I'd love to see it someday."

Mrs. Riley nearly swooned. "Well you can come with us next Thursday if your mom says it's all right."

Jillian got quiet and looked away. Madison recognized the look immediately. She'd done it so many times herself. She was instantly sure that Jillian's mother was dead, as clearly as she'd ever known anything in her life. Mrs. Riley noticed it too, instantly flooded with a deep look of dread and confusion, and shook her head. "Just come. I'll get you a note from the Department of Defense. There's no principal in the country who would turn that down."

Madison scowled at Mrs. Riley with devil eyes, unable to stand the thought of a car ride with Jillian, let alone a day with her glad handing. Mrs. Riley noticed but shrugged her off. "I'll give you a ride home, Jillian. It's always nice to meet one of Madison's friends." Those words cut like knives through Madison's ears. She wished that Mia was still around but she'd left long ago. It was just Madison and Jillian, not just on the way home but for a whole day at the NSA. The day she needed to commit treason, betray her country and change the course of the world.

"Are you sure that Jillian can come?" Madison asked. "I mean, it's Take Your Daughter to Work Day, not take your daughter and her friend to work day…"

"Madison!" Mrs. Riley interrupted. "I can't believe that you would say such a thing." And Madison knew she was right. It was incredibly thoughtless. She wondered how she would feel if someone said the same thing in reference to her father.

She'd probably punch that person in the face.

"I'm sorry Jillian," Madison said. "I'm really sorry."

Jillian nodded. "It's OK. I guess you never heard. I try to keep it low profile as much as I can. I mean, she wasn't a war hero so it's not hard. And it was a long time ago."

Mrs. Riley interjected right away. "Well if you girls ever need to talk about anything, please do it. I'm sure you've got a lot in common. I'm so glad you two are friends and I'm so glad I finally get to meet you, Jillian. This is so wonderful." She'd almost been moved to tears. "How about we all go out to dinner together and talk about the NSA. I'm so happy to have someone who's that interested in cryptography to talk to."

Before Madison could even object, Jillian pepped up, "I'd love to." Madison couldn't tell if she meant it or not. It was so hard with Jillian. There was something about her demeanor, the way she always said the right thing in front of the people who mattered yet still accosted Madison in the bathroom. It was like she was always telling the truth and always lying at the same time.

So they went to dinner at a terrible Italian restaurant located in a nearly abandoned strip mall in a wasteland between Baltimore and Washington DC. It was the kind of place that serves troughs of pasta with three different kinds of red sauce that all look and taste the same. No one had chosen to go there. They just showed up somehow and were seated instantly in the nearly empty dining room. Madison said next to nothing while Mrs. Riley and Jillian gabbed on endlessly about numbers and theorems and the security threats to the United States. It was way too boring for anyone to be as excited about as the two of them were. Then Madison's phone rang. It was Graham.

Madison excused herself from the table and walked into the vestibule to talk. "I'm glad you called," she said. "I need to talk to you."

"Did you ever hear the joke about the guy who goes to the doctor and asks…" Graham put on a terrible Italian accent for the guy's voice, "'Do I need new parachutes?' The doctor said, 'Why did you come to me for parachutes? I'm a doctor.' The guys says, 'My feet hurt all the time. Do you think my shoes are too tight? Do I need a new parachutes?'" When Madison didn't laugh, he said, "Do you get it? Parachutes sounds like pair of shoes…" The joke was not going over with Madison. She was not a fan of stupid puns. Graham waited for her to speak, probably hoping for a laugh, but she didn't give him one. "I'm just saying you need to watch how much you run."

"What do you want?"

"First of all," he started, his voice calm and clear, "you need to be more careful about showing up on security footage. I've spent ten hours hacking into various security systems around the country and deleting video of you running around wearing those million dollar shoes you stole." Madison expected him to sound angry but he wasn't, he was straightforward. One of the things she'd started to value about Graham was that he never seemed to make a big deal about what someone else thought of him. He just said what he needed to say and was done. He sounded like he was lounging on some deserted beach in the Caribbean.

"Secondly," he continued, "Jillian Jacobs is coming with you on your little trip and I take it you just found out. That's good. It proves that you weren't trying to read the future. Never do it, Mads. It's bad news. Take it from a pro. Never ever read

148

the future."

"But you obviously did," she said. "You knew that Jillian was coming. Why didn't you warn me?"

"Because I didn't warn you," he answered. "This isn't a world of cause and effect, Mads. The rules you have in your head don't make sense anymore. If you know something is going to happen then it will happen. So never ask. Never ever."

"Are you saying that we have no choice in life?" Madison asked.

Graham groaned. "I don't know in general. I just know in the specific case. If I ask what's going to happen then I have no choice but to do it. Try it out now. Ask what's going to happen for the rest of the night and then try to do something different. I dare you. Don't ask about anything other than the next five minutes."

"Why did you call?"

"You need to make a plan for yourself. You need to start looking up schematics of the NSA. You need to know where your mom's computer is and how you're going to get there. This is serious."

"I can't read schematics!" Madison yelled. "I can't even read *Romeo and Juliet*. I'm fifteen years old. You expect me to save the world but I can barely pass English class."

"This is bigger than I've told you. It's much bigger. This isn't just about the phone. Honestly, I can't believe I'm bringing you into this already but I can't help it. You're important. You are one of the people who will determine the future of humanity, of the universe. I don't know how and I don't want to know…" His calm demeanor suddenly went into overdrive. It was like he was trying to enter into a hypnotic state where his emotions couldn't get the better of him. He sounded like a zen master, a sequestered monk. He was the perfectly voiced sound of Himalayan calm. Madison assumed he was actually hysterical beneath the façade. "You are going to be there when it happens."

"When what happens?"

"Something will change everything in a single moment. It won't happen for a long time. I won't be there. You will."

"But what happens?" Madison asked, trying not to get hysterical herself. She felt her brain tingle in pin-prick shocks. She needed to know.

Graham went back to his shamanic breathing. It didn't help to calm Madison down. "I'm trying to figure that out," he answered. "It's one of the only things I still don't know. But you're missing the big picture here, Mads. I know for a fact that you're going to live for many years. That means you're immortal until then. You can't die. It's more accurate to say that you won't die, but they're basically the same thing. Whatever happens to you, you don't have to fear death for a very long time."

Madison didn't know how to take the news. It sounded important but she'd never really feared for her own death in the first place. She'd inherited that from her father. He never seemed to mind diving headfirst into harm's way nor did she. Neither ever put their own life on a higher pedestal than anyone else's. Hearing those words both liberated her and trapped her.

Madison was supremely confused. "But during the earthquake you said I needed to stay with you or I'd die. But you just said I can't die."

"I said you won't die. What I mean is that you are still just as fragile as any other person, you'll just happen to make the right decisions along the way to stay alive." Madison could hear him suck in a deep breath. "I know it sounds like I'm saying that everything in the world is in the hands of fate but it's not. It's much more complicated than that. You have free will. Just not a hundred percent free will. If you look something up on that phone then it's set in stone. I'd tell you how I know that but it's complicated. I don't understand how it works and I'm a billionaire genius."

"You're a billionaire? I didn't know that."

"I'm not hiding from you, Mads. Just look me up. And while you're at it, ask it what will happen over the course of the next five minutes. Then try as hard as you can not to do what it says you're going to do. It's a fun game. Seriously. A real laugh." Sarcasm dripped from his voice.

He hung up.

Chapter 19

Madison looked at the phone, the heavy brick that she'd been told over and over had immense power: the power to know the past, the present and the future. And somehow it landed in her hands even though she didn't really deserve it and it would ruin her life. Now Graham was telling her that she'd be present for a moment that would change the course of the universe. She felt woozy, not just from the news but also from the eighteen plus miles she'd just run. Her feet were so battered and blistered she could barely feel them. Her legs wobbled like jelly and her head swam through a mixture of happy chemicals released after the long run and confusion that had been brewing since the moment the phone found its way into her hands.

She spoke to it softly, trying to look inconspicuous in the foyer of the nearly empty restaurant. "What am I going to do in the next five minutes?"

The phone whispered back, in the same woman's voice she'd heard from the phone before. It was as if she was a real person ready to have a full conversation without a moment's delay. "You're going to listen to the rest of this message. Then you're going to run outside and yell 'Stop' at the top of your lungs. Then you're going to grab a knife, after which you will tear a woman's dress. Then you're going to scream and cry. You're going to tie a bow with the woman's dress and then sprint down the street. You will continue to sprint until five minutes have elapsed."

And that was it. Madison couldn't believe what she'd just heard. Her heart thumped loudly and her ears rang with the sound of buzzing from her brain. What knife? She felt traumatized even though nothing had happened. She looked outside. There was indeed a woman wearing a dress on the far side of the decrepit parking lot carrying a very expensive purse. A hulking, lumberjack of a man ran up from behind her and grabbed it but the woman held firmly to the handle. The man pulled something out of his jacket. From where she was, Madison couldn't see it clearly but she knew immediately that this was the knife that Charlotte had told her about. She knew what was about to happen. She couldn't breathe. She couldn't even scream out. The world collapsed around her into darkness as she watched.

Madison sprinted outside toward the man and woman screaming "Stop!" as loudly as she could. The man turned to look at her but it was too late. Madison saw the knife sticking out of the woman's stomach, though she couldn't yet see any blood. She couldn't see anything about the man except that he wore a jacket over a sweatshirt with the hood up and he had a long, mangy beard. He ran away with a slightly stuttering step.

By the time Madison reached the woman she was already on her knees holding the knife in her hands and bleeding profusely from the wound. Madison grabbed the knife from her, afraid she might accidentally fall on it. She laid the woman onto her back, took her own jacket off and placed it under the woman's head. Then she did what she'd done at the airport, she ripped a piece of the woman's dress and used it to apply pressure to the wound. But this wound bled more than any other she'd seen. She pressed as hard as she could but she didn't feel like she had enough strength. She wrapped the cloth around the woman's stomach and cinched it as well as she could before tying it tightly. The woman heaved with pain but Madison pushed her back to the ground.

Then Madison heard other voices. Thankfully, she recognized them. It was her mother, running and sliding across the pavement to help. Mrs. Riley had wordlessly grabbed the first aid kit that she always carried with her in her handbag and treated the wound. Madison stepped back, sure that her mother would do a better job at the triage than she could. She looked over to Jillian who already had her phone out and was calling 911.

Everything seemed to be covered save for one thing. The man was getting away. Madison looked down at the knife in her hand covered with blood. She took a moment to wipe a tear away from her face. Then she scanned the area for the man who'd done this. It didn't take long for her to notice him across the street, trying to look casual as he lumbered awkwardly away.

It was rage that propelled her, that and the leftover adrenaline, cortisol and other pops of chemicals sizzling within her skull. They'd replaced her thoughts so that her mind was a blank page upon which terror and fear were a footnote, the rest slowly filling with the repeated phrase, "Get him!"

She sprinted, still with the knife in her hand. He was slow and obvious. It was hard for him to blend in with that purse in his hand. She crossed the busy street despite the traffic, running along the yellow line until there was an opening between the oncoming cars blaring their horns at her. The wet night air singed her throat as she sucked in breaths. Her jelly legs barely functioned but somehow she was able to tell them to keep moving.

The neighborhoods got darker as they ran but Madison couldn't help herself. She'd never seen anything so horrible in real life, only on videos and in movies.

They reached another busy intersection. The man had to wait for some cars to pass by. Madison had almost caught him. There were no police in sight. There was no help to be found in any direction. He stopped in a grassy abandoned lot so abruptly that Madison almost ran right into him. Although he was slow he was at least twice Madison's size and wider than he was fat. He had big hands. Behind his grizzled beard were wide, determined, glass-blue eyes. He spoke, his voice raspy and slow like a sea captain's. "Do you know how to use a knife?" he asked. "I've been cut before by bigger than you."

Every muscle in Madison's body was weak. She almost felt as though she couldn't run away, she'd expended so much energy just getting to this point. The man wore a thick coat with many more layers piled on underneath. Even if Madison could get close enough to use the knife she probably wouldn't even have the strength to hurt him with it. Even if she could, she wasn't sure she could bring herself to do it. She wasn't a killer.

She screamed at the top of her lungs again. It was all she could think to do.

A gas station attendant across the busy intersection looked through the line of cars to see them. Madison screamed and screamed again. She knew she'd done the wrong thing by chasing the man. She was scared. Yet at the same time she felt peaceful, Graham's voice echoing in her head. "You're immortal." And so she lunged at the man with all her might.

The man pushed one arm against her chest and she fell to the ground, the wind knocked out of her. Then the man crouched above her, reaching for the knife, but Madison knew enough to grab his index finger and wrench it back to stop him. He yelled out but only for a second. With his other hand he punched her in the eye.

Madison had never felt anything like it before. Her head went weary for a moment while her eye exploded with pressure as if a thousand bolts of lightning had shot outward from her brain. And simultaneously her world went brown. Not black. She still had a flavor of wakefulness but she was unsure what she saw and tasted. It was a dream world in that moment, a brief respite from all of the pain she felt. When she finally opened her eyes again the man was gone and the gas station attendant was running toward her while screaming into his phone for the police.

She slowly curled to a kneeling position. The knife was still in her hand. She pushed herself up and stood tall on her wobbly legs.

"Are you OK?" the gas station attendant asked.

Madison dropped the knife and felt her body for any wounds. The only thing that hurt was her face, a brutal sting and a pounding headache, but otherwise she felt all right. "I'm fine," she told him. "Which way did he go?"

The attendant shook his head. "Don't worry about it. You're safe."

But she didn't feel safe. She felt cold and sweat stained and vulnerable. She'd never been hit in the face before. She'd never been at the mercy of a man twice her size. It scared her immeasurably.

"I'll find him," she said. "I'll find him and he'll go to jail."

"The police are coming," the attendant told her. "Just stay calm."

Madison's whole body shook. She fell to the ground with a thud. What was she thinking? How was she supposed to take on a man who would stab a woman for her handbag? She felt stupid and lonely and scared. Not only that, but she had her mom to contend with.

Then there was the biggest realization. It was one that she couldn't understand no matter how hard she tried. She'd asked Charlotte, the woman with the nice British voice on her phone, what she was going to do in the next five minutes and Charlotte told her a crazy story that could never have been true. Yet not a moment later she was living through that crazy story word for word. Graham had told her that she had free will which meant that she could choose what she was going to do from moment to moment, but sitting there on the sidewalk with an ever-blackening eye, she felt as though she had no control at all.

When she tried to cry her eyes stung. When she tried to move every muscle ached. When she tried to think her thoughts lingered on the image of that woman keeling over with the knife sticking out of her.

"I didn't have a choice!" she yelled at the top of her lungs.

"I had to help that woman!"

The attendant knelt next to her. "And I have to help you," he said. "Just try to stay calm. The ambulance will be here in a minute. You're safe now. You'll be all right."

Madison shook her head. She'd live, she acknowledged, but she wasn't sure she'd ever be all right again.

Chapter 20

This was Madison's second trip to the hospital in as many weeks. During the ambulance ride all she could think about was her phone which she'd left at the scene of the stabbing when she ran to catch the assailant. She knew she could find him and tell the police where he was and then pick him out of a lineup. She'd seen his eyes. She knew his voice. All she needed was an address and all it would take would be one little question into the phone. That was it. She didn't feel like she needed to go to the hospital. She'd argued with the EMT when they came but after they found out she couldn't stand on her own they forced her onto the stretcher. Still, she made them wait for a police officer to arrive before she let them take her away.

"I'll tell you more when I get to the hospital," she said. "But he was a tall man and he had a beard. He had glass-blue eyes. He wore a bunch of coats on top of each other and he sounded like a sea captain. He had a limp."

That was the best description she could come up with before they wheeled her away. As they pushed her into the ambulance she added, for the sake of thoroughness, "And he has a broken index finger."

It was a long, awkward ride to the hospital. She wasn't really hurt. None of the blood on her was her own. Still, the cops made sure she was safe and in their eyes that meant sending her away. In reality, she figured, the safest place for her to be was with her phone tracking down the man who had done this to her.

Madison sat in the emergency room, antsy to get up and track the man down. But she didn't have Charlotte with her. She just had to wait. While she was sitting, she heard the nurses talking about the woman who'd been stabbed. She walked over and carefully asked, "Is she going to be all right?" It felt like a repeat of Costa Rica except this hospital was quieter and smelled like lemons instead of sea breeze.

The nurse smiled caringly and answered, "We think so. She's up in trauma now. The knife missed the liver and kidneys. It punctured her small intestine but that's the sort of thing they can usually stitch up." She looked at her colleague for a moment and then looked back. "Do you know her?"

"Can you give her a message for me?" The nurse nodded. "Can you tell her that I'll get him. I'll find him and I'll get him. Tell her I promise. My name's Mads Riley and I promise."

The nurse handed her a pen and some paper. "Honey, you can write her a note and I'll make sure it gets to her."

That was the closest to a hero that Madison had ever felt.

When she finally calmed down her mind suddenly fixated on her dreams, on the feeling of dread she constantly felt. The trauma she felt as she watched that woman fall to the ground brought pale white images of dust and debris, explosions and gunshots thundering into her mind. It hadn't been so vivid in years. It hadn't felt so close. She couldn't understand it. She couldn't visualize it. It was a confusing swirl of displaced images. But suddenly it felt as though it wrapped around her. A straight jacket.

An hour later Mrs. Riley finally showed up in Madison's stark gray hospital room. She had to give a statement to the police about the stabbing even though she fought against them to find her daughter. Plus she had to give Jillian Jacobs, her new best friend, a ride home. She looked furious when she saw Madison, more so than either one expected. "I can't believe you!" she shouted. "After we talked about situational awareness, about not putting your life in danger, you decide to go and do it again. And what happened? You could have been killed."

"But I wasn't," Madison fired back. "Daddy would have been proud. I defended myself, broke his finger when he tried to grab the knife. And now I know what he looks like. I know what color his eyes are. We can find him and put him in jail."

Mrs. Riley wept. Like a puppet with its strings cut, she dropped to her knees on the floor. Her whole body was covered under a mass of hair spread out in every direction.

This was the first time Madison had ever seen her cry like that. Even at her father's funeral when they folded the American flag and presented it to her, she hadn't let her tears flow that freely. This time her body rocked up and down with an uneven rhythm. Whatever guilt Madison had for stealing the ruby slippers sank to the depths, replaced by the deeper and more immediate guilt of having made her mother break down in public like that.

But she also felt guilty for another reason. It was the most important reason of all. Madison felt guilty because she knew her mother was wrong to be so upset and she wanted to tell her so. The secret that she held in her heart, the fact that she knew she couldn't die, it plagued her. She was right to have done it. This was her super power and to ignore it would be to let the guilty go free.

"What did you want me to do, Mom?" Madison asked. She tried not to sound defiant or defensive but she felt both. She felt deeply that she'd made the right choice.

Mrs. Riley looked up from behind her curtain of dark brown hair. She shook her head and winced. "You're just like him. You are almost identical in every way." She wiped her face and finger combed her hair. "I never knew whether to be proud of him or to hate him for ripping my heart out every few months when he'd go missing once again for the fiftieth time. Do you remember all of those nights we cried for him, Madison? Do you remember hearing that he might never come back?"

Madison didn't need to remember. The memory accompanied every breath she took. She remembered the sleepless nights waiting for word from someone who might know something. She remembered her stomach eating itself from anxiety. She stared out the window into the night's black sky. "Now I understand how he must have felt," she said. "He knew he was hurting us. He knew it every day. I know he did." She imagined him in the middle of the Afghani hills with nothing but his thoughts and his rifle. She imagined how sick he must have felt knowing that his little girl was worrying about him. "But Mom," she said, "he knew he had a job to do and he knew that he was the best person in the world to do it. He did it because he believed it was the right thing to do. And it was the right thing. Someone told me that he saved the lives of over thirty Americans while he was alive. I think he saved even more Afghanis. Hundreds maybe."

Mrs. Riley put her head in her hands. "This isn't worth fighting over," she said.

"Why would you fight me?" Madison asked. "You know I'm right."

Mrs. Riley shook her head. "You have to remember that I work in the NSA, honey, so there are things that I know that you don't."

That made Madison furious. Thanks to Charlotte there was nothing that she didn't know anymore. Her mom had no business telling her what she did and didn't know. "Daddy always did the right thing. I remember all of the times he stood up for people. He always cared about other people more than he cared about himself. You don't get to say anything bad about him!"

Mrs. Riley was dead faced. Under her puffy eyes were the trails of dried tears and under those the salt of anxious sweat. She'd already gone through all of the feelings that a normal person has in a year within the span of a few hours. "I'm not going to lie to you," she said, all emotion gone from her voice.

"What do you mean?"

Mrs. Riley tapped her fingers against the hospital cart so that their crackling echoed throughout the room. Whatever it was she was trying not to say, Madison wanted her to say it, and soon. She was getting impatient with being told how much she didn't know. It was time to learn some things for real. Mrs. Riley turned to her and for the first time that Madison could remember her mother looked her in the eye and really thought about what she was going to say. "I'm going to tell you something that hurts me every time I think about it. Some of those Afghani kids your father saved grew up. He thought they were good. He thought that they'd like Americans because he saved their lives. But they became soldiers too. Some of them went on to kill American soldiers later on in the war," she shouted, nearly in tears. "So was he really doing the right thing?"

It was uncharacteristic of her mother to yell like that. In fact, Madison had never seen her mom so confused and angry, yet empty all at the same time. She must have been bottling that up deep inside for years.

Madison shook her head. "A life is a life, Mom," she said, trying to be quiet. "You can't let an innocent person die just because you think they'll grow up to be a terrorist. You don't know what they'll become."

Mrs. Riley shook her head. "I don't know," she said as she wiped her face again, finally looking like the professional she'd always been. She pulled Madison's phone out of her purse and handed it to her. "You have a lot of missed calls. For some reason I couldn't figure out how to answer your phone. Did you use my upgrade to get this phone without telling me? I've wanted a new phone for a year."

Madison didn't answer.

"Whatever," Mrs. Riley said. "Anyway, I'm sure your friends are worried about you." She turned her back. "I have to use the bathroom to stop myself from looking like a monster..." she chuckled. "A momster." Madison cracked a smile and laughed back. "I love you, girl," Mrs. Riley said over her shoulder.

"I love you too, Mom," Madison said back.

She checked her phone. All of the calls were from people from school. Apparently word had spread quickly. Everyone from Jillian to Danny to Coach Dipson knew about what happened. But one text message stood out. It was from Graham and it said simply, "I'm sorry you had to find out this way, but that's why you don't mess with the future. Even if it works out well, you lose in the long run."

Madison dialed his number almost without thinking. She felt his presence on the other side of the line almost before the phone stopped ringing. "Hey Mads," he said. "I'm so sorry." He cleared his throat and swallowed. "I want you to know that I didn't realize it would be so bad. I stopped reading the future long ago so I had no idea what would happen."

Madison thought about it once again. When she was in the restaurant reading the description of what she was about to do, she wanted more than anything not to do it. Then suddenly a situation came up where she had no choice. "It doesn't make sense," she whispered. "How could that man in the parking lot know to stab that woman at exactly the same moment that I read my future?"

"He didn't," Graham answered. "No one did. Nothing did. At least I don't think so. I don't really know. All I can tell you is that in the few years that I've been able to tell the future I've never been able to prove it wrong. I locked myself in a room for hours with no possible distractions and asked it what I was going to do. You know what it told me? It told me I was going to sit in a locked room for hours with no distractions. It plays tricks with me. I've tried to outsmart it and I can't, so instead I just stopped asking. But by then I already knew too much."

Madison focused meditatively on the tiny ridges in the ceiling tiles. "What if I was in my dad's shoes? What if I could have looked at each one of those kids in Afghanistan and been able to tell which ones would become killers when they grew up and which ones wouldn't? What would I do?"

Graham sighed heavily, the growl in the back of his throat felt comforting and warm yet somehow distant, like the sigh of a king. "It wouldn't be right to judge them before they've actually done something. The best you could do would be to watch the crime happen and then punish them right away," he said. Somehow Madison trusted that he knew what he was talking about. She agreed even though she didn't know why.

"I'm proud of you, though," he said. "You ran eighteen miles today, you saved a woman's life and you're well on your way to bringing a bad man to justice. That's more than most people can say about their whole lives."

Madison felt uneasy. She pulled the phone away from her ear and bit her lip. She wondered if he knew what she was thinking at that very moment or if he'd neglected to look it up. "I don't like that you're stalking me," she said. "It makes me very uncomfortable. I don't even know you but you know every single thing about me down to what boys I liked in Spain when I was eight. You're saying it's not right to use your power to judge people in Afghanistan. It sure as hell isn't right to use it to dissect the life of a fifteen year old girl!"

Madison was once again aware of the volume of her voice.

Graham didn't answer. She wanted to apologize but she didn't know why. She knew she was right. She deserved privacy. It was creepy that this grown man knew everything about her, even if he was a thousand miles away or even on the moon.

It didn't make it any less of an intrusion. Neither of them spoke for some time.

"I'm sorry." He snorted to himself. "Yet again I find myself apologizing to you, Mads. Everything that has gone wrong in your life is my fault and I just keep digging the hole deeper." He almost sounded like he was crying. Madison felt like the only one holding it together.

"Just stop spying on me," she said. "I have a hot date for the dance on Thursday and I don't want you watching me with your third eye."

She expected Graham to say something but he stayed quiet longer than she expected. Finally he said, "I didn't know you had a date."

"Whatever," Madison said.

"Honestly," Graham insisted. "I don't know everything. I only know the answers to questions that I remember to ask. I didn't ask it about your social life. I don't remember what I asked but for some reason it left that part out. I probably asked it something along the lines of, 'What did Madison do tonight?' And I'm guessing that he asked you out as opposed to the other way round."

That sounded reasonable but she still didn't like it. "You have the ability to know everything. You could follow me around at all hours of the night like an invisible camera if you wanted to. I'd have no way to stop you. It's awful."

"I don't do that," he pleaded. "I swear to you. I promise." Where he usually sounded so in-control he suddenly sounded like a whining child. Madison had never been pleaded with in that way by a grown man.

"I'm very uncomfortable right now," Madison said. "I

think this might be the moment when I decide to take a sledge hammer to this phone and never talk to you again. I really do."

"Then I think you should," he told her. "But just remember this one thing. Jump exactly when I tell you to." He spoke quickly and forcefully like a hypnotist trying to make sure that a phrase sticks in your head so that you never forget. "That's all I have left to say." And then he hung up.

But she had more to learn from it. She remembered the list of things she needed to know. One of them was counter-interrogation. One was about some crazy spy gizmo. She needed to know more. That night she stayed up all night reading about what to do when you get interrogated. She didn't know why she needed to know it, but she wasn't about to ask about the future again.

Chapter 21

Madison could barely walk the next morning. She hadn't done any of her homework and she had a light purple swollen spot under her eye as well as one on the back of her head, which thankfully was hidden. People watched in disbelief when she boarded the bus in the morning but nobody actually asked her if she was all right. She didn't really know any of them but she'd come to realize that they all knew her and they'd begun to expect that she'd have some crazy story to tell each day. She sat near the back, as far away from everyone as she could but she could still feel them looking. Like most people would, she pulled out her phone to pass the time, but she didn't actually want to use it. She just stared at the blank screen in front of her with a distant look on her face. Today was the day she'd destroy it. She'd decided. She just hadn't had the chance to do it yet.

Walking through the lobby doors, yet again every eye was fixated on her. Mia squealed and a shiver cracked through Madison's nerves. Mia ran up and gave her a giant hug. "Oh Mads!" she screamed as she hugged with all her might. "Stop scaring us. When did you get to be so crazy? You can't chase down a mugger on your own. I mean, look at your eye! Next time something really bad is going to happen." Usually, Mia would have thrust into a hyperbolic explanation of the bodily injury that Madison might suffer. The fact that she didn't made Madison much more nervous.

"You don't even want to know how many posts there are about last night," Danny said. "It's ridiculous. Every single person in this building wants to know what really happened and you didn't even post a status update. That's so inconsiderate, Mads."

Madison melted into the corner, her non-descript t-shirt and jean ensemble that she'd meant to hide behind suddenly felt like insufficient covering. It wasn't just some people staring. It was everyone. She should have expected as much, especially since the story had gotten inflated slightly by the echo chamber of high school Internet gossip.

"Is it true?" Danny asked. "Did you really save that woman's life? Did you run after a guy who was three times your size and then get away with it? According to Jillian Jacobs it was even more heroic than the earthquake." Then he leaned in closer and whispered. "Is all of this craziness on account of that spy phone you took from your mom?"

She nodded. "I have to give it back," she lied. "Just like the slippers. I have to give everything back."

A strong hand tapped her on the shoulder. By the warmth she felt trickling through the fabric of her shirt she knew immediately that it was Patrick, lightly brushing his hand in support.

Danny nodded and puffed out his chest. "What's up, Patrick," he said. "I think I might be beating you in *StarX* right now. You better watch out."

Patrick nodded and smiled to Danny but turned quickly to Madison. He pulled gently at her shoulder, twirling her toward him. He didn't flinch when he saw the swollen bruise on her cheek. Instead, he brushed the back of his hand down her good cheek while looking deep into her eyes. He whispered so only she could hear, "You're amazing." Then he leaned in to kiss her but she couldn't move on account of the tension and excitement and fear. She couldn't even pucker her lips. She just received this tender, willow, awkward kiss on her cheek but also touching gently on the corner of her mouth.

"Do you want to see a movie with me tonight?" he asked, his voice bright and uncharacteristically chipper. "My host brother can drive us. He's a lad."

Danny spurted out his thoughts before Patrick was finished speaking. "Madison never goes out on Mondays," he said. "Her mom won't let her do anything. It's like this set thing they've had ever since she came to this school."

Madison's whole body sank. "It's true," she said. "I can't go out on Mondays. I'm sorry."

Patrick looked baffled. He tried hard to comprehend, his little Irish stammering providing the cutest display of confusion Madison had ever seen.

She breathed in deeply and held her breath. She was still reeling from the pseudo kiss they'd just shared. "It's just that I have this class that I really can't miss. I made a promise a long time ago that I'd do it and I can't back out now."

Patrick shrugged. "Well can I come to your class then? Whatever it is I'm sure I'll have a brilliant time with it. I love learning."

Madison hadn't ever told anyone what it was that she did on Monday nights. It was personal to her but it didn't need to be a secret. She wrapped her arms around Patrick and nestled her head into the crook of his shoulder. "That would be the greatest."

"So what is it?" Patrick asked.

"What's what?" Madison asked back.

"What class do you take on Monday nights that's so important?"

Madison glanced around. She'd already said too much in front of too many people to stop now. She smiled, trying to be meek. "It's just this training that I promised I would do. It's called Krav Maga. It's like kickboxing. I'm not good at it." Patrick took a step back. He looked genuinely speechless. Madison continued. "It's just for self-protection. I started a long time ago."

"Well it's paid off," Patrick gushed. "You are the most badass girl in the world, Maddy. This Krav Maga must be special if it made you who you are today."

"You should come," she said. "The class starts at seven."

Patrick smiled. "Right," he said. Then he pointed to his broken leg, "But I hope this doesn't get in my way." Madison immediately felt stupid for neglecting his cast. She usually didn't talk enough to put her foot in her mouth so she found herself at a loss. As she was about to say something the bell rang. Everyone scattered.

"I wish I had the same lunch period as you, Maddy," Patrick said as he walked away. "I barely ever get the chance to talk to you, but you seem like the most brilliant person in the world." He took a few steps and then turned back. "I'll see you after you finish up with lacrosse practice."

Madison stood stock still in her place. She watched Patrick's hair wave along as he walked as if it were blown by some unseen fan during a photo shoot.

"You do Krav Maga?" Danny asked. "Why didn't you tell me? I do martial arts too. We could have sparred. Tai Chi. It's the most badass because it's the slowest."

Madison rocked on her heels, not listening at all to Danny. "He said I'm brilliant."

"If you ask me it's a tie," Danny grumbled. "I'd rank you about even with Neil deGrasse Tyson, but I see what he's getting at." Madison wasn't listening at all.

She still stood slackjawed in awe as Patrick disappeared around the corner. "I even get to talk to him later today."

Danny laughed. "And I'll bet you if you talk to him for an hour he'll only say one thing smarter than a third grader." Danny rolled his eyes. "Maybe half a thing."

"How do you know?" she asked.

"*StarX* doesn't lie," Danny said. "Nobody could have a character that dumb and have even a quarter of the IQ needed to assemble a worthwhile thought."

Madison took off at a half gallop to get away from Danny. "Is that all you ever think about, Danny? That stupid video game? You know some of us have real lives."

"Well some of us have real brains," Danny yelled after her.

Chapter 22

Madison kept to herself for most of the day. She didn't have much to say to Mia and Danny at lunch. Instead she sipped her water as she pawed at her school bought portion of chicken with arugula salad and Spanish style quinoa pilaf. If there was one thing to be thankful for at Shackleton High it was the food. The international flair that characterized every facet of the place, from its Basque and Bauhaus inspired architecture to its eclectic music, infused the food with an unexpected kick of authenticity compared to other school lunches she'd tried. Government schools were the worst, often serving foods that varied only in the shade of brown to which they'd been fried. She quickly checked her email. Someone had sent her a post from Jillian Jacobs. It was the most insufferably self important thing she'd ever read. She could barely finish. This would not be a good day.

Lacrosse practice that afternoon was a joke. Half of the girls couldn't even walk, let alone Madison and Jillian who could barely stand and hold their sticks at the same time. Instead, they were paired to do a sitting drill where they passed to each other while sitting on the cold grass. It would give Madison a chance to scream at Jillian for ruining Take Your Daughter to Work Day.

At first they said nothing and just tossed the ball between their well-laced lacrosse sticks which extended two feet above their heads. They stared each other down, neither one wanting to break first and act nice.

After a while, though, Jillian started interrogating. "Are you insane?" she asked. "What were you thinking last night?"

Madison shrugged and tossed the ball back. "I just saw it happening. I had no choice."

"You had a choice," Jillian fumed. "You had your phone. You could have called the police. You have some kind of hero complex."

This was the last thing that Madison wanted to hear from anyone, let alone Jillian. It was like she knew it would get to her, she knew exactly what to say in order to cut deepest. So Madison changed the subject. "How long is your stick?"

"Thirty-eight," Jillian answered. "It's scandium. Got an offset head that weighs a hundred and eighteen grams. I strung it myself." She smirked. "What about yours?"

"I don't know," she answered. "I don't really know anything about sticks. I just went to the store and bought one."

Jillian nearly fell over laughing but since she was already sitting down there was nowhere to fall. "Are you kidding me? You almost made the traveling team and you don't even know how to play?" She was so pompous.

"I know how to play, I just don't know about sticks," Madison asserted. "I'll learn. Besides, the stick doesn't make the player in any sport."

"You playing attack?" Jillian asked.

Madison shook her head.

"Oh my God! This isn't fair! Why do you have to compete with me on everything that I care about? I've been playing since I was five. This is one of my many trump cards for getting into college. I deserve this more than you. I deserve to be popular more than you do."

Jillian slung the ball right at Madison so hard she thought it would take her head off. She ducked out of the way and watched it bounce across the field. "I don't care," Madison said. She didn't even try to go get the ball because she was so sore. She wanted to tell Jillian that she didn't ask for there to be an earthquake and she certainly didn't ask for that woman to be stabbed. She put down her stick and pointed to her eye.

Jillian groaned. A girl ran up meekly from behind Madison and handed her the ball that Jillian had winged at her. "Here you go," the girl said.

Madison was speechless. It was strange to be suddenly popular. Ordinarily nobody gave her anything but suddenly people went out of their way to help. "Thanks," she said. "That was really nice of you to grab that."

"Oh," said the meek girl. She did something that almost looked like a curtsy. "Anytime." Then she ran away. Madison heard a giggle after the girl had run twenty yards or so and caught up with her friends.

"You don't have to thank people all the time," Jillian scoffed. "You didn't have to run after that homeless guy. Maybe that's why you keep doing stupid things. You just don't think enough."

"It wasn't stupid!" Madison shouted.

"You know it was stupid!" Jillian growled, trying not to sound like the angry one. "And so was diving into that cave for your phone and so was beating up Arlo Henderson. You do stupid things, Madison. I'm not ashamed to tell you to your face."

And to that Madison had no comeback. She cradled the ball in her stick, twirling it back and forth slowly just as lacrosse players are supposed to. She was pretty good. She hardly ever dropped it. "So," Madison said as she tossed the ball back to Jillian, "Next Thursday we'll be together all day."

"I like your mom," Jillian said.

Madison snapped. She wanted to say that Jillian lied to her, acted like they were all best friends. Madison shook her head. "Do you ever tell the truth?" She was truly screaming. A lot of the girls looked over at them.

Coach Dipson ran over as well as he could given his permanently extended legs. He got between the two of them. "No!" he shouted like a grouchy child, "I won't have my two star freshmen fighting!"

"We're not fighting, coach," Jillian sweetly squealed. "Madison was just caught off guard at how quickly we've become such good friends. Just a few weeks ago we hardly knew each other and already she's my deepest confidant. Isn't it funny how time flies?"

Coach Dipson looked mystified. "Be careful with your eye," he said to Madison, as if he really needed to remind her of the deep purple crescent that had developed. She'd been thinking about it all day. Coach Dipson dashed away in an unsuccessful attempt to look useful.

They didn't talk for the rest of practice. They just tossed

the ball back and forth, staring each other deep in the eye. It wasn't until coach blew his whistle that they rose to their feet, their legs numb from sitting. It wasn't a good idea from the start for them to sit, but that was how Coach Dipson worked. He gave instructions that made sense in his head and then he made sure he saw them through till the end. To put it mildly, Shackleton did not field the best girls lacrosse team in the state, despite the talent of the players.

After the team came in for a cheer, Madison walked with Mia to the buses which were parked diligently in a meandering driveway behind the fields. Most of the kids at school stayed after for sports so any without cars took the bus home at 5:30. Madison could have walked home but her legs were still tired enough that she decided to ride.

Mia kicked her cleats against the concrete curb to get some of the dirt off. Her legs were just as sore as Madison's but no one seemed to care about Mia's wellbeing, especially compared to Madison's. "Mads," she said, "I love you. You made my life better. I had fifty girls cheering me on yesterday. It was the first time in my life that I ever felt like I was part of a team." Her voice shook, accentuating her lisp. "I'm worried about you. You're acting weird. You don't seem the same anymore, Mads." She sat down on the curb and grabbed her sketchbook from her bag, just like she always did. "These are the warning signs that happen to people before they have a nervous breakdown and run away from home, live by the Potomac and get dysentery from eating out of a can of old soup they found."

Madison sat down next to her. She pulled out her phone and wondered if now was the time to smash it on a rock. "I know," she said.

She remembered back to her first day at Shackleton High School. It was a monstrous place.

Madison had stayed in the corner of the foyer each one of her first five days at Shackleton, trying not to get noticed. She didn't make any friends. She barely had conversations with anyone. She kept to herself and watched as people paraded around like goddesses among goddesses. Sure, there were a few anti-establishment types but they seemed just as preoccupied with living up to the standards of their respective subculture as the rest of the kids. The Goths had to look the most Gothic. The punks had to look the most punky. The gangsta kids looked like gangsters. They all spent mountains of cash and loads of time working to fit in with the people like them. Madison didn't fit in either, but at least she wasn't trying to. She sat on the curb next to Mia who drew in her sketchbook unrelentingly.

"When I first saw you I knew you needed a friend," Mia said. "You were sitting in the corner. Everybody else was either talking to someone or playing a game. I could tell you were listening." Mia flipped back through her thick sketchbook to the first page. It was a charcoal drawing of the foyer with Madison sitting cross-legged in the corner, her face stern and her mouth open. Madison didn't usually like to look at herself at all, whether in the mirror or in photos or on video. But she'd never actually seen a sketch of herself before. Instead of scrutinizing her features, or ignoring them, she contemplated the look on her face. She remembered that day, the first day of school. Every coiffure and designer t-shirt was a banner saying, "We're better than you." Madison's other schools were all on military bases. The kids there knew how to listen. They liked spitting and playing in the mud. At Shackleton the only thing that anyone seemed to care about was looking perfect. She remembered the outfit she wore and the way she'd flat ironed her hair for an hour that morning only to realize that everyone else had spent hundreds of dollars on their hairdos and hers couldn't possibly compete. Since then she'd always just let it lay where it lay, frizz and all.

Mia and Madison had come a long way in the few months since they first met. Usually Madison found it so easy to talk to Mia. She could say anything and Mia would get it, she'd laugh, she'd be excited. But she suddenly couldn't get the air out of her lungs to talk. It took all of her strength just to come up with a topic of conversation. "That's beautiful," Madison said, looking over Mia's shoulder at the sketch in her notebook. It was a picture of Madison, her eyes crunched together in defiant slits.

Mia began to tear it out of her notebook. "Do you want it?"

"No…" Madison said. "You should sell it or something."

"You're right," she said. "You're popular now. I could probably get good money for this. People pay for pictures of celebrities." She rolled her eyes, her goofy smile was like a fishing hook it curved so wildly. "Or I could just sell it to Danny," she gibed.

That caught Madison by surprise. She'd never really thought about people wanting to get to know her. She figured there was barely anything about her that was interesting. It was hard to be the person that everyone seemed to want to get to know. "You're my best friends."

Suddenly Mia looked up from her sketchbook, her smile wiped away and a scowl in its place. "Then why did you ask us to steal from America the other night, Mads?" Mia asked. "I didn't think you were that kind of person."

It was a strange way to phrase it. "I'm sorry, Mia," Madison said. "I didn't think about it."

"It's dangerous for me," she growled. "If I break the law I'm gone. Same with Danny! I thought we were a team." Mia wasn't a citizen, Madison knew. She was legally in the country but it still said Brazil on her passport. She had a lot more to lose. If she was found breaking a law she could be deported, not just sent to juvenile detention. She might have to go back to Brazil.

"Why didn't you give me this speech when we were there? We talked about it beforehand. We talked about saying yes to things," Madison said. "I didn't force you to do it."

Mia turned away and scrawled even more feverishly in her sketchbook. She drew an intricate sketch with sharp lines and wild curves that almost bled color despite the fact that they were black and white. Madison looked again at her phone. It was like the only way to fix everything was to use it but the only way for things to go back to normal was for her to smash it right then and there.

Then Patrick Sutton sauntered up on his crutches and sat on the curb next to Madison, his leg completely outstretched in the cast. He looked over to Mia's drawing. "That's really good," he noted even though he was barely able to see the page. Mia nodded but kept drawing.

"So Maddy," he said. "The buses don't leave for another ten minutes. What do you think about walking me home? I think we live in the same direction. Just follow Lera Road, right?"

Madison nodded. She stood and helped Patrick to his feet.

"I'll see you tomorrow, Mia," she said.

"Have fun," said Mia, her eyes never leaving the page in front of her. As Madison started walking she glanced over her shoulder to gauge what Mia might be thinking, whether she was so angry about the Smithsonian that she'd never forget about it. Should she tell Patrick to walk by himself?

She thought about it obsessively as she led Patrick in silence down the busy street away from school. Her anxiety doubled as she realized how serious this was, to be next to him.

Patrick eventually burst out in a fit of emotion and asked, "So what was it like to fight an old homeless guy?" His face was red with excitement and probably from sunburn.

Madison had to think for a second. It wasn't like anything. Nothing in her life even came close to the feeling she had at that moment. Not even the earthquake came close. She deliberated more and more and the only answer that came to her was one she didn't want to share so instead she said, "It was scary. It was the most scared I've ever been."

Patrick was remarkably agile on the crutches. He did this sort of dance as he moved down the sidewalk and he occupied surprisingly little space given the fact that he was such a large person made even larger by the crutches. "I don't think I would have been as brave as you were. I really don't." Then he got excited again, like a boy suddenly remembering the next present to ask from Santa. "But the police have their eyes out for him. Because of the description you gave, they think they might actually be able to find the guy. And you got out with just a black eye."

Madison remembered how much it hurt to receive that black eye and said, "Thanks for your sympathy." It was the first time she'd really challenged Patrick and she was afraid he'd get mad, but at the same time she thought he was acting pretty insensitively. Like always in that sort of situation, she feared that Patrick would hate her, yet she knew she was right. Usually, though, the fear would've won out.

"I'm sorry," Patrick said. "You just seem so rugged, I feel like I can treat you like one of the blokes I knew back home."

That didn't make Madison feel any better. He just wasn't very good at expressing himself, if he actually did like her. "That's what you get when you grow up on an Army base," she said. "You get really used to guy stuff."

Patrick raised one of his crutches into the air. "That's so great! Like what? Do you love sports? Obviously! I mean you're brilliant at it. What about zombie movies?"

Madison hated zombie movies. In fact she hated almost all movies but violent ones especially. They gave her nightmares. But then she always had nightmares, so it didn't make much of a difference. "I'd go to the movies," she said. It sounded well-phrased in her mind for a few reasons. Firstly, she didn't actually say she liked zombie movies, because she didn't. Also, it was a not so subtle way of reframing the question into a request to be asked out. It wasn't often that Madison felt smart, but at that moment she truly surprised herself.

"That sounds like fun," Patrick said. They walked on a bit further in silence. They both realized that they hadn't actually asked each other out.

"What was Ireland like?" Madison asked.

Patrick smirked. "Wet and dark," was his first answer. "My family had nothing when I was a boy, then my dad got a good job with the government and we moved into a big house.

We traveled the world for a while but he didn't think I was getting a good education in Turkey so he sent me here." He did a little jig on his good foot and his crutches.

Madison laughed and imitated his jig. Ireland was one country she'd never been to. She'd never really been anywhere cold in her life. It was all seaports and deserts and planes in between. "Where did you learn Spanish?" she asked. It seemed odd that an Irish boy would be so good at it.

Patrick shrugged. "I won prizes back home. I don't know if I'm anything special. All I've ever done in my life is read, write and play football." He laughed to himself. "And watch zombie movies." He held out his bum leg again and put on his over-the-top accent, "And here's me gimp leg to show that the leprechauns can still get to me here."

Madison tried to get a good look into his eyes but she couldn't hold up her courage enough to keep looking at him as he turned to her. She saw the spark of his eye but she couldn't quite get anything else.

"My house is around the corner," he told her, suddenly. "My host family isn't home yet…" He motioned with his head. "Do you want to see the place?"

Of course she wanted to. There was absolutely no reason not to. She stopped walking in her tracks. The first thing she thought when he said that, the first dire, awful thought in her head was that Graham would be watching her. She didn't have any intention of doing anything foolish. Even being alone in the same room, doing whatever they might do together, she could feel the prying, ever-present eye of Graham over her shoulder.

"I have to get home," she said. "But I'd love to walk with you just to see what it looks like."

He smiled, put his eyes to the ground so that his hair drooped over his face, and kept on down the road, filling her ear with the clicking sounds of his crutches against the sidewalk.

They arrived at a wide three story, white clapboard house with a perfect garden in the front under a canopy of tall oak trees. It was a step down from Carolyn Kaplan's house, but not much of a step. It wasn't flashy or pretentious but it was big enough to catch your eye from the road. Patrick pointed with his crutch, "That's my room in the corner there, in case you ever feel like bringing a ladder and surprising me in the night."

Madison laughed and nodded, but she wasn't sure if her nod meant that she wanted to get a ladder or she was just acknowledging that what he said was funny. It was better to just let a laugh be a laugh.

"My old house in Ireland could fit in that thing five times over," he said. "And I have two brothers and three sisters over there. This house is just me and my host family. It's mad."

She stepped closer to him, somehow ready for a kiss, Graham be damned. He bent over awkwardly, having to keep balance as he did it. She held him up and pushed her lips to his for the final contact.

And she could tell it was Patrick who felt weak in the knees. She walked away slowly trying not to look back. Eventually she couldn't help it. She said, "We'll pick you up for Krav Maga tonight at six thirty," Madison said. "I know you can't do everything with that broken leg but that makes it even better practice. In a real fight you never know what might get broken."

Chapter 23

Mrs. Riley was happy to have someone to bring to class. She didn't ask if Patrick was Madison's boyfriend. She didn't interrogate him about his past. In fact, she didn't embarrass them in any way. Madison assumed this was because her mom had already made a profile of him using her sophisticated software and she already knew everything she needed to know. After the earthquake she probably knew everything there was to know about everybody, if only just as a precaution.

There they were at the gym along with a dozen other fighters. It was a squat room with a low ceiling and mirrors on all sides like a converted ballet studio, except that instead of a wooden floor there were protective mats covering every square inch. The mats were firm but judging by the force with which some of the fighters threw each other they could protect people pretty well from a fall.

Madison wore baggy sweats, not quite ready to display her body to a crowd, much less to Patrick. For his part, Patrick wore sweats over his cast and a t-shirt that said "rumble" on it.

Mrs. Riley wore her yoga pants with a clingy tank top which made her slender frame look terrifying with its visible bulges of rope-like muscles. To first see her in her normal work cardigan you'd never imagine this dowdy woman in librarian glasses could throw men twice her size across the room, but that was what made her so effective: surprise. Not that she'd ever used her skills in real life. She'd spent her entire professional life behind a desk. Better safe than sorry she would say.

"When did you start these classes?" Patrick asked her.

Mrs. Riley answered mid-stretch. "I was working in Jerusalem. I had a lot of time on my hands."

"What were you doing there?"

"Oh," she said. "The same thing I do now."

"What do you do?"

She chuckled and answered, "Math." Then she walked away happily to begin punching a bag in the corner.

Madison rolled her eyes and hit Patrick in the shoulder. "Mom doesn't really answer questions about what she does. It's got something to do with national defense and codes. Nobody in the world understands it but her. When I ask her about her day the only thing she's allowed to say is, 'It was good.'"

Patrick tried to stretch but he had a hard time with his cast on. "Do you mean it's top secret?" he asked. Madison just shrugged and nodded. "What does that have to do with math?"

"I don't really know," answered Madison. She started jumping in place as she spoke. "It's really complicated. See, all these countries have their own armies and none of them want to let anybody else know what they're doing with those armies. So whenever they talk on the phone or send an email they use a code."

Patrick tried to understand but the vacant expression on his face showed he still wasn't quite sure. "Codes like the things in the newspaper where they take a famous quote and change the letters. Like instead of the letter *a* they write *x* and instead of *b* they write *j*?" He focused off into the distance as if to recall a vague memory. Madison could see why Danny might think he was an idiot with a face like that. Then it dawned on him and he said, "It's called a cryptogram."

"Right," Madison agreed. "Except my mom does that with codes that are literally a billion times more complicated than that." She looked over at her mom who was busy tossing a life-sized dummy across the room. "She can solve one of those cryptograms in the newspaper in less than a minute. I don't know what it has to do with math exactly but if you ask her I'm sure she'll explain it to you for hours and hours whether you want to know or not."

Patrick nodded to himself with the same dumb looking expression on his face. Madison assumed it was his thinking face, it just unfortunately looked like everybody else's dazed and confused face. "She traveled around the world for that?" he asked finally.

"Yeah," she said while punching into the air in front of her. "That's how I grew up. We'd be in one country for a year or so and then we'd move."

"Did you live in Israel?"

"When I was a baby. That's where my parents met." Madison jumped up and down in place momentarily as a warm up, trying to focus as she did it, a struggle with Patrick around. "Actually, it's a funny story. They were in Krav Maga class together. He asked her out because she was the only girl who could take him down." She found herself taking on Patrick's expression. It was contagious, but it kind of helped her think. "I guess that's why it was so important to them that I learn it too."

He looked almost embarrassed to hear the story. "That's brilliant compared to the way my parents met. Neither of them ever left County Cork until my dad got the job in Turkey. Those are the only two places they've ever lived."

"Do you miss Ireland?"

"Barely remember it."

"What about Turkey?"

He nodded. "They were nice people but I barely ever got out to see them. Dad doesn't much like the place. Doesn't much like anything."

That sounded so sad. Madison didn't know what to say but she couldn't help but ask, "Does he like you?"

"I think so," Patrick answered.

Madison couldn't imagine having a father who didn't tell her he loved her every chance he got. She also couldn't believe anyone could help but love Patrick.

Then the class started. Patrick did his best to fight along despite his broken leg. He couldn't do any of the throws but he could at least punch and move his body as if he were fighting. He watched Madison intently as she sparred with the other women in the class. It was brutal. Everything happened very quickly. The movements were precise and focused without any wasted energy. After a while, Madison caught his eye and looked away, blushing. It was exactly the opportunity Mrs. Riley needed to knock her to the ground with a thud. Madison had to crawl over to the side to catch her breath.

Patrick came up to her, this time looking decidedly impressed. "Wow," he said. "You're not kidding about your mum. You said she threw your dad across the room?"

"She's pretty badass," Madison answered.

"But so was your dad," Patrick said. "He must have been a gentleman and let her do it."

Madison had nothing to say to that. Everyone was acting as if they knew everything about her dad just because they saw one picture in the school paper and because they knew he died in combat. They all seemed to assume he was a macho soldier. They acted like he was perfect. Actually neither was true. So many nights she'd fallen asleep curled up into him as he read to her on the couch lulled by the cool calm of his voice. She'd never heard a hint of anger from him. And that was his biggest weakness. She remembered all of the times she'd heard her mom shouting at him, especially when he was scheduled to deploy in some distant warzone not to be heard from for months. He'd just sit there and take it, never raising his voice and barely defending himself. Madison had caught him crying to himself about it more than once. But they always made up. They always stayed a family.

She finally said, "I'm sorry about your dad."

"Why?" he asked. "He's still alive."

"It's a shame he isn't nicer."

"I'm sorry about your dad," he returned.

"Don't be," she said. "I'm not sorry for a single second I spent with him so there's nothing to be sorry about."

There wasn't much more to say for the rest of the evening. They talked about plans for the semi-formal and the limo. Madison tried not to think about her dad but it was too late. She'd pictured his face and that was enough to pull her away, even from the cutest boy in school.

Chapter 24

Mrs. Riley dropped Madison off at home to start her homework while she went to pick up dinner. Madison locked the door behind her and dropped her backpack in the kitchen before rushing up the stairs to her laundry-filled room. She hadn't cleaned her clothes in a while, given that she was so busy. There was a musty smell from some unwashed lacrosse socks but she didn't know where they'd disappeared to. She grabbed Charlotte, determined to finally get some answers, and went back downstairs. This was it. If there was anything she needed to know for the rest of her life, now was the time to find out.

The first thing she did was copy down the code that Charlotte had given her before. Even though she wasn't sure she would use it, she was sure she wanted to have the option. It was her mother on the line after all.

The second thing she did was find the name of the man who'd punched her, the man who stabbed that woman. She got his name, where he slept (he was homeless) and where he would be every day for the next week. That was a no-brainer. She had to know.

The third thing was trickier. It wasn't clear what she needed to know, but she knew that she should make solid plans for her trip inside of the NSA, so she started to work on that. The phone screen was too small to see everything that she needed so she asked Charlotte to email everything to her so that she could look at it on the big screen of her computer. She downloaded floor plans, she asked about ways she could get past the security checkpoints. Everything had an answer, as always. It never failed. She wished it would. She wished it would just for once tell her, "There's no answer."

Then finally she decided to talk to it. The phone had said its name was Charlotte, so she decided to just treat Charlotte like a person on the other end of the phone.

"Charlotte," she said. "I need to know about Graham. Who is he?"

"Graham Clarke was born in Carmarthen, Wales in 1974. He was educated at the Shipley School near Essex in England. From there he went to Cambridge University to study Computer Science and Land Economy. He founded his first company, Panacea Software, when he was twenty, two years before he was scheduled to graduate. Panacea went on to become one of the world's leading software companies with three of the most popular interactive titles developed in-house…"

"What are you talking about?" Madison asked. "I don't care about any of this. I just want to know who he is. How did he make you?"

Charlotte went on. "Panacea also became an instant success with myriad applications software for various platforms including mobile…"

"I don't care, Charlotte! Who is he? Why didn't he tell me he was a billionaire when we met?"

"He wanted you to find out for yourself. At this moment he'd implore you to look up Graham Clarke on Wikipedia and check the picture so that you know it's him."

Madison hadn't even known his last name up until that moment. She realized how willfully ignorant she was, how much she'd pretended this wasn't happening to her. She sat down and grabbed a tablet from the table to look at while she spoke to Charlotte. When she saw the picture, it really was Graham except that, instead of looking like a rockstar, he looked like a smartly dressed businessman in a grey suit.

"If he's such a great programmer," Madison began, "he could have faked this Wikipedia page. He could fake anything, couldn't he?"

"Almost every computer that is connected to the internet is capable of being exploited. He can crack any code in the world."

"With your help, right?" Madison asked.

Charlotte paused for a moment. "No," she said. "I'm just a voice. I believe that you mean that he could break the code, which is true, but I am not necessary to that process."

"Who are you then?" Madison asked.

"I'm the voice that Graham gave to this system. My name is Charlotte."

"You told me that already," Madison groaned. "Why did he call you Charlotte?"

"My voice and personality are based on someone he knew named Charlotte Earlham who grew up in Oxfordshire, England…"

"Shut up!" Madison yelled. "I don't care where she was born. Just tell me why she's important to him."

Charlotte answered without emotion, but with the kind of honest, realistic voice that a doctor would have or a scientist. She sounded so real but yet somehow flat, distant. "She was the love of his life."

And that, suddenly, was an answer worth hearing. Madison sat back and thought about this person who'd given her this gift of the future. She glanced at his bio on Wikipedia and saw the dollar figure that estimated how much money he had in the bank. Given that he could control every bank in the world, the number seemed way too small. Life presents quandaries, but not like this. It's not normal for a fifteen year old girl to judge whether or not a fortyish guy is using her. He told her that she was the only person who knew. How many other girls had he said that exact same thing to?

"What happened to the real Charlotte?" Madison asked. "You said she was the love of his life. What happened to her?"

"She was murdered," Charlotte answered. "By a woman named Ellen McCrae."

Madison almost fainted. Her heart raced and her jaw locked. Every muscle contracted. She'd known about Graham's involvement in deep, sinister, underhanded acts, but she hadn't considered murder. She remembered the gunfire she'd heard while she talked to him over the phone. She thought about the collision of her life with Graham's. Why had he chosen her? Was it just because her mom was in the NSA? There were probably a lot of other ways that he could have deleted that file. Why was she so special? Suddenly, instead of having no idea what questions to ask she was filled with too many questions. But enough was enough. Graham told her that she didn't have to do anything. She didn't have to break into the NSA. She didn't have to know the future. She'd already been hurt.

"Does Graham really have my best interests at heart?" she asked.

"He believes that he does," Charlotte answered.

Then she heard the garage door open. Her mom was home from work. She had one last question she had to ask before her mom walked through the door. "Should I destroy this phone tonight?"

Then Mrs. Riley walked through the door. Madison silenced Charlotte before she could answer. Mrs. Riley didn't seem to notice and shouted, "Hey honey! I forgot to ask earlier, how was lacrosse practice?"

Madison wasn't sure what to say. She stared at Graham's picture on her tablet and shrugged. "I don't know."

Mrs. Riley shook her head. "I'm going to complain to the school administration about that coach of yours. What's his name? Chip?" She took off her jacket and hung it by the door. "I don't like what he's doing to you girls."

Madison shook her head. "Please don't, Mom." She grabbed the tablet and walked upstairs. "It's really not that important."

Mrs. Riley called up after her, "I brought home Thai. I got that fish you like. The one that still has the head."

"Thanks Mom," Madison shouted back. She wanted to say "I love you," but it just sounded too weird and out of character. Her mom would be onto her for sure if she said that.

Chapter 25

The next day when Madison got up and looked in the mirror she saw that wallop of a black eye and thought about covering it with makeup. She wanted to forget about what happened entirely. Her own makeup selection was limited so she checked through her mom's. All of the colors were a half shade too light for Madison. She pulled them out of the makeup bag anyway. But as she brought the cover-up toward her cheek she stopped and looked at the bruise again. She never wore makeup to school, why should this be the first time? So again she rode the bus with a black eye.

At school, everything looked slightly different than she expected. She couldn't tell what was different, whether it was the birds or the rays of sunshine peeking through the dreary clouds, but where there had been quiet the day before, suddenly the lobby burst forth with loud, clamoring voices. It wasn't so different that she worried, but somehow there was a palpable irreverence in the air. She liked it.

Then she saw something that she knew had caused all of

the commotion. As she walked up the stairs from the bus to the lobby, there was a large banner stretching across the far wall. In tall, straight letters it said, "*StarX* banned on school grounds." There was more text underneath but Madison didn't bother to read it.

She wouldn't have expected a full-on rebellion about a little game, but here they were, nearly rioting in the hallways. It wasn't as if they could ever have played during class. What made it even more strange was that they singled out a game. Why didn't they just block everything? You already weren't supposed to use phones during school hours. What was the difference?

She found Danny sitting dismally in their corner, staring at his blank phone. Mia came up to Madison and whispered in her ear. "I think he wants to play in protest, but he can't quite get up the courage."

"Danny, stop" Madison said. "You can still play when you're at home."

Danny shook his head. "You don't understand, Mads! I was ranked. Top thousand plebes in the world. I could become an extra. They actually pay you to play the game at that point. If I can't play in the mornings or on the bus or at lunch then I'm done. Someone else will take my spot."

"Why today?" Madison asked.

"The Supreme Court said it was OK for the state of Wisconsin to ban *StarX* for everyone under eighteen by using retina scans."

"But we don't live in Wisconsin," Madison said, still confused by the whole business.

Danny shook his head. "It's the beginning of the end,

Mads," he said. "Every state can do it. People are saying this thing is evil even though it's no more evil than the Internet was or the printing press. It's truth."

Mia took Madison aside. "I've never seen him like this," she said. "Not even when I first met him in ESL and he didn't talk for a week straight. I've never seen him this depressed."

"It's a stupid game, Mia," Madison said. She turned to Danny. "It's a stupid game!"

"No!" Danny shouted. "It's an assault on the rights of anyone under eighteen. It's saying that we aren't smart enough to make our own choices. It means that it's impossible for us to engage in the dominant cultural discourse of our generation and I'm not going to stand for it!"

Firstly, Danny must have practiced that speech. Secondly, she thought he looked silly getting so irate about it. But then she noticed that there were a ton of people who'd turned to him. They'd stopped their own conversations and were listening just to him. Madison felt good that for the first time in a while, she wasn't the center of attention.

"We must protest!" Danny screamed. "They can't put us all in detention. I say that every person in this room has to take out their phone and start playing, right here, right now. If every one of us bands together to play this game right now, then we'll send the administration a message. We'll tell them that we won't bend to their will. That we're bigger than they are!" The crowd gathered in a wide circle around him so that everyone could see. He raised his hand. "Text everyone you know and tell them that we're organizing a sit-in. Everyone at Shackleton High, sit down where you are! Text your friends at other schools! Tell them to sit and play! This will be on national TV.

The world will hear about this! We have a voice!"

Then he sat down where he was with his legs folded and turned on his phone to start playing. He didn't even look up to see if anyone else had joined in. He just went for it.

Madison looked around. At first it just looked like everyone was texting, but slowly she saw people drop to the floor and sit, right where they were. People in the hallway yelled, "Sit and play!"

Mia sat. Hannah Chanel sat. Suddenly Madison was one of only a handful of people around her left standing. Even though they weren't organized, they suddenly were unified. Madison had never seen anything like that before.

Danny looked up from his game and sneered at her. "I've been laying the seeds for this with all my fans on *StarX* for months. They knew that this would happen someday soon. I know they're with me. I can see it in their eyes when I play. I thought you were a fan too. Haven't you been paying attention? Are you with us or against us, Mads?" His eyebrows raised in condescension. "You have to say yes or no."

Madison's face went flush and her hands felt numb. She had no idea why this was so important. Somehow she'd managed to miss the biggest cultural phenomenon in years. So important that every single person in the school, it seemed, was willing to risk all sorts of punishments in order for his or her voice to be heard.

"I'm going to go talk to Principal Hayward," Madison said. "Maybe I can get him to lift the ban."

"He'll know what we're doing. You don't have to explain it to him." Danny shook his head. "You're either with us or against us."

"I need to go," she said. She turned and waded through the masses of sitting teens, all staring at their phones at the same time. Down every hallway and in every stairwell were kids playing that stupid game. Only a hundred or so out of the thousands of students actually had the wherewithal to go against them. She got sour looks as she stepped over people, like she was a union buster, a scab. But she wasn't. She just didn't understand. It was beyond her. There was no video game in the world that could be so important that everyone had to guard it so carefully.

Then she made it to the principal's office. She saw him frantically debating with teachers. Even the superintendent was there, yelling inside of the glass office, waving his arms. There wasn't much she could say to him that would change his mind.

So Madison looked down at her phone and wondered what all of the fuss could possibly be about. But as Patrick had noted before, she didn't have an app store. She couldn't play if she wanted to.

Then Madison heard a murmur spread through the hallway. It sounded as if it started from the lobby. As the murmurs got closer somebody yelled out, audibly, "Keep playing when the bell rings!"

And on cue, the bell rang. About half of the people who were sitting down playing their games looked up, unsure if they should obey the rules or keep up the protest. Principal Hayward strode out of the office with his jaw clenched. He had a southwestern vibe to him, a bolo tie and an old sports coat. He looked like a cowboy who'd just popped a squat on a cactus.

"Go to class!" he fumed. A few people near the door stood up. They looked over to Madison for reassurance that they were doing the right thing by standing. She didn't know, but since she wasn't sitting at the time she felt like she might as well not start, not with the principal as angry as he was.

"Go to class!" He hollered, his big round white eyes staring out of his face like saucers of milk. His skinny bald head sat atop his skinny neck, the entrée to the wiry frame that was a collection of intimidating spindles. He turned to Madison, unsure if she was the ring leader or just an onlooker, but he knew she stood out. He'd probably seen her face on the evening news or been shown a picture online after the earthquake. She'd never spoken to him though and she doubted he'd realized who she was. But the way he stared, Madison felt like she needed to say something.

"I don't get it either," she said to him.

"Get in my office!" he screamed in his impossibly deep voice. He wasn't talking to anyone else, just her.

The hallways were filled wall to wall with students staring intently into their phones, occasionally taking a brief hiatus to watch Madison and the few stragglers who were indecent enough to be standing. Madison slowly crossed through the hallway. She could feel a few people around her stand as though they'd given up with the protest, but most people stayed put.

Chapter 26

Principal Hayward retreated into the depths of the cavernous administrative offices. They looked like they were relics of antiquity, the wall hangings were yellowed. For such a rich school they really didn't take care of their principal. It might have been on purpose, Madison thought. Maybe they wanted the students to feel out of place, out of time. Sitting in that uncomfortable chair in the office lobby, glancing from one to the next harried secretary scurrying about to answer emails and ringing phones, Madison felt like the calmest person in the room. She hadn't done anything wrong. She hadn't sat when the rest of them sat. She hadn't even encouraged them. At the same time, she didn't really think all of this was such a big deal. Compared to the insanity in the office her relative convalescence felt absolutely glacial. She considered pulling out her phone to warn Danny she was going to be interrogated but Principal Hayward's booming voice called her into his office.

There was a long corridor before her with offices on either side. Principal Hayward's was at the far end. Madison slowly walked toward him as he typed things into his phone, grumbling under his breath. When she reached his office he stood behind his desk, leaned toward her and stared into her eyes until she looked away.

"Who started this?" he asked. Madison just shook her head. This was her test in counter-interrogation. Her objective was to save Danny from getting in trouble. That was it. She could say anything else, but she wouldn't dare rat out a friend. Even if she wasn't sure she agreed with Danny, she couldn't bear to rat him out.

"This is a nationwide protest," Madison said. She really didn't want to lie. One of the things that she'd learned from her mother's interrogations was that a lie was easy to deconstruct. You had to remember a lie. The truth is simple. She kept that in mind.

"Where did you hear about it?" Hayward growled. Veins popped out of his neck.

"In the lobby," Madison said. "Everybody sat down at the same time. They all just started playing."

"Why didn't you?" he asked.

"I don't play," Madison answered. This brought her back to her comfort zone. It was an irrefutable truth. It was so definite and so personal that Hayward couldn't possibly rebut. He would just have to move on. Madison felt her muscles relax. Then she saw Hayward motion to somebody out in the hallway. She knew who it was before he even walked through the door because of the swoosh of his balloon style nylon pants. Hayward grabbed Coach Dipson by the arm and sat him in the chair saying, "I need you to find out what she knows, Chip. Do it fast." Then Hayward rushed out the door as if there was a fire in the hallway that he needed to stomp out with his foot.

"What did you do, Riley?" Coach Dipson asked anxiously. "You can't get in trouble. I almost put you on the traveling team. Work with me here."

Madison rolled her eyes. "Coach," she said, "I'm here because I'm the only person who didn't protest. Now tell me if that makes any sense."

"Come on," Coach Dipson pleaded, his slight drawl peaking the pitch of his voice while simultaneously elongating his vowels. "This will make Shackleton look really bad. Not only that but all of us in the office, we get paid to keep this place in line. It's our job. We need your help."

Madison felt sorry for him. She always felt sorry for him. He was such a pathetic sort, always trying to look proud and stoic but really you could see the disappointment on his face with every passing moment. And it wasn't an angry disappointment, it was this pathetic, whining expression that wouldn't look good on anybody, least of all a man who basically wore a clown costume every day.

Madison said, "They think it's got to do with free speech. I don't understand it. I don't play."

"You don't play *StarX*?" Coach asked, almost in awe. "I thought everyone played."

"I barely know what it is," Madison groaned.

"It's amazing," Coach said. "It's this place where everybody in the world comes together to make stories. Everybody is a star. It's the greatest. You should really start."

Principal Hayward burst through the door huffing. He'd taken off his sports coat. Sweat spots appeared on his light blue shirt by his neck and under his arm pits. "Did you break her?"

he asked Coach Dipson.

"She doesn't even play," Coach answered.

Hayward spun Madison in her chair to interrogate her, only a foot from her face. She could smell the coffee on his breath and she could see in his teeth the last remnants from the eggs he'd eaten that morning. "Who started this?" he asked again. "I know how popular you are. Popular girls are all the same. You want to hold onto it with everything you have, even if it means lying and ratting out your friends. So if you don't tell me what I want to hear in the next thirty seconds, I'm going to serve you with an in-school suspension that will mar your transcript like a big red blot. You tell me everything you know right now."

Madison could hear some commotion in the hallway but it still seemed eerily quiet. She couldn't see through the office to the hallway but she had to believe that it wasn't on her shoulders. She insisted, "I have never played *StarX*."

"Who told you about the protest?" he screamed. "If you don't tell me right now then I'll consider it an offense. Just give me one name."

The first name that came to mind was Jillian Jacobs, but she knew that was unfair, and too obvious a lie anyway. It would have been easier if she'd just heard it through the grapevine, but the fact was that she was there at the source, the exact moment that it happened. She knew Danny started it. She knew why he started it. She, in fact, had all of the details and was probably one of the only people at school who did.

"Everyone," she said forcefully. "Why would I single one person out when there are hundreds of kids out there and each one is doing the exact same thing? It's you against three thousand."

"Detention," Hayward said forcefully. "With me, in this office."

Coach Dipson stood up and shook his head. "Wait a second. That means she'll miss practice."

"I don't care," Hayward griped. "I'm cancelling all after school activities for today. I'm cancelling everything that these kids care about and we're reconfiguring the school routers to block the kids from using this game and we're doing it today, not next week like we planned." He picked up the phone on his desk, a very old looking beige piece of work that had blinking white and red lights. He dialed a number and waited, tapping his knuckles against the table.

"Hey Danielle," he said behind clenched teeth. "Do you have kids sitting in your hallways right now?" He rolled his eyes and sat back in his chair. His groan was like a bellow, a full-throated exhalation of every last breath in his chest. He sounded relieved, or at least less angry.

Madison looked around the room at the diplomas on the walls and the certificates: Mount Saint Mary's, University of Maryland and Hood College. They were all schools in Maryland. She checked his photos. There was a picture of Ocean City, Maryland on his wall where he held a three foot tuna. There was a picture of the Baltimore skyline. There was a map of Deep Creek Lake out on the tiny western sliver of the state. It was as if he'd never left Maryland in his entire life, or at least as if he was so obsessed with this tiny, insignificant corner of the country that he took pride in all of it, even the part that's only a two mile wide slice between Pennsylvania and Virginia. Didn't he know there was so much more to the world?

She wasn't even listening to his frantic phone calls anymore. It seemed like he hung up or changed lines every few seconds, barely even enough to get a full sentence out. It struck her that he wasn't actually doing anything. He was frantic, agitated and resolute, but he still hadn't made a single decision about what to do with the thousand kids sitting in his hallway like barnacles on the hull of his school.

Coach Dipson was on his cell phone as well. He was even more agitated, probably because he'd been told that practice had been cancelled. No doubt he was plotting some way for the team to work out even though activities were suspended.

Principal Hayward pounded the phone down against its ancient base so hard that the little bell inside of it dinged. "It started here!" he yelled. He licked his lips while his roving eyes occasionally rested on Madison before rolling maniacally in his head. "Who did this?"

He looked like a lunatic. A man unhinged, like he could beat someone in the face for answers.

That brought Madison to her second counter interrogation strategy. *Threats don't mean anything until they've been carried out.* She didn't care what kind of crazy things Hayward threatened he would do, she knew he wouldn't actually do any of it, not as long as kids were still protected.

He stared straight at her, right in the eyes. "Give me your phone," he said.

Madison hadn't seen that coming. Whoever texted her would be implicated and they'd get in trouble. Luckily, Danny hadn't texted her. He didn't need to. Other people got the word out. He just had to yell it for them all to take up the cause and start texting up a storm.

But it wasn't right for Hayward to ask for her phone. It was a matter of civil liberties. Of justice. "No," she said.

"What?" Hayward asked, his squawk carrying the low tone of a trombone. "You don't understand, Miss Riley. You're on school grounds. I can confiscate your phone if I want to. It's part of school policy."

Madison shook her head. "You don't know if I have my phone on me," she said. "You'd have to search me to find it." She tilted her head and peered through her narrow bangs. "Are you going to search me even though I haven't done anything wrong?"

Hayward looked over to Coach Dipson. He gulped loudly, as if he'd just carried a mouthful of water so deep there might have been a goldfish in it and he needed desperately to swallow it all at once. "I'll suspend you if you don't give it to me right now."

A threat is still a threat until it's been carried out. "No," Madison repeated.

"Phones have to be turned off during school hours," Hayward said. "Is your phone off right now?" Madison knew it wasn't. They didn't have the number for Charlotte...but other people did. Hayward was the kind of person who would go to everyone at Shackleton and ask for her number. She couldn't give up Charlotte under any circumstances but she couldn't think of a way to stop him.

Hayward turned to Coach Dipson. "Chip," he said, "Go into Ms. Riley's file and find her cell phone number. Give it a call. If we hear it ring then she's broken the rules and we'll be able to confiscate the phone."

Then came the next strategy, the counter threat. Madison

lifted her chin and looked down the length of her nose. She smirked. "My Mom works at the NSA and she has friends all over the government. She's friends with the Deputy Attorney General…" Mrs. Riley talked about that whenever she wanted to throw her weight around. Madison had never met him. She didn't even know his name, what he did or what he was like. She just knew that he was important.

"OK," Hayward said, reclining in his chair, taking a deep breath afterward. "I know you know who did it. By the honor code you're required to tell me. I can serve you with an in-school suspension for any honor code violation, including that one." He smirked. "So give me a name." He nodded. "Give me one name."

Last line of defense: it's better to lie than to continue to evade. She looked Hayward right in the eye, her face stone cold even though her innards twisted into deep, threadbare knots.

"I did it," she said. "I started the whole thing."

Chapter27

The in-school suspension room was a compact dungeon with no windows. The desks were spaced just far enough apart for everyone's elbows to knock against each other if anyone tried to do anything, especially put their head down to nap.

Madison sat staring ahead of her at the over-muscular back of one Arlo Henderson. He'd obviously served in-school suspension before because he'd brought with him a near perfect collection of sports magazines and books on baseball strategy. Madison, on the other hand, had only the school work that she'd brought in her backpack, which didn't include her history or math textbooks which were still in her locker. That was all she had to keep her company for the next six hours locked in a tiny room with only brief bathroom breaks and the chance to stretch one's legs at lunch time.

She half-wanted to slip Arlo a note but she didn't know him well enough to have something to say. Maybe she should apologize to him for the incident at the pool. There wasn't much that she could do to alleviate the problem, but why not attempt a truce before the war even began?

She scrawled an apology on a tiny slip of paper but before she could hand it to him, she saw beneath his foot a tiny slip of paper slowly making its way across the floor, propelled by an anxious rumbling of his left leg. It eventually slid to her with a flourish.

Madison had never been good at looking natural in these situations. In fact, the last several times she'd attempted to pass a note in class she'd been summarily punished. In Spain, where she'd attended a school that still condones corporal punishment, she'd had her knuckles slapped raw by a metric ruler. She was half-tempted not to pick it up but given her situation, the fact that she'd be in that room for a long time and the fact that she'd have to deal with Arlo at some point, she decided it was best to find a way to grab the paper. Besides, it would be yet another chance to heighten her skills at espionage.

The old pencil drop wouldn't really do the job. It was an obvious ploy that would draw attention to her instead of diverting it. Instead, she decided it might work to use the lack of space to her advantage. It was underhanded, she realized, but if she could make someone else in the room make a scene then she could use the diversion to grab the paper.

She did the first thing she could think to do. She turned her head and very loudly sneezed in the direction of the tall, angry looking older boy next to her. She assumed that he would give the biggest reaction, given the scowl already resident on his brow.

"Yo!" he yelled, recoiling.

While Madison pretended to wipe her nose, she grabbed the note. The older boy skidded his desk backward away from her. "Cover your damn mouth!" he screamed.

The monitor at the front of the class, Madison hadn't yet learned his name in the solemn quiet of the room, ran straight over and got right in the boy's face. While he yelled, Madison read the note from Arlo. It just said, "You're in so much trouble."

Meanwhile, the monitor kept yelling at the tall boy next to her. "Do you want to go again, Kale?" he growled.

Kale sneered even more deeply. His puffy jacket hung off his shoulders like a toga. He was lanky but everything about his clothes made him look bigger. The extra folds of his clothing gave weight to his shoulders even though his neck looked as spindly as Madison's.

"*Thanheduaiak khukan nyak*," the boy said under his breath. That only made the ornery suspension monitor angrier. He obviously didn't like it when people spoke in other languages, assuming that they were cursing him under their breath. In this case though, Madison was pretty sure Kale was playing with him. She wasn't sure what language it was, but it sounded familiar. Definitely Asian. It sounded like Thai but with a strange accent. Whatever it was, there were no curse words in it.

Kale had said something like, "You work too hard." She had only learned a tiny bit of Thai when she was there for a month with her family during her Dad's last furlough. It was a nice month and Thailand was beautiful. Just thinking about it brought her to another world.

"What did you say?" the monitor asked him.

Madison almost couldn't help but translate for him. "He said that you look stressed out," she blurted. "Or something like that. I know he didn't curse at you if that's what you're thinking." She usually wouldn't have spoken at all but she was suddenly more willing to let go of her inhibitions.

Kale seemed surprised, not just because Madison might have sort of understood him, but also because the goody two shoes next to him was speaking up, diverting the attention away from him.

The monitor shot his glare toward Madison. He shook his head angrily. "Are you covering for him?" he asked.

"I don't know him at all," Madison replied. "I've never met him before." She looked around the room once again, for the millionth time in the past two weeks, to realize that every eye was on her. "I just speak a little Thai."

Kale grumbled. "I'm Lao," he corrected, a slight bitterness in his voice.

"Sorry," Madison said in response. Whatever language he spoke sounded like what she'd heard in Thailand, so she'd just made the assumption. She'd long ago realized that it wasn't nice to say someone was from the wrong country, but at the same time Laos and Thailand were so close together she figured it wasn't the worst mistake in the world.

"Shut up!" the monitor shouted. "The next person who talks is going back to Hayward's office."

Before either of them even had the chance to speak, an announcement came over the intercom. It was Principal Hayward's voice. He sounded like he was trying desperately to be calm even though Madison could tell he was petrified. "Attention students. All confiscated phones will be made available only after the one week waiting period that has been laid out in the student handbook. We are instituting a new policy of confiscation on sight effective on the entire school grounds. If anyone is seen using a cellular telephone of any kind they will be served detention and the phone will be taken immediately. Do not test this policy. We have already confiscated over three hundred phones. We will not hesitate to confiscate more. That is all."

Everyone in the suspension area appeared to be in shock. They'd all been in the room since before the school day started so they hadn't seen any of the sit-in. It was all news to them. They were cut off from the world entirely. There could have been a nuclear war outside and they would be the last to know about it.

Even the monitor looked puzzled. "Three hundred phones," he mused. "What happened?" Madison wasn't about to start talking. "Seriously," he asked, "does anybody know?" Madison still said nothing.

Coach Dipson poked his head through the door. He motioned to the monitor. "We need all hands on deck," he said. "We'll lock the door in here and let them sort themselves out. We have bigger fish to fry."

And so the monitor left without another word. The tiny room erupted in confused talk and worry. "Holy—" Kale shouted before Arlo cut him off.

"You know, don't you?" Arlo screamed at Madison. "Carolyn said this was you and your Chinese friend."

Danny is Japanese, Madison thought, but this wasn't the time to correct him.

"How did you know?" Madison asked.

Arlo pulled out his phone. "I've got an app for occasions like this. It vibrates Morse code. I got most of the story but you gotta give it to me straight. What did you do?"

Madison shook her head and took in a deep breath. Was this another interrogation? "Started a movement," Madison answered.

"What?" Arlo yelled, "A movement to confiscate all our phones?"

"What am I supposed to do after practice?" one of the girls shouted at her. In fact, everyone in that room was standing and staring at Madison, furious with her, about ready to beat her into the ground. These were the worst kids in school and here they were in a locked room with no supervision.

And the fact was, she still hadn't done a single thing wrong. Her life had slipped completely off the rails. Then another thought crossed her mind.

I can't die.

Chapter 28

Arlo Henderson was probably the tallest freshman at Shackleton High, but Kale was at least three inches taller and two scars tougher. Madison wasn't sure if she'd made a friend in him but at least she wasn't completely alone. Besides, what was Arlo going to do, really?

"You won't hit a girl," Madison said in Arlo's face.

A girl in the corner of the room yelled out, "I heard she already beat you once, Arlo." Everyone laughed. It wasn't helping Madison's cause.

Arlo's hands clenched into fists. His back extended so that his head inched closer to the ceiling. "Madison Riley couldn't beat a dead raccoon, even though she looks like one with that black eye. That doesn't make her tough."

Kale stepped forward. He said, "Lay off, Freshman," to Arlo and laid a firm hand slowly on Arlo's chest. For a moment it was a stalemate. The other boys started to push all of the desks into the corner to make room in the center for a fight. It was quiet.

Madison stepped forward. She wasn't going to let Kale fight alone on her behalf. If there was an actual fight, she was ready for it.

"Who here is tired of all the attention that this Riley chick is getting?" Arlo asked the girls around him. "She takes credit for everything that happens around her. I was there. All she did for Hannah was grab some ice. She didn't save her life. She saved her from a concussion. I've had like ten concussions and I'm fine."

"I can tell," Kale said snidely.

Arlo pretended not to listen. "But she gets in the school paper for it." His short, dirty blonde hair radiated, backlit by the lights above. His cheeks were flushed. Madison could tell that he was just barely keeping himself from lashing out. "And she didn't kick my ass. She pushed me into the pool. It's all lies."

Madison looked around the room pleadingly for support from the other guys in the class but no one aside from Kale stepped forward. None of the girls stepped forward either.

"We have a locked room and no adults," Arlo said. "This is the only chance we'll ever have to get revenge on her for screwing us over so bad. She's the reason there are no phones on campus." He spun in place. "I won't hit a girl, but I'm willing to bet there's a girl in here who's up to it, and I'll hold back anyone who tries to get in the way."

A pretty looking girl came forward. She had a rough demeanor, the swagger of someone lacking the genetic code for fear. She cracked her knuckles as the rest of the crowd stepped back. Madison turned back to Kale and said, trying to match what she'd heard of his accent. "*Chuay lua,*" she whispered as well as she could. It was the closest she could get to saying help, but she may have offended him by speaking Thai instead of Lao, making him yet another enemy. But he didn't back down from Arlo. He shucked to the side and faked forward, just to make Arlo flinch, which he did. Suddenly people were yelling for a fight. Arlo and Kale squared off against each other, each taking a fighting stance.

"Who's taking Riley?" Arlo asked with a bit of unease in his already shaky voice.

Four girls came out into the ring, each one with an angry snarl.

Kale snarled back.

Madison said, "I guess it's four against one. If each of you four chicas never saw three filles get stomped by one scrawny little girl, you're in for a show." She didn't know where that line came from. It just burst out of her with complete confidence. She had to play it back in her mind for a second to make sure it even made sense.

The pretty, swaggering girl stepped forward and threw a surprisingly balanced punch at Madison, though it was easy enough for her to step out of the way. This girl knew how to fight, Madison was sure, but what style she brought was uncertain. It wasn't street fighting. Her stance was like a traditional boxer but her face was too pretty to risk smashing in with a glove.

Madison grabbed her wrist and wrenched it back behind her but the girl twisted free. The crowd had begun to chant, "Jade, Jade, Jade, Jade!" At least Madison had a name for her now.

Jade thrashed back at her, this time less poised, less agile. Madder. Madison dropped her shoulder into Jade's stomach and rammed her back into the crowd. The room echoed loudly with screams and shallow wails from all around. Madison felt other hands on her, other girls with less fighting experience but with a raw sense of entitlement to her body. They began to grab at her hair and her shirt. She knew better than to thrash about. She picked one girl from the mob and knocked the back of her knee with her hand. Another girl was off balance as she pulled Madison's hair so she was the next to meet the ground face first. Then Jade came back, by far the most able of the fighters. Everyone stepped back again to give Madison more room, now much more aware that she had a strong will and power behind her punches.

Jade smirked. "I heard your dad was a SEAL," she said. Madison said nothing, instead looking for a weakness in Jade's stance, some point of entry for an attack. "Did he teach you to fight?"

Another girl jumped out of the crowd. Madison dropped to her knees and threw the girl over her shoulder kicking. Of course that gave Jade an opportunity. She rushed at Madison full force, knocking them both to the ground. Madison fought to stay on top, her knees banging hard against the linoleum floor. She worked to get her arm behind Jade's head, trying to get control by pulling Jade's elbows in the opposite direction from where they're supposed to go but Jade wriggled toward her. She was too strong to be taken in by Madison's arm holds.

So Madison jumped to her feet and stepped back. "Enough!" she shouted. "What if we get caught fighting like this? We'll get expelled."

Arlo got right in Madison's face. "I won't get expelled," he said. "Because everyone in this room is going to get my back when I tell Principal Hayward that you started this."

"I won't," Kale said. He stood up straighter than he had before. Even his skinny frame couldn't hide the fighter inside of him. He was ready to take Arlo on just as much as Madison would take on Jade. The rest of the room was dead quiet. Kale looked at Madison. "How do we get out of this?"

Madison put her hand into her pocket and pressed the button to call for Charlotte and ask her one last question, out loud so that everyone could hear. "How do I get out of this?"

Charlotte answered clearly and succinctly. Madison listened as she ducked and jived to avoid Jade's attacks. Charlotte said, "Throw this phone as hard as you can at the sprinkler above Kale's head. It will trigger the fire alarm which will unlock the door. Go out the door, turn right and walk five doors down. On your right will be the security room by the main office. Wait until the security guard exits. Then enter the room, pull the computer marked SE-072 from the wall and take it outside with you. Dismantle it and destroy the hard drives inside."

Madison knew better than to second guess, so with all the force she had, she hurled Charlotte at the silver sprinkler above Kale's head. A deluge of cold dirty water splashed over all of them, soaking each in seconds. Charlotte flew to the far side of the room both from the force of Madison's throw and the force of the water. When it smashed against the far wall it shattered flamboyantly with a loud crack and sparks flying out of it, more of an explosion than Madison thought a phone should make. She ran over and grabbed it but the seemingly indestructible phone's screen had cracked and the bezel chipped open. Instead of a river stone it had become an open clam shell. It wouldn't turn back on. She picked it up and shoved it in her pocket, her heart sinking through her stomach. There was no more fighting now that everyone was drenched.

Madison pushed through the crowd to the door. The door had unlocked automatically when the fire alarm sounded. The fire alarm screamed in her ear when she reached the hallway.

Madison vaguely remembered what Charlotte said but wasn't quite sure which computer she had to destroy. Of course, all of the in-school suspension students followed her as she ran with purpose down the hallway to the security room. They waited in silence as the security guard exited and half of them piled into the security room after Madison.

It was a modest room with a few shelves with computers and six monitors on the wall, all showing four different views of the school for a total of twenty four different camera angles. It was Jade who found SE-072. She pointed to it. "Is this it?" she asked.

Madison grabbed it without thinking and pushed her way back out into the hallway, down the stairs and finally to the parking lot. There was chaos. Everything was cacophony. Everything was out of balance, as if the school had truly turned to anarchy. And she had no way to stop it.

It didn't actually take that long for the police to show up, and for two different camera crews to descend on the scene. Also two fire trucks, a news helicopter and the entire security staff of Shackleton High. Madison watched from within the crowd, cold from the soak she'd just received from the sprinklers. As she brushed her hands across her chest to warm up, the supposedly orderly lines that had been rehearsed during fire drills became swirling streams of people, all trying to find out what happened on this strangest of school days.

Madison knew it was all her fault, as did everyone in the in-school suspension room. In addition, they had no reason to keep quiet about the whole thing. She was as good as expelled, so the brief moment shivering in the parking lot felt stretched out like the last note of a song resonating on a lone string.

Then suddenly Jade and Arlo came up from behind, themselves shivering. The rest of the in-school suspension students loomed like a mob around her.

"Who was that?" Arlo asked. "How did they know how to get into the security room?"

Madison shrugged. It wasn't time to tell the truth yet.

Jade considered the computer under Madison's arm. "Do you have someone on the inside? Do you have surveillance on the school? Your dad was a SEAL. Your mom's in the government."

They were above all scared of her. Madison looked at each of them in turn, her hands trembling. "Will you help me crush this thing?" she asked, pointing to the mini cube of a computer under her arm.

Kale was the first to grab it and chuck it to the ground. It dented slightly but didn't break open the way they'd expected. He kicked it. Then again. A half dozen feet started stamping on the thing in turn. Slowly but surely the box burst open and the circuit boards fell to the ground. Madison didn't really know what a hard drive looked like so she just kept breaking each part, one by one until it was all twisted metal. There were two pieces that were harder than the rest. They were identical, rectangular boxes, about the size of a DVD case. Madison picked one up and checked the scratched writing on the side. "3TB Hard Drive," it said. Madison tried to bend it and flex it. It was nearly indestructible. She handed it to Arlo. "I need you to either break this open or throw it farther than you've ever thrown anything in your life, into the bushes. Onto the roof. Any place where they won't find it."

He stared at her.

"You're in deeper than you realize," she told him. "This is a matter of national security."

He deliberated momentarily, the heavy hard drive bobbing in his hand. With a sneer he tossed the hard drive across the street into a neighbor's yard, at least a hundred yards. "I'm so glad you play baseball," Madison said as she handed him the second hard drive. "Throw it in the same place." He gave the second one a good toss but it didn't make it, instead busting open in the middle of the road, thankfully avoiding any passing cars.

Of course throwing hard drives is the type of thing that people notice. Madison had to hide the computer at her feet as well. She roused her entire in-school suspension troupe together in a huddle around the device. "My cover's blown to all of you but if you keep your mouths shut we can get through this," she whispered. They stared at her rapt, half their mouths drooping open with raw consternation. "I need one of you to put the computer case in your backpack, someone else put the circuit board in hers. If we all work together then we can keep this out of the national headlines and make it a local issue instead of an international incident."

She regretted saying the words as soon as they left her mouth. There was no way this plan was going to work. How would these kids keep their mouths shut? There were too many of them. On top of that, security was bearing down on them rapidly and if they started hiding bits of computer then it would surely be noticed. Madison hoped that the chaos all around would make enough of a diversion that they could quickly gather up the pieces without anyone seeing.

"If I tell you who I'm working for they'll put me in prison, it's top secret." Madison said. "But I will tell you it's a matter of national security. There's someone listening to everything that I say or do, so if anything happens to me, they'll know about it and they'll know who did it. They can read your emails, your texts and your posts online. Don't tell anyone about any of this."

The one thing that Madison hadn't counted on was the fact that these kids knew better than anyone how to get away with doing the wrong thing. They quickly formed a human wall between Madison and the outside world. Jade and Kale helped her grab the pieces from the ground and stow them in any available backpack or pocket from the group. It was over in seconds, long before the guards got there. And the police as well.

Madison's crowd parted begrudgingly as the cops pushed their way through. She smiled politely at them, her damp bangs covering her eyes. "How can I help you, officer?" she asked.

The policeman grabbed her by the arm and pulled her away. It was like a maze of bodies all parting to allow her passage. Television cameras photographed her wet face and dress, the bruises on her arms from the fight and her stiff posture, standing as upright as she could to try to see over the crowd to look for Danny, wondering what he thought of her ordeal. And for Patrick.

Jillian Jacobs was there to lend a wry smile and a discourteous shake of her head. Carolyn Kaplan stood next to her with a meaner look, a cold meander of her eyes and an upturned red eyebrow. Hannah Chanel looked more confused than anything. Her bright yellow eye makeup made it look like she was permanently wide eyed. But there they were. The three meanest girls in school together again and with a shared agenda to get to the bottom of this riot. They knew, as well as everyone at Shackleton High, that Madison Riley was at the bottom of all of this. It was obvious. They just needed some way to prove it.

Being led by police escort away from the school she hated, Madison realized that she'd truly reached a different phase in her life. She was no longer primarily a student. She'd become, more than anything, an operative. The second highest profile operative in an organization that consisted of only two people. And it felt good.

Chapter 29

The inside of the police station was an efficient looking office with a couple of bored men and women clicking at their computers. Madison watched them glance up at her periodically, their distrust of the people who came in, even a fifteen year old girl, was a clear sign that they were on edge. So when Mrs. Riley stormed in, flailing her arms over her head, cell phone on speaker, they thought immediately that she was just another lunatic. "This place is getting its pensions slashed in five minutes if I don't see my daughter. I'm saying this on order of the Department of Justice!" she screamed.

The Department of Justice is a big deal. Huge, in fact. Mrs. Riley made sure Madison knew it. They oversee the FBI and they're involved in every aspect of federal law. Mrs. Riley knew how to bring the big guns and knew how to name drop, so she showed up at the police station with the Deputy Attorney General on the phone, second in command at the Department of Justice.

"This is outrageous," Mrs. Riley complained, her hair flying in frizzy waves in every direction. "Why is my daughter in a police station rather than the principal's office? Is she in danger? Has she been charged? Her principal is an idiot, but I wasn't expecting him to stoop so low as to arrest her."

"Ma'am," the officer behind the desk started.

Mrs. Riley cut him off. "Ma'am nothing," she said. "I literally have the Deputy Attorney General of the United States of America on the phone and he would like to speak to the highest ranking member of this police force immediately."

The cop put his hands up to calm her down, but when that didn't work he motioned to the big office to his left. Mrs. Riley disappeared.

"You're mom's a fighter," he said softly.

Madison nodded. "A bruiser," she said. Then she thought about her black eye and said, "She didn't hit me though. I got this from a homeless man." The officer didn't seem convinced.

Madison waited a good long while until her mother re-emerged from the office. She looked down at Madison, "If you don't tell me everything then neither one of us is going to sleep until I get it out of you."

The cop gave Madison a knowing nod.

They didn't speak in the car, probably because they'd had to fight past television crews just to get onto the open road. Madison wondered if they'd be camped out at her house. She thought one last time about what she'd actually done wrong. For starters, she'd lied to her principal and said she'd instigated the sit-in. Second, she'd gotten in a huge fight with four other girls and won handily. Third, she set off the sprinkler and in turn the fire alarm, which she was sure was against school rules. And finally, she'd stolen a computer and destroyed the hard drives just as Charlotte had told her to.

And now she was without her saving grace. She no longer had Charlotte to fall back upon, just a cold brick of a phone that had cracked almost in half. All she had, sadly, was her mom, who was about to give her an interrogation the likes of which she'd never experienced.

When they got inside the house, Mrs. Riley pointed straight at the couch. "Sit down! Now!" Madison walked slowly and purposefully over to the couch and sat on the end, taking up the least possible amount of space on the giant sofa. Mrs. Riley sat in the armchair opposite. There was a buzzing in Madison's ear as if she'd lost her hearing temporarily like after a rock concert. It would come and go but she couldn't shake it.

The living room was narrow with bright white walls and simple molding by the ceiling. The centerpiece of the room was the stone fireplace with a deep mantle and brass grating in front. The couch and two chairs sat in the middle of the room while two other chairs nestled in a nook between tall bookshelves with a wide window in between. The room was quiet and peaceful. The first thing that many people noticed was that there was no TV in the room. In fact, if someone were to search the house, they'd find it hard to even locate a television. This was Mrs. Riley's way. She was austere about media, as with other, less daily issues. The only stimulation in the room came from the art on the walls, oil paintings with various levels of abstraction from juvenile cave style paintings to geometric, almost architectural pieces. If one wasn't an art critic one might think that Madison painted them, but for someone with an education, they represented a sizeable investment in paintings that looked like they were drawn by pre-schoolers.

Mrs. Riley pulled out her phone and held it up like an exhibit in a trial. "Why is a phone so important, Mads?" she asked. "Is it for video games or is it for personal protection? If you're in a dangerous situation, this is your best friend. The first chance you get you call 911. Do you hear me?" It was a rhetorical question, of course, but one that Madison still wanted to answer. If she had Graham's phone the first thing she'd do is ask Charlotte for help.

Mrs. Riley continued. "Yet you just pushed the administration at your school to ban cell phones on campus no matter what the situation. It takes about twenty seconds for the average phone to start up. That's twenty seconds during which you are not in contact with the authorities."

Madison nodded. The buzzing in her head grew louder. She debated with herself about whether or not to tell her mother that she'd in fact taken the fall for something Danny did. He was a friend, but was it worth lying to her own mother to protect a friend? She'd already been compelled to lie about her dealings with Graham and with Charlotte, she didn't want to do any more.

"I didn't start the sit-in," she said. "I lied to Principal Hayward about it."

Mrs. Riley studied Madison's face. She accepted that almost instantly as the truth. Then she leaned in closer. "Who were you protecting?" she asked.

Madison's first thought was Graham. She didn't want to turn her phone over in case the authorities got hold of it and realized her connection to Charlotte and to Graham. Her hesitation spoke volumes to Mrs. Riley. She squinted and gazed into her daughter's eyes. "Danny Kai," she said knowingly. "I've heard him talking about this stupid game before. You let yourself get into trouble in order to save him." She shook her head. "Do you realize what you've done?"

Mrs. Riley looked around. "This is one of the few times I wish there were a TV in here. I want to show you what's on the news. I want you to see how deep a hole you've dug for yourself." She pulled out her phone and swiped across it with wide gestures. She finally found the video she was looking for and she handed it to Madison.

Of all things, it was Madison's picture on CNN. Of all the pictures that they could have used on TV, they chose her school portrait, an oversaturated photo taken in the gymnasium where her head was shiny, the squint in her eyes was too angry and her smile was too wide. It wasn't hideous, but seeing it, even on that tiny screen, was mortifying. Then she realized what it said underneath her photo: "Instigator of National Protest."

Madison couldn't believe it. Danny was right. The protest had gone viral. According to the news report, tens of thousands of students sat down just before school and played *StarX* on their phones until school officials started grabbing them out of their hands. Fights broke out. There was almost a riot in a Philadelphia suburb. And it was all getting blamed on her. Even if Danny stepped forward and took responsibility no one would believe him. Madison had much more cache with the students at Shackleton. Everybody knew it. It was obvious.

The CNN correspondent was talking but Madison was too overwhelmed to understand. As she slowly steadied herself, she again heard her life story repeated. Living almost entirely abroad, the death of her father, her mother's station at the NSA, her gift for languages. It was as though they were simply reading Jillian Jacobs' article about her on national television.

Madison took a deep breath, still hearing the buzzing but finally realizing that it wasn't coming from inside her head, but instead from above her. She looked up. Mrs. Riley looked up too. Madison shook her head. It was her old phone, the one she'd used before Graham had given her the new one, echoing through the floorboards as it vibrated in her room. It must have fallen off of her night stand after all of the calls.

She shook her head. "My phone's probably been ringing off the hook ever since we got home," she said.

"Everyone you have ever known is calling you as we speak," Mrs. Riley said. "I'm glad I have a government issued phone. I bet my other cell phone is blowing up just as much as yours."

The incessant buzzing sounded exceptionally loud in that moment of silence. Both Madison and Mrs. Riley tried to ignore it but it just wouldn't stop.

"Wait a second," Mrs. Riley said. "You didn't even bring your phone to school with you today?" she asked. "How can you be the ringleader of a viral social media protest if you didn't even bring your phone?" She chuckled to herself. "We are going to fight this. Even if the school tries to expel you, we're going to make sure nothing bad happens to you. I don't care what favor I have to call in, we're fighting."

Madison nodded. It wasn't even worth trying to dissuade her mother from a fight. It was ridiculous. But she counted herself lucky. At least she didn't have to answer any questions about Graham or about any of the other things she'd been lying about. She wasn't even sure if her mom knew she had in-school suspension.

Then Madison realized something. Her eyes bulged open and her teeth nearly chattered. "It's Take Your Daughter to Work Day tomorrow, isn't it?"

Mrs. Riley rolled her eyes. "Of course it is. I'm taking my daughter to work in the midst of a media firestorm." She nodded to herself, thinking things through with her customary rapidity. "But you're coming. If you're not going to school then I'm giving you an education whether you want it or not."

Chapter 30

It was the night before the big day. Madison looked at the bag of items she'd amassed since learning her place within the world of espionage. It was lucky that she'd made Charlotte email all of the information about the NSA to her personal account. She had floorplans and lists of over a thousand steps of what to do between that moment and the moment she pressed enter after finally entering the code on her mom's computer. Instead of looking at the screen, she was tired of screens at that point, she opened the document and hit print.

She rifled through the pages of typewritten instructions. She inspected the magnet, the pens, and the liquid helium container. It was time to figure out how it all worked. First was the list of things that she needed:

1) HX1-7271 superconducting electromagnet
2) 17-AFF-1899 RFID spoofer capable of 128 bit encryption
3) Three hollowed out ball point pens
4) Spring Semi-Formal Outfit

Madison had pens at least. She found some on her desk and pulled them apart. The ink was in a thin plastic cylinder connected to the point of the pen. Madison realized that if she just pulled it apart then ink would spill everywhere. She grabbed a plastic bag from downstairs. She held the point of the pen and the ink cylinder inside of the bag with her hands clutching it from the outside, almost as if she was picking up dog poop. She grasped the cylinder in one hand and the point in the other hand and yanked. It wasn't easy to pull them apart. The two parts were glued together pretty tightly. She worked at it for a while, twisting and pulling. Then pop, they came apart and sprayed ink all over her shirt and on her jeans. A bit splattered on the floor.

"I hate you, Graham!" she screamed out loud to no one. "Why can't you do it?"

But she kept going. After the third one she'd gotten the hang of splitting the pens, but she still hadn't forgiven Graham. Those were her second favorite pair of jeans.

She still didn't have the RFID spoofer, nor did she know where to get one. On the internet it said, "Radio Frequency Identification (RFID) is a system that uses radio waves to transmit information including unique identifiers for people and equipment." It sounded fancy but it turned out it was just a tiny radio antenna that sent out a little code that a sensor could use to tell who was wearing it. They were everywhere, apparently. The government could use the RFID to track you. She'd seen things that looked like the pictures of RFID that she'd found online. The pictures showed a white box, about the size of a phone but a little thicker, and it was stuck to the inside of a window. Her mom had two in her car. One of them paid for tolls, Madison knew, but the other one was for getting into Fort Meade. So what she was looking for was a small radio transmitter that could easily send a fake signal that would trick the people in the NSA into thinking she was someone else.

Then she tried to look up "17-AFF-1899 RFID spoofer" but she couldn't find that particular model online. She didn't have time to buy one online and have it shipped anyway. She needed to know what it was so she could figure out a way to make one.

A spoofer is a device that fakes an RFID signal. There were instructions online showing how to build an RFID spoofer but they were incredibly long and they required all sorts of computer parts and wires. She couldn't build one. She didn't know anything about radio waves...

So she gave up. At first she didn't know why it made her feel so good to give up but then she realized. Charlotte had taken care of her every other time she needed something. There was a huge list of directions in front of her that she hadn't really read. The answer was probably somewhere in there. So she just moved on to the next step.

The instructions said that she had to take the HX1-7271 superconducting electromagnet apart and put each of the three pieces in a separate hollow pen.

The electromagnet got cold when she used it at the Smithsonian. How was she supposed to do anything else if it made her hand go numb? Again, she looked online to learn about superconducting electromagnets...they need to be really cold. Only liquid helium, which is apparently crazy cold, could cool it down enough to use it. She also learned that if she wasn't careful the liquid helium could freeze her hand so quickly that it would fall off in a few seconds.

Madison sat back on her bed and threw some dirty laundry across the room. "I could have had my hand frozen off, Graham!" she yelled into her empty room. "Why does this have to be so dangerous?" The amount of resentment welling up started to overwhelm her. She started to resent her mom for working at the NSA and needing to be saved in the first place. She started to resent technology because it made things like RFID and superconducting electromagnets something she had to worry about.

Then she thought about it another way. If she had to figure all of this out on her own she never would have been able to do it. Her mom would die and she'd be helpless. It all looked pretty complicated, but all she really needed to do was bump her mother's computer over and quickly type in a code without looking suspicious. National security and her mom's life hung in the balance over a few items in a gym bag.

The list of things she needed to do from that moment until the final push was twenty pages long with a small font numbered list from one to 1,102. It seemed as though every third step was: "Practice code 10 times – record time." This felt like a special kind of torture. She had no choice but do each of these steps exactly as they were laid out, in the order they were laid out. Yet at the same time it seemed like the absolute most boring task she'd ever undertaken.

But she started. She quickly completed steps one through 137. They were mostly just practicing the code, making sure everything was in the bag, testing the electromagnet and hollowing out pens in order to hide the thing from the NSA guards.

Then came step one hundred thirty-eight:

138) Answer call from Jillian Jacobs

Madison stared at the page for a moment but she'd gotten used to this kind of thing so she turned to her phone and saw, as expected, Jillian was calling her. She'd almost forgotten that they were going together to Take Your Daughter to Work Day. She picked up, careful not to sound too disappointed. "Hey Jillian," she said, her voice like a death rattle.

Jillian had returned to her crackling, low voice, the angrier one. "Are you an insane person?" she asked. "Do you know how many times I've called you today?" Madison didn't answer, but Jillian didn't really wait long enough anyway. "So you finally did it. You finally made the national news. I guess any press is good press, isn't it?"

"Did you get credit for giving your story from the school paper to CNN?" Madison asked.

"Yeah," Jillian answered, as if it was the stupidest question she'd ever heard. "Of course I got credit. When they showed the text from my story on screen it said my name in tiny letters at the bottom."

"So you owe me," Madison said, finally feeling a little bit of nerve to stand up to Jillian.

"No, you owe me!" Jillian shot back. "I made you, remember. I wrote that article. I did the work to get on CNN. A reporter doesn't owe anything to the subject of her piece. That's like saying Woodward and Bernstein owed everything to Nixon. It's ridiculous." She was almost out of breath but she just kept on talking as if her life depended on it. Madison could barely keep up with the pace of Jillian's speech but that didn't stop her from talking. She sounded like one of those singers who doesn't rhyme but instead talks so fast you can't even tell the difference. "And I have to spend the whole day with you tomorrow, sucking up to your mom and pretending not to be completely flipped out about the fact that I've allied myself with the craziest girl in school."

Madison cut in. "Do you really hate me, Jillian?"

"Hate you?" Jillian asked, shocked by the question. "No! What are you talking about?"

Madison waited a second to speak, unsure if she was even talking to the same Jillian Jacobs she knew from school. It seemed like a foregone conclusion that Jillian hated her. Who in their right mind would think that they were anything but bitter enemies? "Jillian," Madison began cautiously. "You've been so incredibly mean to me over the past few weeks…"

Madison was cut off by a flurry of guttural sounds that made Jillian sound like a cross between a gibbon and a chimpanzee. "That…no…see…that's just who I am, Maddy. You just have to get used to it. I'm forceful. I get what I want. I don't hate you anymore than I hate anyone else."

Madison almost wished Jillian had said yes, she did hate her. It would have made so much more sense. Why would anyone treat her so badly if she didn't even hate her? Then Madison had to ask herself if she hated Jillian. It felt like the next logical question. The only answer she had for herself was that she kind of did. Jillian had intimidated her, she'd yelled at her, she'd bullied and browbeaten and cudgeled her. She'd blamed her for things that she hadn't done.

"Call me Mads," she said quietly.

"What?"

"I like to be called Mads, not Maddy." She said.

Jillian softened. "I always liked Lee. It's a girl's name too.

I never liked the Jill sound, a hard consonant. I'd like something softer. My name used to be spelled with a G but we changed it because people would call me Gilly like the gills on a shark."

It was the first human thing that Madison had ever heard Jillian say. In fact, it was probably the first human thing she'd ever said to Jillian. "I love sharks, and dolphins too," she said. "I used to swim with them when my dad was stationed in Japan."

Neither of them said anything for a moment. For Madison, it didn't feel like the right time to become friends with someone like Jillian. She was too used to her being an enemy, not quite ready to even contemplate her as a friend.

"What time tomorrow?" Jillian asked.

"We'll pick you up at six in the morning," Madison said. "Text me your address."

"See you then."

There was another awkward pause. "Bye Lee," Madison said.

"Bye," Jillian returned. Then Madison slowly pressed the end call button, almost positive that Jillian would have one more thing to say to her but happy when the call ended on its own.

Had Madison read further in the directions, she'd have seen the next phone call coming, but since she was already overwhelmed she hadn't brought herself to turn the page yet. So when the phone buzzed in her hand with Danny's face on the screen, Madison nearly dropped it. Charlotte didn't have any pictures of her friends stored. It felt strange to suddenly be looking at Danny when she wasn't expecting to see him. She didn't know what to say to him. Was she mad? Should she blame him for everything that happened to her? He hadn't forced her to take the fall but all of these problems were on his account.

"Hi," Madison said blandly, trying not to allow her emotions into her voice, though sadly, that meant that she sounded cold and put off.

Danny said back, just as coldly, "What's wrong with you?"

That was the second time in as many conversations that someone had asked her that. It wasn't a fair question in the first place. If there was something wrong that Madison was aware of she'd have corrected it. Whatever the problem was, it was obviously beyond her notice. "I saved your butt," Madison answered.

"You what?" Danny blurted in shock. "You saved my butt? By taking responsibility for the movement that I started?" He was sadder than Madison had ever heard him. Despite Danny's depressive dress and goth haircut, he was cheerful most of the time. "You just can't let other people get the spotlight, can you? Now you're on TV, you're all anyone talks about anymore. How did you convince Hayward it was you who did it? I'm not even convinced you've played *StarX*."

"He cornered me," Madison yelled back. "I didn't sell you out. I kept my mouth shut."

"That's so noble of you, Madison. Everything you do is so noble these days. You're everybody's hero, even us nerds who play a video game all day and never have time to save ourselves." The high pitched, almost ear piercing tenor of his voice told Madison that he'd lost control. He was probably pacing around his room knocking the action figures from their shelves.

Gone were the days when Danny would calm himself with his glacially slow Tai Chi moves. Now he was a warrior.

"It's your fault!" Madison screamed. "This isn't a first amendment thing. The school can make the rules they need to make, including blocking websites. They didn't do anything wrong."

"Who are you?!" Danny squealed. "The Mads Riley I know cares about issues and about the bigger picture, not just saving people in the moment. You're so caught up in the moment that you forgot who your real friends are, now you just want everyone to love you. Well I'll tell you something, Mads. They'll turn on you. You think they like you now but after your thirty seconds of fame they'll drop you like an old YouTube."

"I don't care what people think!" Madison shot back. "I never said I did. I just couldn't be the one to get you in trouble."

"I wanted to get in trouble! I wanted to be the one to talk to the news crews because I wanted to make a bigger issue about this. The president of the United States is involved. Congress is holding hearings tomorrow because of a probe launched by the Attorney General. It's a big deal. I want to put my mark on it and here you are, someone who can barely put together two coherent sentences on the topic of *StarX* and suddenly you're the voice of our generation. Who do you think you are?"

Madison couldn't believe what she was hearing. He hadn't thanked her for saving him. All he did was blame her. "Fine," Madison said. "I have homework to do and I won't be in school tomorrow. I'll see you on Friday."

"What about the dance tomorrow night?" Danny asked. "I heard you were going with your new boyfriend. Did you decide you were too cool to be seen there?"

Madison had totally forgotten about the dance. She didn't have the details on where to meet him. She didn't have a dress. Patrick was planning a big entrance. Would she even be back from the NSA in time?

"I'll see you there, then," she said, and then she hung up. She had work to do. She had to save her mom.

Chapter 31

By step 238, Madison was ready to fall asleep. Luckily, step 239 said to set a timer with an alarm for thirty minutes and step 241 said to take a nap. But in between there was a step that seemed out of place. Step 240 said the following: "Step 240: ask yourself whether or not you're doing the right thing."

The right thing? Why, in a list of a thousand steps would one of them be to question the whole enterprise? But she was tired and grumpy and wanted that nap so badly, she did just as it said. Madison looked at the page, she thought about everything that had happened to her since she'd gotten the phone. For all of the work she'd put in, all of the risks she'd taken, she hadn't quite dealt with the single most important one. Was it right?

She crumpled the paper up into a shriveled ball and threw it across the room. She was done. If Graham had so much power, why couldn't he just save her mom? If he could do anything, like predict earthquakes or give her a perfect character in *StarX*, why couldn't he be the one to break into the NSA? Why did it have to be her? Why would he ask a fifteen year old kid to put herself on the line? How big of a coward was he?

She wanted to call and ask him, but she'd lost the phone and with it Graham's number. She wanted to call and scream at him with all her breath. But she was tired. She climbed into bed and fell asleep on top of her covers. And then she dreamt her only dream.

It was filled with explosions and yelling, with clouds of dust and blinding flashes of light. It was so familiar. But this sleep-deprived nap brought forth the images more intensely than her usual drab re-imagining of the traumatic experience of first seeing the video.

She had a moment of clarity. A familiar voice that she never would have expected.

The alarm brought her to an instant standing position. Her hand reached out like lightning to silence it. Her heart pounded. She looked over at her computer in the corner of the room and the thumping in her chest pumped out an angry rhythm of discord. But she knew she had to do it. She walked over and turned it on, her hand shaking.

The video was no longer online. It was removed by the government, and rightfully so, because it showed such horrible images. But she felt she had to watch. She sifted through the folders on her computer until she found where she'd buried it. She'd wanted to delete the video so many times but she just couldn't bring herself to let it go.

The images were grainy, they were shaky, taken by the helmet camera of an infantryman not even thinking about what he was recording. The view shifted from a dark hallway to a third story window looking upon a desolate desertscape where a lone man could be seen in a tiny beige guard post that amounted to a metal shack with no back end. He was barely a few dots in the image, a blurry dark figure you could only tell was a person by the way he moved. He jutted from side to side and peeked out of the busted window just long enough to take a few quick shots with his rifle. The camera panned up to see four white vans parked beyond the compound's wall, just fifty feet from the meager guard post.

The vans created an effective barricade behind which at least ten men hid. At one moment all was silent. Then there would be a flash from one of the broken van windows and a crackle of gunfire. The man in the guard post stayed still mostly. He moved deliberately, his rifle only momentarily lifting high enough to fire a few quick bullets at nothing in particular.

Someone off camera was talking into a radio, "Mortar fire stopped six minutes ago. A car bomb…we need help—"

Then an earsplitting series of pops resonated so loudly that the camera shook and dust flew up from the windowsill. It was the infantryman, the one who held the camera. He fired his rifle at the white vans. Then it was quiet again. Almost silent. But there was a crackle in the air like the sound of wind mixed with the roil of distant thunder.

Then a pop and a cloud of dust erupted among the scrub brush beyond the vans. The infantryman behind the camera pulled back into the hallway and the view went almost completely black, but soon adjusted to the darkness of the hallway. He yelled at some other people, cursing in a thick British accent. More pops. More crackling gunfire. When the camera caught a view out of the window everything was pure white but the camera slowly adjusted and the guardhouse came back into focus. The man inside remained crouched, barely visible. The infantryman shot another few rounds, again with earsplitting pops accompanied by dust spraying up from the windowsill. Another pop and puff of dust erupted near the white vans. The camera once again turned to the hallway as the infantryman ducked for cover. Some men in dusty formal suits ducked nearby. Madison tried to see their faces but she couldn't quite make them out in the dark hallway.

The camera looked back out of the window to see the man in the guard post cautiously inching along the ground, hiding from the insurgents while trying desperately to move to the other side of the guard post. Another explosion popped nearby.

The camera panned back into the hallway. "Are you hurt?" the infantrymen asked the men in the suits. They said nothing in return. More pops of explosion burst from the desert. The infantryman ran through the hallway to another window to get a fresh perspective. The guardhouse was more visible. From this new view the smoldering remains of a fifth van could be seen. It had blown up before the video started and what remained was barely recognizable save for the hood and windshield.

This was a better view of the guard post and now the man inside was much more clearly visible. He wore a camouflaged uniform with various patches on the sleeves and a helmet with complicated electronic equipment attached to it. He clutched his rifle at the ready. He looked calm, almost peaceful. His motions were slow and elegant, despite the explosions all around him.

He did something surprising, something that Madison still couldn't quite understand. He grabbed a second rifle from a rack on the wall of the guard post. He fiddled with its mechanism, rigging the trigger, and he appeared to drive a stake into the ground. There was rope involved but the picture was too blurry to understand how it was used. Finally, he pulled at the rope. The gun began to fire on its own toward the vans. Then the man stood within the guard post and hobbled slowly backward, obviously wounded. He fired a few shots when he could but mostly just made his way toward the building from which the infantryman filmed.

Another few loud clacks echoed through the hallway as the infantryman laid down his own round of fire upon the vans. It wasn't clear what happened to the man from the guard post, so the infantryman turned to the men in the suits and yelled, "He's wounded! Go and help him."

One of the suited men stepped forward and, in a posh British accent, screamed, "We're too important! You go and help him!"

The infantryman shouted back, "I have to lay down suppressing fire!"

So the man in the suit reluctantly sprinted off down the corridor and down the stairs at the end of the hall. The infantryman shot a few more rounds out of the window.

Madison paused the video and replayed the last few seconds. She listened to the voice of the man shouting, "We're too important!" She paused to try to get a look at his face. She played it again. She was absolutely positive who it was with his chiseled jaw and rock star swagger. She wasn't surprised she hadn't noticed it before. She'd only ever been able to sit through the video once. But there he was. Madison sat back in her chair in disbelief. She turned to her stack of instructions and saw step number 242: "Step 242: watch video of your dad giving his life to save Graham Clarke."

Step 243 should not even have been written. It was so obvious. All it said was, "Step 243: cry."

Chapter 32

Before anything else, before any rational, productive thought Madison could have had, she replayed again in her mind the look of revulsion on Graham's face as he was asked to risk his life to save her father. Why hadn't he tried sooner? Why hadn't he been the first to run out to the guard post with guns blazing to save him?

That wasn't the Graham she met at the airport. The Graham she knew, or thought she knew, was the first to dive in to help others even if it was dangerous. Yet in the video he clearly did not want to save anybody.

She felt so sick. Every time she remembered that video she imagined what her dad must have felt while he crouched alone in that guard post with mortar shells exploding next to him and people shooting at him with machine guns.

But looking at her father this time, he looked so calm. She hadn't noticed before the way he moved so slowly and patiently. She hadn't noticed his face which was barely visible as he walked. It was the same face she'd held near her own, the face she'd rested her head against and felt the scruff of his five o'clock shadow. He didn't look angry.

Since the airport, she felt she had a taste of what it had been like to save people in a crisis, the calm that can take over when you know that what you're doing is important.

If Graham had listened to that feeling instead of cowering in a corridor, her dad might have lived. He was a coward. He was self-important and smug. When she saw the video the first time, she felt absolute revulsion when she heard those words: "We're too important." This time she knew it was coming, and she knew that the man who said it would eventually help, but those few seconds felt like an eternity as her dad suffered.

So was she doing the right thing?

Step 250 was to try the code ten times again. She typed it in once:

[tab]   stockmadisonquenchinvegle   [enter]   [alt+tab] [alt+f4] [tab] Pike, Connor [enter] [tab] [tab] [dn arrow] [dn arrow] [enter] [shift+tab] x77 [enter] [enter] [enter] [ctrl+alt+del] [rt arrow] [rt arrow] [enter] [enter]

She tried to break down the code a little bit more to understand it better. [tab] was just a key on the keyboard. "stockmadisonquenchinvegle" was probably her mom's password. Her mom always told her to make really long passwords with four random words because they were easy to remember but really hard to decode. Then a few more keys on the keyboard and then "Pike, Connor," which was probably someone's name. Then a few more buttons and then "x77" which was probably some NSA code to delete the file.

How could she possibly type all of that into the computer and make it look like it was all an accident? It would be so obvious to anyone who was watching that she was actually doing it on purpose. Who was Connor Pike? Why was his file so important?

But, like all homework, Madison realized that she shouldn't get bogged down into details when there was so much more to be done. The more she considered it, the less comfortable she was with this project. Why was she supposed to do this on blind faith? Why wouldn't Graham just tell her exactly what was happening and why she needed to delete the file? She'd been asking these questions all along but kept going without answers. Now it felt like it was too late to get them.

Madison scanned through the list to see if there would ever be a step that said, "Receive call from Graham Clarke." It all looked like the same things repeated over and over again. It was all just learning the code and preparing her bag and packing everything perfectly. It was late, she was tired and there was just too much on her plate.

Then her phone buzzed at her. It was a text message from Patrick Sutton. It said, "Pls txt to let me knw if yr coming." Madison hadn't read her text messages. There were just too many to deal with. She hadn't listened to her voicemails. It turned out that Patrick had left a total of ten voicemails and twenty-seven texts. They started out giving elaborate details of the entrance they were planning for the semi-formal. He'd rented a limo and they were planning to have a choreographed dance and loud thumping music. Most of the texts were sweet but near the end they began to sour. He started wondering if she was ignoring him on purpose. The texts got angry. Then he started to plead with her to let him know if she was coming.

She'd screwed that up too. She immediately texted him

that she'd be there. But she started to wonder if she could even make it, given how tired she was. How could she do it all? She read the plan she'd created and studied steps that were vaguely stated. There was one step that said: "Step 1029: look at camera to your right and smile." Why did she need to do that? What was so important about looking at the camera that it needed its own step? She had so many questions and no one to answer them and the one person who could do it was someone she'd only met once in her life and talked to on the phone only a few times since.

Madison listened to a few more voicemails. A lot were from people she barely even knew. They had phone numbers she'd never seen before, numbers that she hadn't saved in her contacts list. She scrolled through the calls. They were endless. Mia had called. Carolyn Kaplan. Hannah Chanel.

Near the top of the list was a voicemail from several weeks ago, the day she'd flown to Costa Rica. She didn't have her phone with her so she didn't check her messages, and ever since then she'd been using the phone that Graham gave her so she hadn't even remembered to check for messages. But, even though she hadn't put him on her contacts list his name was in her messages clear as day: "Graham Clarke."

Madison pressed play.

Chapter 33

"Hi Madison," Graham's voice grumbled through a bit of static. "You won't get this for a while but I have to leave the message now…it's a long story, but they'll be tracking me by the time you need to hear this so I won't be able to call then." He laughed to himself. His speech halted from time to time as if he wasn't sure what he was going to say. "It gets complicated to plan the future and this was the only way I could think of to get this information to you.

"I'm in an airport in Costa Rica and your plane is about to land. From where I'm standing today I haven't met you yet. I saw you at your father's funeral but we didn't speak. There's going to be an earthquake here and I'm going to save your life. From there your whole world will spiral out in all directions and it will feel like you don't have any control over anything.

"But that's not true. You have control. I know it seems like fate is spoon feeding the future to you but I swear to you that it's not that simple. Here's how it works: if you know the future, you can't change it. It's a strange but simple fact. However, there are things you can change about it.

"I don't know if you've realized this yet, but I was there when your father died. I was the last person he spoke to. He told me that he had a daughter." He paused for a long time, completely lost for words. He sounded almost scared to speak. "You see, I knew your father was going to die that day in Afghanistan. It was set in stone. But what I didn't realize was that if I'd acted just a little bit more quickly I could have gotten the infantryman with the camera over to him so that he could tell you just how much he loved you. Or I could've turned the bloody camera off so you would never see that video at all. But I missed the chance.

"When he died I felt like it was my fault. I could've done more and I didn't. So I started helping people. I started using this magic bit of technology that I'd developed to do good for people all over the world. It started with little things but eventually it got bigger and more important. For instance, I know that there's going to be an earthquake in a few minutes, but I don't know if anyone is going to die. I made it a point not to ask that question. So now I can be here, ready with first aid to help whoever it is that's wounded. I can't stop the earthquake. That's impossible. I can't tell people ahead of time because no one would believe me. There's no safe place for people to evacuate to so I just have to be here to save whoever I can. I have to be here to save you.

"So that's my life. I try to ask the right questions of the future so that I don't know too much. I've made that mistake, such as with your dad, and I regretted it ever since.

"This device I'm about to give you, it can tell you the future but it can't tell you everything. I don't know if you've noticed yet but it can be very coy. I've actually noticed a pattern in the things it will tell you and the things it leaves out. The more that you have control over the situation, the less it can tell you about what happens. For instance, in the situation of the coming earthquake, there's no stopping it. The forces under the Earth are too great and no matter what anyone does it's going to happen. But in a situation where you ask it who you're going to fall in love with or something like that it suddenly gets very cagey indeed. It's almost as if there are certain parts of the future that are within your control and certain parts that are set in stone before they happen. This shouldn't really be a surprise. The Earth will spin whether we want it to or not. No matter how much we try, humanity would have a very difficult time stopping it. So too with certain big events. You just can't do enough to change their course. But there are loads of things that we do have control over. There's so much in life that we can change. You and I are going to save lives today, Madison. We're going to be heroes, just like your dad.

"Now, I said that I try to use this technology for the cause of good. But there are other people in the world who don't want that. They want to use it for governments or for war or to control people. I can't let that happen. You need to help me stop them. There are people within your own government who are onto me and who want to steal it away. They're very close to finding me out. I need your help to stop them. I'm going to ask you to break into the NSA to delete a file for me. It's complicated, but I need to make sure that the government doesn't realize that there are two people, Connor Pike and General Orson Crawley, who know about my device and are using the power of the US Army to take it from me. If your mother cracks the code that they've been using then their files will be available and I'll have everyone in the world looking over my shoulder.

"They're the two people who I'm most afraid of. They get closer to me every day. I need your help to stop them. I know they think they're going to use this technology for good but I don't trust them. That's why you have to do this Madison. Should I call you Madison? What do your friends call you? I'll look that up before we meet.

"The last thing your father said to me was, 'I'm fighting for my daughter. I think about her every day. She's all I dream about. I just want to go home.' He asked me to promise him that I would look after you. That's what I'm trying to do, although I realize that in doing so I'm putting you through absolute hell. I'd prefer that you know the truth about the world so that you can tackle it head on. I don't want to coddle you and look over your shoulder. I know that's what your dad would have wanted.

"We have the chance to save your mom, but only by keeping her in the dark. If she learns one thing about this strange conspiracy that this general is undertaking then she won't stop until she's figured it out. We can't let her do that. She's too smart for her own good and she doesn't listen to reason. She'd tell all the wrong people and get thrown into a stockade with no food and water. But this general is unhinged. He would find a way to kill her and cover his tracks. If you do everything right, we'll get her out of this.

"I want to keep my friends safe but I can't always do it." He sounded almost tearful. "After I'd discovered this device that can tell the future I only told two other people about it. They're both gone now. I wanted to save them just like I wanted to save your dad. I couldn't. One of them told me before she died, 'Now you have everything you ever wanted. Your power is almost absolute. But you can't beat fate, and you can't change people. You've won the war for the world. You're its king. You're just not its ruler.'"

He paused for a long time.

"Well, I see that your plane is at the gate so I have to say cheerio for now. I don't know when you'll hear this message, and I'm not planning to look it up. Some things are better left up to us, don't you think? Goodbye Madison, and good luck."

Madison hung up the phone. There was so much more she wanted to know. But that phone message was enough to propel her through each of the steps in an absent minded stupor to the point where she didn't even think about step 521. "Step 521: put your pressed semi-formal dress into your bag with the ruby slippers." By that time she was just too tired and too anxious to realize what a bad idea that was and she was too excited for the next step: "Step 522: sleep." Only five hundred eighty steps left until it was finally over.

Chapter 34

Madison slept well, if only for the few hours before her mom's wake-up call at 5:30. So much depended on being perfect. Or maybe not quite perfect, but at least perfect at following directions. Maybe it was just the bravado of having the best directions in the world, but her morning came briskly. She showered and dressed in a pair of khaki pants that fit her well. She knew she'd be doing a lot of moving so she made sure not to wear anything too tight or too loose. Her top was an understated navy polo with pops of cobalt around the collar. Her shoes were her normal pair, a dressed up sneaker that didn't get in her way but also didn't look like an ensemble that Frankenstein's monster would wear. Altogether it was a normal outfit, nothing to make her stand out. She might even look like an intern if nobody knew better.

She brushed her cheeks briefly with some foundation and ran a few dark highlights above her lashes. She'd learned to do this from Mia whose makeup selections tended to be overdone, but at the same time she knew how to put the stuff on. Mia had at least seven siblings that Madison knew about, possibly more. It was impossible not to learn, even though Mia wasn't really the makeup type.

"Is this the outfit I wear to save the world?" she asked herself looking in the mirror. "I feel like I should have a cape or something."

After a quick breakfast of scrambled eggs, they were in the car toward Jillian's house. It was on the other side of town, in the opposite direction of the NSA building, making them set out fifteen minutes earlier than they would have normally. Already Jillian was cramping her style.

Madison found Jillian's house, a surprisingly small brick home with a modest front yard and a porch swing. It didn't seem like the pretentious house of an overachiever, much less the house of a girl who wore designer clothes every single day of the year, but it was nice enough. Madison walked slowly up to the door, not wanting to actually knock but also not wanting to wait.

Before she could even reach the front door, Jillian burst out at a jog. She sidled up to Madison and grabbed her arm with a fake laugh. She spoke through gritted teeth as they walked to the car. "Thanks for picking me up," she said.

"I like your house," Madison returned.

Jillian rolled her eyes. "Debatable."

They got situated and began the long drive across eight lane freeways filled up completely with cars, most of which crawled along at a snail's pace. Once in a while the traffic would free up for a minute, enough that they could burst ahead with unremitting speed until a moment later the speed remitted once again as if they'd never sped up in the first place. Madison stared out of the window at the people driving beside her as they clutched their steering wheels in white knuckled anger. She looked over at her mom, who herself clasped the steering wheel with vice grips.

"Is it always this bad?" Madison asked.

Mrs. Riley smiled. "This is nothing," she said. "I've been through hours on this highway. I get five different kinds of traffic reports and I plug a Bayesian analysis through the data with a Gaussian algorithm. I can usually get through as long as I don't get caught in a bad patch between exits."

"That's so interesting," Jillian swooned. Madison felt sick hearing her overindulgent crooning for approval. "Do you mean that you can predict how the traffic will be using the day of the year?" Of course Jillian would know what her mom meant.

"That's right," she said. "It's an interesting distribution that I've found over the years. Given the traffic report, the day of the year, the weather, and the road construction, I can accurately judge the best route to work 230 days of the year. It's partially based on the Riemann zeta function." She laughed to herself as if imagining a joke she'd heard years ago. "I validated the formula over the past four years of driving to a correlation of point nine eight as the Pearson coefficient for a day like today."

"Pearson coefficient," Jillian chirped. "What's that?"

"Oh," Mrs. Riley began, "don't get me started on Pearson coefficients." Madison hoped that she'd follow her own advice and not get started but it was already too late. Her interest had been piqued. "You see, Jillian, Pearson coefficients are…"

Madison couldn't stand to listen. It wasn't that she found her mother boring, but when she started to go off on tangents related to obscure mathematical principles Madison had just heard too many PhD level equations that her mom never really explained. Madison didn't even listen anymore. After a while she'd drift off to think about boys or books or the vacations she'd go on someday and she'd retain absolutely zero mathematical theory. It was a pity, in a way, that she wasn't more interested. She knew very well that her mom was one of the smartest mathematicians in the world. She could have learned a lot from her. Instead she could barely finish her math homework, it bored her so badly. She could barely stand to look at any equation, let alone one that her mom had told her about.

But whenever Jillian would talk, Madison would be stirred out of her musings to listen in. Jillian would say something like, "That's so interesting," and Madison's ears would ring inside of her head and she'd look over her shoulder as if to suddenly gape at the gorilla in the back of the car. Jillian didn't seem to notice. "That's the best explanation of statistical dependence I've ever heard in my life," she said. "You should be a teacher."

"I've thought about it," Mrs. Riley said. "I'd love to think about going into a professorship. Sometimes I'm just not sure if what I do is worth it."

"What do you mean?" Jillian asked.

"Well," answered Mrs. Riley, "It's a rough commute. I just would rather live where we are. Shackleton is a great school." She stared blankly out of the window and Madison could see in the twinkle in her eye that she dreamed of far off possibilities. Then she snapped back into place. "Of course I love my job. I love that I get to go in there and play a high stakes game of numbers." That was how she always described her work: a high stakes game of numbers.

"Mrs. Riley, you're such a great mom to do all of this traveling," Jillian said. Madison flipped around again to stare Jillian down. They shared a quick look but Madison just scowled and watched the road ahead. She couldn't get angry at Jillian for saying something so nice but she could definitely get mad at her for sucking up so clearly. It was so obvious. Jillian's eyes looked like saucers and her mouth a half moon. A ridiculous farce that Madison saw right through. Somehow, though, despite all of her training in lie detection, Mrs. Riley didn't seem to notice how much Jillian cowed to her. How could someone who was usually so perceptive be caught up with a girl as transparent as Jillian?

She didn't really have the strength to find out. She had too much to think about for the next few hours, let alone the possible plot for Jillian to unseat her as her mom's favorite daughter.

It felt like forever until they reached the entrance gate of Fort Meade, the giant base on which the National Security Agency sat. The traffic going into the gate was incredible. So many cars had to pass through every day. They had an intricate system of electronics to accurately identify every car that entered the facility in addition to the RFID that Madison had read about earlier. She'd always seen the bar codes and transponders in her mom's car and wondered what they were. She was surprised to see what they actually meant in the eyes of the national intelligence community. Breaking into her mom's office would be hard enough, but having to get through the million layers of security required just to reach the front doors was mind boggling. It was no wonder Graham needed her help. Who else could do it? Of all the spies in all the world, only a fifteen year old girl could get through the gates without arousing too much suspicion. And even once through the gates she'd have to work incredibly hard just to do the simple task she'd been assigned.

She wondered if she even had a chance, looking at all of the cameras and barricades. There were guards armed with assault rifles and military trucks painted in camouflage. This was one of the most secure places in the country and all Madison had was a couple of gizmos in her purse and the knowledge of exactly where to be and when. That last part was something that no spy had ever had quite as accurately as she did. She hoped it would be enough.

They finally reached the parking lot, a good half mile away from the shining black glass building sitting unflinchingly in the distance.

It was quiet as they waited. Jillian finally said to Mrs. Riley, "I'm so impressed by your devotion."

For a moment Madison wanted to turn around and scream at Jillian, but she stopped herself, not because she didn't want to upset Jillian but because she was shocked by what she said. Madison had always thought about it from her own perspective, never seeing her mother's side of things. Madison felt guilty. She didn't ask to go to Shackleton but she was aware that it was the best school within an hour drive from her mother's office. If she'd had any compunction about proceeding on the task in front of her, it vanished. She had to save her mom, regardless of the difficulties. It was official. She had arrived.

Chapter 35

They made their way through the parking lot to the main entrance of the building. The faceless black glass tower loomed over them. Busy professional types flocked from every direction to enter the building in a huge flood of people with expressionless faces. A few kids accompanied their parents, many of them as young as ten, but for the most part the crowd was male, suited and angry.

The entrance was a concrete bunker style hut jutting out from the building. A very complicated series of bollards and buttresses preceded it with an austere sense of grandeur and a military weightiness. For some reason, in an atmosphere like that the "Visitors" sign was exceptionally out of place. They followed the few other families into the visitor's entrance to be processed.

This was not the setting that Madison expected. Unlike the military style exterior, the visitor's entrance was a lavish area with crystal chandeliers in its center and more woodwork than could have been chopped from a single forest. There were two giant insignia of the NSA, a circle with an eagle holding a key, one inlaid into the marble floor and one hung dead center on the far wall with gilded letters. The one on the wall looked like a six foot wide coin that weighed a thousand pounds.

The visitor's entrance opened up to the actual entrances to the building which were contained behind thick bulletproof Plexiglas. A person would swipe in, walk through a rotating door like the one at a department store or the airport. A million little things had to happen just for one person to get past the gate. Madison knew she had to get through that door. She had directions to do it but she wasn't sure it would work. But it wasn't time yet.

"I'll see you for lunch," Mrs. Riley said. "I have to do some work in the morning but I'll see you soon."

"I love you, Mom," said Madison, thinking she'd be a changed girl before the end of the day. She almost wanted to apologize for what she was about to do.

It could only be ruined by one person, coming in sideways in order to break up the moment. "Have a good day Mrs. Riley," Jillian said, her face all screwed up with overeager interest. Mrs. Riley waved and turned to go through security. They both watched as she hit one checkpoint after the other. The whole process took almost as long as the line at the airport, but it was more streamlined and more practical. Madison listened to hear the respectfulness of the security guards as they processed her.

Madison lumbered along with her gym bag filled with all of her clothes for the dance, just as she'd been instructed to. It made her stick out, but no more than the backpacks adorning all of the other daughters. The daughters to work girls all huddled together, a group of twenty or so, all quietly gazing around the room at all of the nervous energy of the place. None had ever seen so many suited, anxious people in one place.

"Hi, I'm Doctor Jean Yedidya," the guide told them. Her thin face widened out to a broad forehead above which a tightly bound shock of blond hair pulled into a spherical bun at the back of her head like the top of a bowling pin. "You must be all of our angels here for Take Your Daughter to Work Day. Thank you so much for coming."

"Unfortunately, we can't give you the clearance levels you'll need in order to pass through those doors. You'd need to be pretty important to get back there. Instead, we're going to take you to all of the non-essential spaces." She looked each girl in the eye momentarily as if to both intimidate them and size them up. Madison knew this tactic well. "This is the first time we've participated in Take Your Daughter to Work Day. We've had a lot of bad press here at the NSA and we want people to know that we're good people. We're just normal people trying to do our jobs." Madison nodded. Dr. Yedidya didn't seem entirely convinced of what she was saying.

Dr. Yedidya moved on. "Firstly, we're going to go to the cryptography museum to show you how the work is done. Then we'll come back and have lunch with your folks and then we'll take a tour of the rest of Fort Meade." Her smile was military issue.

Jillian leaned toward Madison to whisper, swiping at her own disastrously tight hairstyle. "I can't believe how close we are to the magic. You know I've heard that there is more intelligence in this building than the entire rest of the world combined."

Doctor Yedidya went on. "We process data through many types of computer systems, some housed in this facility and some housed elsewhere. It is all protected to an astonishing degree." She looked lovingly up at the building towering above them. "This building could be hit by a nuclear blast and the Department of Defense would not lose a single file."

Jillian and Mads were taken on a brief tour of the lobby while Mrs. Riley headed up to her desk to check in. Their tour guide seemed very smart but very OCD. She tossed off orders and gave darting looks to any dawdlers. "I don't make time for those who don't follow directions," she said at one point with her chin stuck out and her eyes darting rapidly from one face to the next.

The tour boarded a van which wound across the parking lot and over to the cryptography museum where they housed all manner of old devices for manipulating data to make or break codes. Some were old hulking supercomputers that are slower than Madison's old phone. Some weren't even computers but instead used wires and dials to crack codes.

It was all very boring. Madison and Jillian were the only two people in the group who seemed to know each other and they maintained an icy silence. The whole trip felt eerie and dim. There wasn't much to talk about and even less to see. While Madison was preoccupied with her plans for the rest of the day, Jillian stood in rapt attention as the tour guide talked about the code algorithms that were used to confuse the German Panzer tanks in World War II. She took notes, even.

This was the first moment when Madison had to implement a part of the plan. There was an item that she needed from the museum, the RFID Spoofer, and it was behind a locked door. It was probably the most important part of the plan because it was the only thing that could stop her from being spotted later as she skulked through the bowels of the main building posing as people who were twenty years older than her. Getting behind this door would require much more finesse than any other she'd sneaked through. Before, she'd just waited until someone walked through and then sneaked by, but this time wouldn't be so easy. What she needed to do this time was much harder. She needed to trick someone into letting her in.

She went over to Jillian. "Are you actually interested in this?" Madison asked loudly, so that Dr. Yedidya could hear.

Jillian rolled her eyes. "I can write an article about this in the school paper and put the clipping in a college application." Jillian curled her lips in response, a little too focused on the weird piece of equipment in front of her. "This is the original Enigma machine that the Germans used in their U-boats. It's still not that easy to decode."

The machine looked like an old typewriter, far from impressive except for its antique value. Madison looked over Jillian's shoulder at her notes. They were intricate and detailed, with equations interspersed. "You seem like you care," she said.

"I seem like a lot of things," Jillian bit back like a scared tigress.

"No you don't," Madison said. She looked at Jillian's face and the slight hints of fear in her eyebrows. She'd learned enough from her mom's mind reading techniques to know when someone is scared. "It's OK if you really like this stuff," she said softly. "I won't make fun of you. I mean, I'm a huge nerd. Not a fashion nerd or a sports nerd or any of the other popular types of nerds. I'm just a regular old girl who likes stuff."

Jillian studied her notes and quickly turned the page as if to erase the last few moments from her life. "That's why I'm stronger than you. I don't like anything."

"Wrong," Madison said, trying out some of her mom's lie detection techniques. "You just pretend not to like them but I can see it on your face. You're serious when you talk to my mom about statistics. Someone told me recently that math is beautiful. It's a language with as much poetry as Shakespeare and as much music as the Beatles. If you pay enough attention, everything turns into song." Jillian subtly nodded in agreement.

They stood there staring at the display case, Madison quietly mulling over the fact that they'd gotten closer to each other despite their better judgments. The place was quiet save for the chatter of some of the younger daughters in the group who all seemed bored out of their minds.

"It does," Jillian agreed. "You know, I've actually spent nights alone reading textbooks online." She was embarrassed to say it, but Madison was glad to hear her open up. Also, it was imperative to her plan that Jillian do so. Dr. Yedidya watched fondly over Jillian's shoulder as she spoke without really thinking, a strikingly candid muse. "You know our tour guide, Dr. Yedidya, she's kind of a legend in cryptography circles. She was one of the first women from the NSA to be taken into a warzone. She saved a lot of lives during the first Gulf war."

Dr. Yedidya cleared her throat and startled Jillian. They smiled at each other, both a bit embarrassed. "You know," Dr. Yedidya said, "I work at the museum now, so I can show you something special from my time in Kuwait." She motioned for them to follow her into the back of the building.

The back of the museum was fairly unimpressive, a cinderblock structure that reminded her of chemistry class. But in the back was a display case that looked unfinished, as if they were still trying to make it look right. It showed pictures of Dr. Yedidya herself hunched over a computer squinting. She started explaining all of the decoding that she'd done over the years. Jillian watched in rapt attention. That let Madison's eyes wander around the room to look for the spoofer.

Unfortunately, the directions were again somewhat vague. She hadn't seen a picture of the thing but instead only knew it was disguised to look like a tube of lipstick. She glanced around the room. She wasn't even listening as Dr. Yedidya talked about her work during the war. She didn't even try to look like she was paying attention. Luckily, Jillian was paying enough attention for the both of them.

Then suddenly she saw something that fit the description about ten feet away. It even said "*Chanel*" on the side. She whispered hopeful thoughts under her breath and inched carefully toward it. She moved slowly with her right hand to grab it as she quickly moved her left to scratch her head, a misdirection tactic she wasn't sure would work.

"It's time to go," Dr. Yedidya said at last, cheerfully. They walked out of the back room and the group came together to quietly get back into the van. They were carted around the rest of the fort, looking at the giant satellite dishes and the barracks. It might have been interesting, had Madison not been so nervous, carefully running through what she'd already seen in order to truly understand what she was up against. She had almost three hundred steps still to complete before the end of the day.

Then came lunch. They waited for Mrs. Riley in a tiny café by the entrance to the giant black building. All of the girls waited by the entrance for their parents to show up, most of them still not having spoken to each other. The atmosphere felt so rigid and nervous that when Jillian and Madison spoke to each other in their quiet, guarded voices they could hear their echo within the tiny room. Dr. Yedidya spouted facts periodically, mostly limited to the security of the place, which only made Madison feel worse and worse.

"Every square inch of this building is monitored by camera," she said. "Every person in the building wears a tag on their badge that can tell the security staff exactly where they are within the building." That, Madison assumed, was why she needed the RFID spoofer, to make the computers think that she was someone else. Dr. Yedidya seemed so proud of a fact that would make Madison's life harder, so much so that Madison could feel the blood rushing to her face with a full range of fury and fright. But Dr. Yedidya just kept going. "There are fifteen different levels of security within the building and no single person has access to every room." She took a moment to twiddle her thumbs and then went on, still with an absent stare in her eye. "In most buildings, if there's a fire, all of the doors open so that emergency personnel can fight the fire, but since this is a government building on a military compound, it's exempt. Even if a missile hit the side of the building, everything would continue to function without any problems. In fact, the systems in this building are more complicated than those in the Pentagon."

One of the little girls in the corner raised her hand meekly. Dr. Yedidya called on her like a teacher. The little girl looked around to make sure people were listening and then quietly asked, "What would happen if a terrorist attacked this building?"

Dr. Yedida smiled. "Well," she began, "if a terrorist made it through the checkpoints, and was somehow able to get past the ten doors between the entrance and any important systems then they still would not be able to transmit anything out of the building. They'd have to get through eye scanners, fingerprint scanners, some of the most important computers are not even connected to the internet. No information can be sent out, and no one can get in to access it. They only talk to other national security networks no matter what."

Madison had been told as much by Graham, but it felt good to hear someone on the inside confirm that he wasn't lying.

After more waiting around, Mrs. Riley finally came down to greet them. They all got their food and sat together at a small group of tables. Once again, Jillian and Mrs. Riley went wild talking about math as if it were the most interesting subject that any human could possibly discuss. After a while, Madison couldn't take it.

In the midst of Jillian's fawning sentence about data structures, Madison blurted, "I'm really impressed by you, Mom." She was overcome with emotion, suddenly feeling for her mother in a way that she didn't expect, a fear for her and a sense that she was the only one who could save her. They all went quiet. Madison felt like she had to explain. "This is an amazing place. Thank you for bringing us."

"Thank you, Honey," Mrs. Riley said.

Madison wanted to tell her how scared she was, and how much she loved her, and how intimidating the building was—how it made her feel so small. But instead she just looked deeply into her mother's eyes and smiled.

"I'm impressed too," Jillian said.

Madison shot her a look of contempt before standing sharply to take her food to the trash. She didn't care if Jillian hated her. She was too overwhelmed to worry about anything but the task at hand. They met back in the lobby. Madison awaited what she knew was coming. She tried to look surprised when her mom broke the news. "I pulled some strings and got you both temporary badges with non-classified security clearance," she said. "I can take you on a short tour away from the group."

Madison tried to look surprised and she ended up looking almost disappointed. She wished it wasn't all happening. This was the official start of the operation. She could feel her hands grow clammy with sweat.

Jillian looked positively ecstatic.

Madison felt the bag on her shoulder for the devices she'd put inside. They were small, three pens and a container of lipstick, but she knew their outlines well enough to get them at a moment's notice. The next hurdle was to get them through security. Then the fun began.

Chapter 36

Of course Madison's giant bag set off the scanners. She expected as much. With five items in her bag that could have landed her in a military jail, she'd be disappointed if they found nothing.

She emptied the contents of her bag onto the counter with complete confidence, absolutely sure that the pen-sized implements she'd brought with her would be undetectable by the guards. There was enough in there to make them search for a while, what with her dress. She wanted to explain that it was for the dance but the guard didn't seem to care. He didn't even ask about the ruby slippers. Everything had worked out properly so far and there was nothing to make her think circumstances were changing. But she couldn't help but look at the three pens, the one which was the actual electromagnet, the second which was the battery and the third which was the vial of liquid helium cooling agent. They were heavy, but not so heavy that you couldn't believe they were just plain pens.

The officer smiled, his closely cropped hair made his

smile seem out of place, like wrinkles on an infant. "Try not to bring so much stuff next time," he said. *It probably helps to be fifteen when breaking into the NSA*, Madison thought. He grabbed her phone and put a tag on it. "You can't take this in with you either. Anything with a camera on it is prohibited." Like a coat check at a nice restaurant, she was given a little slip and told that she could collect the phone when she came back out. At least Jillian had to do the same. He'd noticed the obvious things, the phones, but completely missed the real dangers, despite the billions of dollars of security.

She collected her stuff and started to do some of the items on her checklist. The first was to turn on the spoofer, the piece of equipment that would make the sensors think she was someone else. Jillian and Mrs. Riley were up ahead, talking up a storm about the facilities so she had time to figure out quickly how to program it. There was a numeric keypad but the keys were comically small, almost to the point where you needed a toothpick to push them. Luckily, her mom and Jillian had such a good rapport that they wouldn't have noticed if Madison was acting like an ape and throwing bananas behind them. She entered the first number that she'd memorized: 587898422. Easy enough as a start. She hoped she'd gotten it right. There were so many things that she needed to memorize. That was simply first on the list.

"Now we won't be able to go to my desk," Mrs. Riley said, "but I can show you around the low security floors of the building."

Madison chuckled. "If we make a wrong turn will we go to jail?" she asked, hoping to make a joke.

"That's not funny," Mrs. Riley said back. "Don't joke

about that." Madison felt her skin crawl as she realized more and more what she was doing, how deep she'd already gone.

They walked slowly through the corridors. Everything felt narrow and closed in. Even the desks were behind monstrous cubicle walls. If you didn't know any better you'd think there wasn't a single person working in there, just floors and floors of maze-like office space. "Where are we going?" Madison asked.

"I got permission to let you both sit in on the low security network operations center," she answered. "You'll love it."

She opened a set of double doors upon a room unlike any that Madison had ever seen in real life. It looked like something out of mission control at NASA. There were rows upon rows of people working behind computers all looking in the same direction, each row two steps higher than the one before. On five movie theater sized screens at the front of the room were projected numbers, tweets and weird graphs. One showed a map of the weather and another showed news feeds from a bunch of different cable networks.

"Wow," Jillian said candidly, her mouth opened wide.

"For once I agree with Jillian," Madison said. "This is awesome, Mom."

Mrs. Riley said, "There's a guest terminal in the corner that you two can share. I have to work with low security network operations up front." As she started to walk up the stairs toward the back of the room, Madison stopped her.

"I'm sorry Mom, but I've got to go to the bathroom."

Mrs. Riley nodded. "Take a left out of the door and you'll see it," she said. "Just knock when you come back and I can let you back in." And so Madison left, free at last to wander the halls.

She walked slowly down the hall trying to look inconspicuous. The stairwell down to her mom's floor was cattycorner to the entrance to the bathroom without much else in the vicinity. It was unlikely that anyone would see her but then she remembered what Dr. Yedidya said. Every square inch of the building was monitored by camera. Looking around, she couldn't see anything that looked like surveillance equipment but this was the most technologically superior building in the world. If they wanted cameras to be hidden, they'd be hidden.

But she couldn't worry about that. It was time to act. The first thing she had to do was drop her ID badge somewhere because it could be used to identify her. She already had the spoofer and she didn't very well need two identities. She pulled out the spoofer and quickly typed in the second code that she'd memorized. This would be her identity for the next part of the trip. She pressed the spoofer to the door and the lock clicked open as if the spoofer was a keycard. This was the point of no return. She pushed with a full heave of her body and waited for a moment with the door slightly ajar, wondering if she should turn back.

"What's up?" asked a cheery voice from down the hall. Madison turned to look with a start, letting the door swing closed. It was Jillian, eyeing her with the same reserved expectancy that she always had, like she could see through to Madison's soul.

"Nothing," Madison answered.

Jillian motioned to the spoofer in Madison's hand. "What are you doing?" she asked.

Madison dropped the gizmo into her gym bag and shook her head. This wasn't in the directions she'd been reading.

She'd planned and practiced the whole thing in her mind. There was no step about dealing with Jillian in the hallway. Had she missed a page?

Jillian's calculating look melted into incredulity, the coldness into quiet. She shook her head. "I knew it," she said. "There was something about you that just wasn't right this whole time. I knew you were a terrorist."

Madison gasped. That was the last thing she expected, especially from someone as conniving as Jillian. To be called the bad guy by her was like being called a gangster by Al Capone. "Is your mom in on it, or are you acting alone?"

"What?" Madison asked, unable to even formulate a decent rebuttal.

"You knew too much," she said. "At the earthquake, you had that app on your phone that you dove back into the hole to get. Nobody in their right mind would do that if it was only to get a picture of their dad. I should know. I've lost a few pictures of my mom over the years. I wouldn't die for them." She came closer, almost in Madison's face. "And then there's your character in *StarX*. I looked you up. You're at 92 and you've only logged ten hours of playing time. That's literally impossible. And there's no way you could be in better shape than me unless you were trained by some government to be a killing machine. Nothing about you adds up. I'm just glad I was here to report you before you breach national security."

Madison stepped back and shook her head furiously. "No," she said, "you think that you understand but you don't. Trust me."

"Trust you?" Jillian laughed. "Why would I trust you? You stole my boyfriend, you made me look bad in front of everyone.

You hate me. I can see it in your eyes whenever you look at me and now I know why. It's because I'm the only one who sees through you, Mads Riley. I'm the only one who knows who you really are."

Madison grabbed Jillian by the arm and pulled her through the door into the stairwell. Madison locked Jillian's arm behind her in a hold she'd learned in her Krav Maga class. "You're not getting away, Jillian, until you understand what's going on." She pushed Jillian against the wall and whispered in her ear as she squirmed. "I'm doing this to save my mom," she said. "I can tell that you like her. She's a good person and she's in trouble. There are people who want to kill her. Someone told me that I need to delete one file and if I don't then she'll die."

"I don't believe you," Jillian said.

Madison pushed harder. "I just got through a locked door in the NSA, Jillian. Do you think I could've done that if I wasn't connected somehow?"

"You're a traitor."

Madison let go. The two girls stared at each other, gauging the next move. "You're right," Madison said. She thought about her dad and how much he'd done for his country and about all the time she'd spent wanting to be anywhere else but America. Was she a traitor? She didn't know anymore. She started to cry. Jillian just stood there.

"They're going to catch you," Jillian said coldly.

Madison nodded. "That's fine," she said through her sobs. "As long as Mom's OK." But really, Madison hadn't anticipated getting caught. Before, when she'd done something like this, Graham had been able to cover her tracks, but in this case it was impossible. Even he couldn't break into the computers in the NSA. That was the whole reason she was there, to do the one piece of hacking that he couldn't. She would be caught, she was sure. The only question was how deeply she'd be in trouble when she was.

After a few moments, Jillian touched Madison on the shoulder. "Tell me the truth. Is this a hundred percent guaranteed to save Mrs. Riley from getting killed?" Madison nodded earnestly. "This isn't right," Jillian said. "We should just tell someone. We should tell someone important. There's got to be a government official that we can turn to who can help."

"It's a government official who wants to kill her," Madison said. "There are people within the government trying to do bad things and I need to stop them."

Jillian turned to walk out the door. "I'm telling someone. I can't just let you go."

"No one will believe you," Madison said. "You have no evidence. You're just some delusional girl who thinks she's better than everyone else. Or at least that's what they'll say about you."

But Jillian just kept on walking. The door closed behind her. Luckily, what Madison had to do wouldn't take much longer. After she was finished, she wasn't sure there was any way back.

Chapter 37

The trip down to the high security level where her mom worked was only a few flights of stairs. She was underground now, somewhere deep within an even bigger maze of tunnels and endless offices. She'd memorized the way to go, down one set of stairs, stop, change the spoofer to pretend to be someone else, go through the doors and down a long hallway, change the spoofer again. It was all very complicated.

On edge after her encounter with Jillian, Madison realized she hadn't really worried about getting caught before. Everything else had worked out so smoothly when she had the phone. When she broke into the Smithsonian there weren't any problems. This was different. It was a suicide mission.

All of the trust she had for Graham started to fade. Who was he? Why did she think he was helping her? It was all coming to a head as she neared the final door before she'd make it into her mom's office. But of course it wasn't that easy.

This was where things got tricky. The next door had a handprint reader on it. To get through, Madison would have to use all of the tools that she'd collected. If there was anything that she was going to get in trouble for doing, this was it. This was treason. This was a crime punishable by being locked away in a military prison. Or worse.

Then there was that word: traitor. Jillian had spoken it in Madison's ear with whispered excitement, like a girl tattling on her to the teacher. Traitor.

But this technology, this ability to see the future, it was something that Madison could tell immediately was dangerous. In the wrong hands it could cause wars, or be used to enslave the human race. Even if someone wanted to use it for good, how would they? What would they do to change the future? As Graham had said, it's delicate work. You have to carefully plan in order to only know what was necessary. What if someone didn't have that kind of restraint? What then?

The door she had to bypass was unique. It was bigger than the other doors and had a massive latch comprised of a foot long metal lever as thick as a broom handle. It stood central to the office space surrounding it. It had no window. There was a black box to the right of the door with the outline of a hand and a keypad. It was in clear sight of everyone around. She would have to get everything ready in the far corner of the office before walking over so that she could just go right up, break the lock and walk straight through as though nothing was strange about doing so. At least she'd used the electromagnet before. That time it hadn't gone well but this time might be better, though the directions were vague compared to those at the Smithsonian. It just said to put the magnet together, point it at the divot in the side of the handprint reader, release the liquid helium, and let the thing do its magic.

Madison skulked into the corner of the office. She finally found a cubicle that was empty save for a stack of old computers, the huge beige kind that sit under the desk with wires snaking out of the back. She stepped inside of the cubicle and pretended to be fixing one of the old computers, as if the spoofer and the magnet were tools.

The HX1-7271 superconducting electromagnet was still hidden inside the three pens she'd hollowed out the night before. She took them apart while still in her bag, just like she'd practiced. Her clumsy fingers fumbled them. Her hands shook with nervous energy. It took forever for her to stick them together until they finally clicked into place. She held the magnet by the liquid helium canister, the little toe of the peace sign, because she knew it wouldn't get as cold as the part she'd held before. She was ready to go.

There was so much to keep handy as she walked back to the giant door. She tried to look inconspicuous, but couldn't help feeling as though all eyes were on her. She was walking right down the center of the office in plain sight. She made sure not to make eye contact with anyone, she just kept her sights focused on the door and its handprint reader, trying to visualize exactly what she needed to do. Luckily, everyone seemed too absorbed in their computer screens to notice her. They, like her mom, seemed pretty good at tuning out everything but their work.

When Madison got to the door she slung her gym bag behind her, keeping it in place with her elbow. Her hands were completely full. The sequence began. She held the spoofer up to the card reader, held the magnet up to the handprint reader and got ready to push the button on the magnet, the tip of which was pushed into the tiny divot between the door and the hand-print reader. The next step was to drop the magnet and press another code into the keypad to the right. She wasn't sure it could be done by anyone, let alone someone who'd never touched the equipment before, especially without being noticed by an office full of people.

She couldn't afford to think. Instead she just tapped the button on the magnet. Unlike the popcorn popping sound at the Smithsonian, this sounded like a huge crunch. The electromagnet leapt from her hand like a missile through the card reader. The lights dimmed and flickered out through the whole floor. There was a crackle on the other side of the office, by the stairs. That was the popcorn sound, which made everyone look in the opposite direction. Madison had her opportunity. She typed the code into the keypad and pulled the metal handle, opening the heavy door to a completely dark room.

After she stepped through, the door closed behind her. She walked forward into the almost total darkness, lit only by exit signs, navigating by sound like she'd practiced so many times before. This office was easy to navigate. The room was oddly silent though. Even the computers had shut down, but the air conditioning still wheezed cold air into the room. Madison used the sound of the airflow to point her in the right direction. It was a straight shot from where she stood to get to her mom's office on the far side. About ten seconds after the lights had gone out, they suddenly flashed on again. No one seemed to notice her, they were too busy freaking out about their computers turning off. Mrs. Riley had once told her that the computers in her office had stayed on 24/7 for fifteen years. The workers had no idea what to do without them.

This was a nice, very modern looking office. The walls were divided into square panels. Some of the panels were bamboo, some were frosted windows and some were clear. It almost felt like the room was a living game of Tetris with shapes being built from other shapes. But it also had a very Zen feeling to it, exactly the opposite of her mom's personality. Madison half-expected to find a lotus pond in the corner with a burbling fountain.

She was doing everything perfectly according to the script down to the exact step. She hadn't missed one. But she suddenly drew a blank. She couldn't remember what to do next. She looked around her for clues and suddenly the next step came to her. There was a tiny black dot in the corner of the room that she realized was a camera. She remembered, right at that moment, number 1,029: "Look at the camera to your right and smile." It was amazing. She couldn't help but smile because it meant that she was on the right track. Everything was clicking into place.

And there she was at the tall glass door leading into her mom's office. She walked briskly inside and stood behind the black oak desk. Unlike the office in the attic of their house, Mrs. Riley kept this space immaculately clean and perfectly ordered. Each of the square shelves held books which were aligned with a strong mind for Feng Shui and balance. Her work station had a flow. There were two tall stalks of bamboo growing in a shallow vase in the other corner. Her mother had found a way to perfectly mesh science and nature within this office. Madison wished she'd seen it sooner. It gave her a brand new appreciation for her mom's taste.

There was also a laboratory style chamber in the far corner, the type where you put your hands under a sheet of plexiglass and work on an experiment while all the noxious vapors are sealed inside. Madison never expected her mom to have something like that in her office. That had nothing to do with math. But Madison was learning that a lot more things were math than she had thought.

What surprised her most after everything she'd just done was to see her own picture staring back at her from her mother's desk. It had been taken a few years before. She couldn't remember smiling that widely, as if it had never even happened. She could barely smile at all anymore.

Another picture was right next to it. It was her mom and her dad standing on a beach together while she played in the sand in front of them. She saw the smile on her dad's face. The picture was taken in the south of France when they were on vacation after her dad's third tour of duty. His smile, like hers, wasn't as wide as she would have liked. He looked sad, like he'd seen a few too many awful things and couldn't get them out of his mind. It was a feeling, she imagined, amplified from her own memories of the video she'd seen of his death in Afghanistan. She couldn't get rid of the things that she'd seen. She couldn't go back. It was probably just the same with him.

But she'd come too far not to finish the job. She put her hands on the keyboard and typed away, just as she'd been instructed to do, the strange code that she'd been given. She didn't know what it was doing, but the screen seemed to pop between a few different functions. It pulled up a series of two reports. They both showed the same man's face. He wore a uniform and had all kinds of commendations and medals. The name on the file was Connor Pike, who she kind of recognized. He was a slender man with striking features, a former Army soldier. Then she saw his current title: Deputy Attorney General of the United States. More times than she could fathom in the last two and a half weeks, she'd experienced a revelation that completely undercut everything she thought she'd known. This would have shattered her world if she'd learned it earlier but suddenly it didn't seem like a revelation at all. This must have been the man her mom was talking to on the phone in the police station.

Next to him was a picture of General Orson Crawley, a fat old man with a bushy white mustache and an angry bald forehead. She hadn't seen him before, and she hoped never to see him again. She finished the code and stepped back. It was done.

She took a deep breath and wondered what to do, how to get out. Her first thought was to walk right back the way she'd come but she hadn't planned out the directions so she had to think about them for a moment. Then she saw the brigade. It was at least fifteen men, all wearing army uniforms coming straight toward her and in front of them all was the man she'd just seen on the computer screen, General Orson Crawley. The man who Graham worried might kill her mother was less than fifty feet away.

Madison wanted to run but had nowhere to go. She wanted to hide but he'd already seen her through the office window just as she'd seen him. It was too late to save herself. She had no phone, no way to call for help. She reached out for the phone on her mom's desk and dialed zero, hoping that some operator somewhere would pick up, but before she even heard a voice, the door opened and General Crawley was standing there, two armed guards on either side of him. He glared down at her and pulled the phone from her hand. "You have a lot of explaining to do," he said.

Madison shook her head. She was not about to talk without a fight. She'd finally finished. It wasn't time to give up yet.

She realized that for the first time since she'd gotten to the NSA building she'd made a mistake. Instead of pushing the monitor on the computer to the ground she just typed the code. In an act of bold defiance, Madison flung the computer to the opposite side of the room, staring right into Crawley's eyes.

He didn't flinch.

Chapter 38

Before she knew it, Madison had a bag over her head so that she couldn't see and no one could see her. She was being shoved down hallways and pushed into a van. No one said anything and Madison wasn't about to start asking questions. She knew enough to stay quiet.

Once inside, General Crawley pulled the bag off and grunted at her. "We're taking you to an interrogation room. One your mother doesn't know anything about."

"I know who you are," she said.

He smiled. "I expect no less from a girl with the most sophisticated piece of hacking equipment in the world at her disposal." He chortled under his breath. "I should think you know a lot more about me than that."

Madison said, frankly, "Not really."

General Crawley leaned forward and stared right into her eyes. "Not really?" he asked. "You broke into the NSA and you didn't even bother to do your homework about the place?"

It almost sounded like a joke. Madison was so uncomfortable and so desperate, she actually laughed out loud in his face. It was the nervous laugh that happens when your brain is so overwhelmed that it can't help but burst out somehow.

"I am the Combatant Commander of US ANTCOM, young lady," General Crawley said with a sharp bite to the ends of his words. "I have complete command over all forces within functional boundary of the Antarctic continent."

"What?" Madison asked. "Antarctica has an army?"

"How do you know Graham Clarke?"

"I've only met Graham once at an airport."

General Crawley leaned closer. "So you admit it? You know Graham Clarke?"

Madison laughed, the fluttering whispers of panic in her brain. "What do you want from me?"

"Young lady," the general groaned, "don't protect a man who convinced you to betray your country."

That was the second time someone had said she was a traitor. Both times it stung but when she'd heard it from Jillian it cut deeper. Graham had already said that this man wasn't to be trusted. He would kill her mother if he needed to. She tried to get deeper into his head, like her mom might. He was nervous, there was a twitch under his white moustache that told her he was also angry. It was strange that she was even looking at him in the first place. If he was so important, what did he care about a high school girl? Why did he come himself instead of just sending a million lackeys to nab her? She asked, "What are you trying to hide?"

He didn't yell. He barely acknowledged her presence, but his anger was palpable. The whole van shook as his rage overtook him. His body shook and the muscles in his cheeks, which he'd obviously worked out over many years of clenching his jaw, rippled under the drooping skin of his round, wrinkled face.

The rest of the van ride was conducted in silence. Madison looked at her shoes as the van skittered along bumpy roads. Like on the bus ride to school, she could feel the gravel path under the wheels and she knew they were heading deep into the fort, someplace far away from prying eyes. She listened carefully to the turns, hoping to find some clue as to what was going on. At least they hadn't left the base yet. She was sure of that.

They parked again. Madison looked out of the door when the General and his men got out. All she saw out the door was another underground parking garage, no sign of the light of day. They closed the door behind them, sealing her in the windowless van with no lights and no food.

Madison couldn't believe this was the same military that her father had worked with for so many years. He'd spoken so highly of the Army commanders and the role they played in his life. Every image she had of the military was of patriotism, of men fighting as hard as they could to save the lives of those around them.

She decided to yell at the top of her lungs, to let them know that she was still there, still a power that they had to contend with. "The fact that you're hiding this from the rest of the Army means that you have something to gain. I mean, Antarctica isn't exactly important to the Army, is it? You want the phone. Graham told me so!"

She listened for a response but she couldn't hear anything. She was just alone in a van, waiting. She'd never been in a place so dark, except for those times when she used to go down to the basement after she'd shut off all the electricity in her house, darker even than her mom's office had been. She knew there would be some noise, some tiny crack in the van that would let her hear what they were talking about outside. She wriggled around the van putting her ear to every window and every seam. There were definitely people talking outside but in whispers.

She waited as long as she could but after a while she gave up. She started humming to herself in a quiet voice, "Somewhere Over the Rainbow" from *The Wizard of Oz*. It was a song she knew very well. She'd seen the movie at least twenty times with her dad. Every time he was going to be deployed they'd watch it together.

He told her, "Where I'm going is a lot like the land of Oz. There's always something to be scared of and you never know what it's going to be. One minute there's a wicked witch, the next minute the trees are chucking apples at you." He laughed. He had the brightest smile. "But I always have people around me who I can trust like the Cowardly Lion or the Tin Man. Even though they're scared, they're always ready to risk everything to save me and I feel the same about them." He kissed her on the forehead. "When I'm there I always tell myself, 'There's no place like home.'"

Madison remembered the sound of his voice as he said that, the peace that he gave her even when speaking about the scariest things in the world. She closed her eyes.

They'd left her gym bag in the van but none of her spy gadgets were left inside. Madison felt through the items in the bag, and was surprised to find that the ruby slippers were still there. She was so tired when she packed the bag, she didn't even register how strange it was to bring the most expensive pair of shoes in the history of the world with her. Since this would be her last chance, she put them on, even though she wouldn't be able to see them on her feet. It might help her remember that moment with her father. She might just click them together so that she'd wake up and realize it was all a dream. In the darkness, she also changed into her semi-formal dress. Maybe they'd treat her better if she wore it. She felt pretty, even with her black eye, she was proud of it. She'd stood up to a monster and lived to tell about it. She was pretty. People tend to treat pretty things better. That was what she imagined at least. Maybe she was just going crazy from solitary confinement.

She listened to the wall again. There were more whispers but they were faint enough that she had no idea what they were saying. "Promise me that you won't hurt my mom!" she screamed. "Promise me!"

There was no response. She was absolutely sure that they heard her. That was the last straw. If she'd thought even once about telling them what she knew, she reconsidered.

She sat back against the seat and closed her eyes, not that it mattered in the pitch black confinement of the van. If she'd had Charlotte with her, she would have probably known some way to get out, but here she was on her own, not only without Charlotte but also without any set of instructions at all. It felt like hours as she waited for them to let her out. No matter how loudly she screamed, they didn't react. They were treating her as if she was five years old and in time out.

The van started to feel smaller and smaller. The world started to feel smaller. The walls were thick steel. She tried to kick out the door but all she managed to do was to pop a blister on her heel that she'd gotten from racing Jillian Jacobs for eighteen miles. She was trapped by some very powerful people and she had nothing to bargain with.

But they didn't know that.

"I know where the phone is!" she screamed.

The door opened as if she'd said the magic words. The light from the parking garage was blinding after all of the darkness, but Madison could see the outline of General Crawley's bowling ball body. "Where?" he asked.

She thought quickly. What was one thing she knew that no one else knew? "The man took it," she said quickly, without even thinking. "The man who attacked me in the street after stabbing that woman. He took it."

General Crawley looked over to one of the uniformed men next to him. The man nodded back, as if to say that the story made sense. "Where is he?" the general asked. "What does he look like?"

Madison tried to remember his face but it was a blur. "I don't know," she lied. "But if you take me there, I can find him. I don't remember the road, but it's by a gas station. If you take me to Route Forty and show me all the gas stations, I'll be able to pick it out for you. He'll be around there. I'll recognize him when I see him."

"That's not how it works," he hissed.

Madison smiled. "If you don't get it right away, you can bet Graham will. Every second you wait is another opportunity for him to get it back on his own."

The general turned to the man next to him and gave a short nod. They all piled back into the car, filling every last inch of space as if they were trying to set the record for most elbows thrown in a fifteen year old girl's face.

"So you're ready to help us?" Crawley asked.

Madison nodded.

They drove off, but instead of the leisurely path they'd taken to get there, they flew like a fireball, each turn skidding across the road. This was a real military operation. There were no jokes anymore. It was for keeps.

Chapter 39

Madison told them the name of the Italian restaurant where the woman was attacked. They put the name into a computer and were determined to get there in the quickest way possible.

The door finally opened to look upon the orange dusk of the hills, a beautiful view of the towns below and past them to the mountains of Frederick and past them to the farmland of northern Virginia. Madison's racing heart told her this might be the last sunset she would ever see.

They escorted her at a run to a helicopter only thirty feet away, its rotors spinning wild gusts of dust into her eyes. They put a set of headphones onto her and started asking her questions so that they could get the exact location where they needed to go. Then the men spoke to each other in some coded language that she'd never heard before. Had her mom been there she'd know exactly what they were saying within moments but Madison wasn't so adept. She understood none of it. But there was a rhythm that she found familiar. Usually, her mother told her, codes take English words and switch the letters around, but it still sounds like English. Whatever language they were speaking didn't have the same intonations and pauses. It wasn't a language that she recognized. She knew enough about Arabic to rule that language out, and it certainly wasn't English.

One of Madison's tricks for learning languages was to pay attention to names. Most of the time people can't translate names so they just say them with an accent. After a while she realized they weren't just talking about the stabber. They were talking about Connor Pike. They said "Coonoo Peek," with sharp syllables. Something important was happening and the general was very anxious about it. Eventually, one of the uniformed men pulled out his cell phone. It was a video from C-SPAN, a direct feed into Congress. She could barely see it over the general's shoulder but it was unmistakable. It was Graham testifying before a congressional hearing.

The man questioning him was a very handsome quarterback type with a chiseled jaw and fierce confidence behind his wry smile. She couldn't tell what he was saying, but she could read the little nametag in front of him. It said Connor Pike—Deputy Attorney General.

He seemed oily, like he'd spent too long moisturizing his face. His skin looked too young to match his streaks of gray hair. His skin was perfect.

"I need to hear this," the general yelled. "Plug it into the radio!"

The officer fiddled with his phone, probably trying to get the Bluetooth in the helicopter to connect. Madison suddenly heard Graham's voice once again, and the image came alive on all of the screens in the helicopter. His dulcet calm hit her softly, making her feel just a little bit safer than she had.

"I believe in protecting children," he was saying. "I think it's very important to make sure that children are kept safe from predators whether they be in the real world or online. I think it's important that they be saved from seeing R-rated movies and from playing violent video games. I think they should be saved from knowing too much too soon."

He looked straight into the camera which in turn made it feel like he was looking straight into Madison's eyes. "But sometimes it's important to tell hard truths to children. I made a game with some hard truths in it. There is death, there's sadness, there's fear. But there are lessons too."

The screen flashed back to Connor Pike whose face was filled with both calm and an eerie resolve, like he was at a firing range aiming delicately at the target, ready to pull the trigger. "Are you saying that children should be able to play video games that depict violence and gore and adult situations?"

"No, sir," Graham said, as calmly as ever. "I think we should do everything in our power to keep those things from them. We need to help children learn gradually and in a way that enriches their lives instead of dropping all of the pain of the world into their laps. My games are the best in the business at censoring violent content."

It was like a staring contest between Graham and Pike. Graham's quiet calm was the complete opposite of Pike's perfect, unflinching composure. Pike leaned closer. "Are you saying that your game, *StarX*, is not filled with material inappropriate for children?"

Madison gasped out loud. Of course it was Graham who owned *StarX*, of course he was the most powerful man in the world. Who else would he be?

"It is absolutely filled with inappropriate content," he answered. "But that content is locked out for kids under the age of eighteen. I defy you to find a child in this world who has found a way to hack into *StarX* to see something inappropriate unless they've stolen a parent's identity." He smirked as the final syllables of his British enunciation ceased echoing through the room. "To be quite frank with you sir, I think that you are attacking my game for some other reason. I think you're concerned about the same things I am." He pulled in a deep breath. "For one, you're worried because the game is addictive. But unfortunately you can't prosecute me for that so instead you're just attacking by whatever means you've got."

Pike leaned forward. "I resent the accusation that I would use this investigation for anything other than its stated goal."

"The problem is," Graham continued, "that I agree with you. It is addictive." There were confused murmurs in the audience. "There was an incident yesterday that really brought this home for me. A high school in Maryland staged a sit-in. Thousands of students all came together to protest the fact that the school forbid them from playing *StarX* in the mornings before class started." He laughed. "They were led by an industrious girl by the name of Madison Riley."

The general turned to Madison in disbelief. He obviously hadn't heard about the sit-in, nor had he realized how famous she was, to the point of being mentioned on national TV.

Graham kept speaking but with more fervor and excitement. "Children do not need to be plugged in twenty-four seven. It's a basic truth in the world. They should go out and play and socialize with real people, not virtual puppets."

He again was looking right into the camera, right into Madison's eyes. She felt her heart race as he spoke. "So I'd like to say something to young Miss Riley." He smiled the same knowing smile he wore at the airport the first time she met him. "Mads, you might think that you're saving the world but right now the most important thing is that you save yourself."

Madison looked around the cabin of the helicopter. All eyes were on her. She shrugged as if she had no idea what was going on but she'd learned enough to realize that she had to take Graham absolutely seriously. She needed to listen to every word he said as literally as possible in order to follow his directions.

Next, he spoke in the same horrible Italian accent he'd used with her in the Italian restaurant before the stabbing. He said, "Grab the pair of shoes from under your seat, open the door and go outside." He smiled a joking, toothy smile. Madison knew immediately what she had to do. She undid her seatbelt cautiously, hoping that none of the military men would notice, and she leaned forward as if she was getting sick, but in actuality she was looking under her seat for a parachute. She could feel a nylon sack between her fingers. It had all sorts of straps on it.

She was ready for what would happen next but first she wanted to make sure the general would find the man who punched her with or without her help. She said, "The man who has the phone is tall. He has a beard and glass-blue eyes. He wore a bunch of coats on top of each other and he sounded like a sea captain. He has a limp and a broken finger." She breathed slowly to calm her nerves and said, "The gas station is on the corner of Route Forty and Sudbury Road. Go find him and put him in jail."

She studied the door, a complex apparatus with arrows and instructions. Operating any equipment in the world for the first time is hard enough, but this was a piece of military hardware and she had to do it immediately with the whole force of her being, and without any instructions from Charlotte. There was a metal cover that said 'Pull cover to open,' then under the cover there was a big red lever. She ran through the steps in her head: first grab the parachute, second step over to the door, third flip the cover, fourth pull the handle, fifth jump.

The next words out of Graham's mouth were crucial. "You deserve to be a normal teenaged girl who can hang out with friends and go outside without having to worry about anything. Trust me, wherever you are, get some fresh air." He didn't need to say anything more. Madison knew exactly what she needed to do. "Seriously Madison. Do it. Right...now!" He yelled it right in the middle of the congressional hearing. Everyone in the helicopter flinched except for Madison. She was already standing, slinging the parachute over her shoulders just like she had with her school backpack a million times. It clicked into place before the military men could even reach out to grab her. She stepped up to the helicopter door, pulled the cover and heaved the big red lever to open it.

Despite their surprise, the officers all reacted quickly. They undid their restraints, driving toward her across the deck of the chopper. The general was closest, and also slowest. He lunged, completely off balance, stepping hard on his left foot to keep upright. That gave Madison the opportunity to stomp on it as she slid the door open. The general's arm collided with her shoulder, propelling half of her body out the door. She was suddenly looking down on five thousand feet of air. She felt his hand grasping the hem of her dress, holding her feet to the floor of the helicopter and suspending her above the open air. She reached back and grabbed his pinky finger with her free hand to pull it back toward his wrist, and watched as she slipped out of his fingers, the chopper blades whooshing above her with hurricane force winds. Her balance was shot.

Without thinking for a single moment, she pushed against the chopper door and slipped back, tumbling weightlessly into an endless black abyss.

Chapter 40

Madison had never jumped out of a helicopter, but she felt calm despite the roar of the wind against her face. She could barely open her eyes from the force of the wind, but she was used to dealing with the world in darkness. It didn't faze her. She quickly checked the various straps on the parachute. There were leg straps which she hadn't connected yet so the parachute wasn't really attached properly, not that they could easily attach over her dress if she wanted them to. Luckily, the dress was plastered to her stomach from the wind.

She'd had one brief lesson about skydiving and for that she was strapped to an Army Ranger. Rather than panic, she remembered her father telling her the key to parachuting, something he'd learned from too many missions dropping into hostile territory. He'd said, "It's the same as flying except you just have to trust the air around you a little bit more." As she tumbled through the air feeling for the strap, she thought about him. She knew she had to pull the chute as soon as possible. She had thirty seconds at most.

She opened her eyes only long enough to see the lights from below her flash slightly like a spotlight. Maybe she'd jumped out of a helicopter only to land on the same military base where they were searching for her. But she didn't let that stop her from snapping the parachute around her leg.

One by one she checked all of the buckles, then she pulled the rip cord. The parachute unfurled above her and caught her more gently than she'd expected. The world below came into focus suddenly in darkened silhouettes. The brightest lights were familiar, the football field at Shackleton High School was lit so bright that the fifty yard line looked like daylight. It was the entrance to the semi-formal. All of the couples would arrive in limos or stage coaches trying to outdo each other with the best entrance. They were all just dots below her as she descended. It felt so insignificant against the backdrop of military generals and helicopters.

Of course Graham would have told her to jump exactly when she was flying directly over Shackleton High. It went without saying that he'd make it all happen as dramatically as possible. That was just his style.

She didn't really know how to control a parachute, but she realized that there were straps above her that she could pull. She tried to remember more of what her dad had said. "I just let the wind tell me where it wants to go. Trust it."

She pulled at the straps. It felt much more natural than she'd expected. Slowly but surely, she made her way down to the field, hopefully at the right speed not to break her legs when she hit the ground. The ruby slippers sparkled brilliant red below her. They no longer looked like a schmaltzy prop but instead were two glimmering jewels under the lights.

And then she touched down to earth, running forward as fast as she could to compensate for the momentum of the fall. She hadn't realized it while she was still in the air, but the entire crowd was cheering as loudly as they would have if she'd just scored the game winning touchdown. She unhooked herself from the parachute harness and stood in the field. People filled the bleachers in their semi-formal dress. It felt, for a moment, like that scene of her parents dancing in Spain. She felt elegant.

Before she knew it she was in Patrick Sutton's arms. She could barely feel his touch she was so overwhelmed. The screams from the crowd muted in her mind. Everything felt dim and distant.

Then she felt Patrick's lips against hers and her knees melted away from beneath her. She grabbed onto him and held him tightly. Her face against his crisply pressed suit jacket.

"That was brilliant. The best entrance in the history of Shackleton High," he whispered in her ear. "Why didn't you tell me you were going to do that? I'd gone mad not knowing where you were."

She wanted to tell him about what happened but she knew she couldn't. She wanted to ask him to save her from the General and whoever else was out to get her. But instead she took solace in his arms, as young and unknowing as they were. At that moment, she just needed someone to cling to.

The stands had emptied and everyone had run onto the field, surrounding Madison entirely. All she could hear was cheering and screaming. Jillian Jacobs ran up to her at a sprint. She grabbed Madison by the arm and pulled her away. "Mads, are you kidding me?" she screamed. "Your mom is crying her eyes out and screaming at military police right now and you're coming to a dance!? I kept quiet about what happened but don't expect me to stay quiet now."

Then Danny and Mia arrived to accost her as well. They wore clothes as bright as neon safety vests. It was the only time she'd seen Danny wear anything but black. Madison realized she hadn't even asked them about their outfits for the dance, or who they were bringing. Obviously they went together and decided to wear the strangest things possible. "Mads!" Mia shouted. "If your parachute didn't open you could have hit the ground at terminal velocity and burst open like a bag of spaghetti. How long have you been planning that?"

"It just happened," Madison said meekly.

Danny huffed. "I guess you managed to outdo yourself," he said before walking away.

Then suddenly the crowd parted. Coach Dipson lumbered up to her, shouting and blubbering and barking. Even his dress pants were baggy enough to completely hide his figure. "You did not get permission for that stunt!" He was livid, almost as mad as the general had been before him. Actually, they looked somewhat similar except that the general had an air of confidence while Coach Dipson never seemed to believe what he was saying. "You could get expelled for this." He grabbed her by the elbow and pulled her toward the school. That didn't sound like the worst thing in the world. Maybe she'd outgrown high school already. She'd already been part of an espionage mission and taken hostage. What more could school teach her? Coach Dipson grumbled in her ear. "I have to call your parents."

"Don't say *parents*," she said, emphasis on the *s*.

Coach Dipson escorted her up to his office as if she was

in more trouble than anyone had ever been in before, but for Madison it was salvation. All she wanted was to get away and let her mom know she was alright.

She sat on a puffy chair in Coach Dipson's office and dialed her mom on his ancient phone. It rang again and again. Finally her mom picked up. "Mommy," she said like a warbling soprano. "I have something very, very, very important to tell you."

Mrs. Riley huffed into the phone, obviously having sobbed just moments before. "Madison, where are you?"

"I'm at school," she answered. "At the semi-formal."

Mrs. Riley didn't say anything for a few moments, enough to give Madison the chance to hyperventilate. The panic she'd felt in the black van was replaced by the equally intense panic of having disappointed her mom. When she next spoke, Mrs. Riley's words were protracted like those of a kindergarten teacher cleaning up the sick of a child. "I had the entire department of defense looking for you." The anger in her voice sizzled. "I'm glad you're safe," Mrs. Riley went on, "but you're too old to disappear like that." The guilt was palpable too, stronger than any she'd felt before.

"I'm sorry Mom," she said. "I think I made a big mistake."

Her mom groused, "I don't know how you did it, Madison." Her rattling voice let Madison know she'd been yelling for hours. "How did you get out of Fort Meade with half of the US intelligence community looking for you? I mean, I couldn't even do that and I work with them every day."

Madison reflected on her time with Graham. He'd worked so hard to help her, maybe he'd been her guardian angel, helping her escape a helicopter, saving her from an earthquake. Maybe he still had her back, keeping her out of trouble. Maybe he'd already made a cover story for her, but without any way to contact him, how could she be sure?

"I was channeling Dad," she answered.

"But why run away like that? Your friend Jillian was as confused as I was. We called everyone you know. Why would you worry us all so much?" She sighed. "Jillian said it was because you're suddenly obsessed with popularity."

Madison started crying. The only way she could think to explain this to her mom was to lie. "Maybe she's right," Madison answered. "I did it because I wanted to make the biggest entrance in the history of Shackleton High." She felt the tears start to flow as she lied yet again to her mom. "So I did what Dad would have done. I parachuted onto the fifty yard line to impress all my friends." She couldn't bear to disappoint her mom even more but she couldn't help it. There was no other way. "I'm sorry."

Another long silence.

"I'm coming to pick you up, Madison." Mrs. Riley hung up.

Madison grabbed onto Coach Dipson and began to cry into his shoulder. "He said he was going to ruin my life…" She could feel her tears wet his shirt.

"Who did?" he asked.

But before she could answer, she turned around to look out of the window onto the parking lot. It was a mess of news vans crowded outside of the school, all waiting to hear her story. She turned to Coach Dipson. "Could you please turn on your computer so I can look at it?" she asked. "I think I'm on the news."

The screen blinked on to the local news site. They were interviewing someone. Of course it was Graham. He was standing in front of the school. She could even see him out of the window as he was being interviewed. He looked as polished as ever, wearing his designer label suit and his day old stubble. "I'm officially going on record to admit my involvement in this ordeal," he said into the camera. "I provided the helicopter. I was the one who faked the theft from the Smithsonian so that the entrance would be as spectacular as possible. I assure you that the ruby slippers were not stolen. I have all of the proper paperwork to show that I have them on loan and have left a sizeable endowment in order to make it possible." It was all lies. He must have faked the paperwork for the shoes after she'd taken them from the museum, just like he'd faked everything else in order to cover her tracks. He was always trying to cover for her, but she felt like he was only making things worse.

The reporter behind the camera asked, "Why did you get in contact with a fifteen year old girl?"

He answered modestly. "Madison Riley wanted a way to raise money for earthquake relief in Costa Rica. I thought jumping out of a helicopter was a great idea. It was wrong of me to make this happen without parental permission. I didn't know at the time that she was a *StarX* master willing to risk her future to save my game. I'm not that self-serving. I didn't mean to make Mads Riley a household name, I think we're all better off now that she is. She's up to the task. Whatever she does next, the world will be watching."

Then Madison started to see what he might be doing. By putting her into the spotlight, Graham was making it that much harder for the general to abduct her again. Being famous meant that she'd be missed. If she suddenly disappeared from the face of the earth, people would notice, not just her mom.

"Coach," she said quietly. "If you ever want me to play lacrosse again, let me make a statement to the cameras out there."

Dipson looked visibly confused. He loved the team, even more than he really should have. All of that machismo he showed on the field suddenly looked like a front. He was insecure. He wanted Madison to like him. "OK," he said softly. "But you have to promise me you won't say anything that gets you in even more trouble. And don't tell them I let you go. Tell them you snuck out."

So Madison got up and walked out of the room, hoping with all of her might that she'd be saved by fame.

She slowly made her way to the bright lights of the TV crews with her head held high. Graham was the first to notice her. He smiled and welcomed her in front of the cameras. He held out his hand and greeted her. "Mads Riley," he said cordially. "It's so nice to finally meet you."

"It's nice to meet you too," she said, trying to sound happy.

Graham looked down on her. "I just want to make it clear, Madison. I made a mistake today by helping you. But if I can work with you, I think we can save the world. We just have to do it in a smarter way."

Madison nodded. "I know," she said. "I think we can too." Lights flashed in her face and she tried her best to smile. She'd never wanted to be famous. She'd always wanted to fade into the background, but here she was on national TV with a social magnate saying she wanted to save the world.

And there was a part of her that believed she could.

Chapter 41

Everything felt as though it returned to normal. Between Graham and General Crawley, everything had been covered up from the government, explained to the news channels and erased from history.

Madison was suspended from Shackleton for a week. The only reason she wasn't expelled was because both the deputy attorney general and the fifteenth richest man in the world gave the principal a call. She saw Patrick at school but couldn't go out with him again. She was grounded indefinitely. Graham didn't contact her again. She'd stopped checking her email because she got so many contacts from people all over the world wanting to talk to her about *StarX*. But she didn't know anything about *StarX*. She barely knew what it was.

Every day she was home she regretted all of the things she could have asked Charlotte but didn't. She had an opportunity to understand the secrets of the world, like the nature of consciousness and cold fusion. She wasn't sure why she hadn't asked more questions. She was definitely afraid of what she might learn. Graham had told her that Charlotte would ruin her life. She got frustrated by how difficult it was to ask the right questions. If she wasn't careful, Charlotte would have given her the entire history of the universe every time Madison asked a question.

What made it worse was that she might have missed her only chance to know. She might never get the chance again. It didn't seem like she'd hear from Graham any time soon, mostly because he'd gotten in a lot of legal trouble over the stunt. Mrs. Riley threatened to sue him and requested a restraining order against him.

At least it was over.

On her way to school each day, she'd keep an eye out for suspicious looking vans or other indications that the government was out to get her, but she couldn't find anything.

So she returned to being a normal kid, acing every test for Spanish and English but barely scraping by in her other subjects. She'd improved her math scores, though, possibly because of the instructions she'd been given by Graham. She still didn't like it, but at least she could relate to it somewhat, imagining the math spoken instead of graphed.

Her mom still hadn't recovered from that night. All that they could do for each other was sit across the dinner table and try to talk casually about their days. Mrs. Riley was fond of telling Madison how happy all of her co-workers were to hear that Madison was safe that night. For Madison that was just a reminder that she'd done something wrong.

"Director Tenant asked me to tell you that he was impressed by your interview on CNBC yesterday," she said. "He thinks you're brilliant. He still can't understand how you snuck out of the building without security seeing you."

The director must have been lying too, or else someone faked the surveillance tapes. How far did the conspiracy go? Madison tried to look cute as she smiled. "I guess it just helps to be young and quick," she said.

"By the way, Madison, you got a package today."

Madison perked up and looked around. "What was it? I didn't order anything."

Mrs. Riley got up from the table and grabbed a cube shaped box about the size of a few books stacked on top of one another. Madison picked up the box. She had no idea what it was. Her mom hovered over her shoulder.

"Oh right," she said, trying to act as though the package was nothing special. "I ordered this months ago. I can't believe it took so long to get here."

She walked over to her mom and said, *"Te quiero."*

Mrs. Riley smiled. "I love you too, Mads. I love you too."

Her mom started clearing away the dishes while Madison opened the box, sifting packing peanuts out of the way. She pulled out a smaller box, a carrying case for glasses. Inside of the case was a brand new pair of very expensive looking sunglasses, like the ones that Graham wore in the airport in Costa Rica. They had a familiar heft to them. They were unique.

She looked on the side of the glasses for the brand name—*Charlotte.*

Acknowledgments

I can't imagine thanking everyone who helped me in bringing this book to the page. I'll go through some names, but I hope that those excluded from the list remember that, like the proverbial goldfish, my short term memory lasts only four seconds.

Colleen, you have been my biggest fan since all of this started. You keep finding new ways to inspire me. Thank you to Brandon for the beautiful cover art. I could not have done this without Brad Pauquette and everyone at Columbus Creative Cooperative. Thank you to our readers, Amber, Ved, Aja, Tej, Eliana, Stephen, Jacob, Shannon and Caitlin. Thank you to our family and friends who gave encouragement along the long road to this point, past strange digressions and awkward moments. Thanks to my teachers.

About the Cover Artist

Brandon Moon graciously provided the oil painting for the cover of *Graham's Charlotte*.

Brandon Moon creates fragmented paintings derived from factual visions. Originally from Jackson, Mississippi, after receiving a BFA in Painting from Delta State University in Cleveland, Mississippi, Brandon continued his studies in the graduate painting program at the Savannah College of Art & Design in Savannah, Georgia. After three years of creating art in Columbus, Ohio, he now resides on the outskirts of Manhattan, furthering his exploration into a personal visual representation of the world with his soon-to-be wife and inspiration.

Drew Farnsworth

Drew Farnsworth lives with his wife Colleen in Columbus, Ohio where they spend their time together cooking, eating, running, pet sitting, making random crap out of old circuit boards, and designing stuff. He's been known to strap things to his feet and slide down hills in the wintertime. In summer, he's far more likely to go barefoot. *Graham's Charlotte* is his first solo novel.

Learn more about Drew at
www.DrewFarnsworth.com

CPSIA information can be obtained at www.ICGtesting.com
Printed in the USA
BVOW02s0706050314

346696BV00002B/7/P